MISS UNDERSTANDING

AUBREY BONDURANT

Camio,
So nice to meet
you at XiiBB221.
♥ Aubrey
Bondur.

This is a work of fiction. Names, characters, businesses, places, events, and incidents are either the products of the author's imagination or used in a fictitious manner. Any resemblance to actual persons, living or dead, or actual events is purely coincidental.

This book is for mature audiences only.

Cover by Marisa @ Cover Me Darlings

Text copyright © 2020 by Aubrey Bondurant

ISBN-10 : 167596064X

ISBN-13 : 978-1675960646

Sign up for my newsletter for all the latest release information HERE

Chapter One

KENDALL

*H*ow could a man that pretty be such a complete dick?

I sat at my desk, positioned outside of my boss's office door in a secluded corner of the modern office space, and opened a secret file on my computer. After he'd complained about the turkey sandwich I'd brought him for lunch, it was time to make a new entry. Was it my fault the cafeteria had been out of wheat bread? Was his stomach so special it couldn't handle country white on a Thursday afternoon?

42. Paper cut on his right hand. Unexpected infection sets in. Cannot jerk off properly for weeks.

None of the entries on my list of how I'd like to see my boss suffer were violent or too long term. After all, I did try to be a nice person. Which is why I'd settle for a minor accident which would moderately inconvenience him or make him have a bad day. Also, I wouldn't mind if it made him uglier in the process. Like entry number fourteen where I wished he'd get a big cold sore on his lush, full lips, or entry twenty-nine where I wished he'd be hit with a bout of acne on his stupid, perfect face.

Typing these things throughout the work week seemed to get me through his barking demands, ungrateful, snobbish demeanor, and general lack of personality.

Yes, Liam "Asshole" Davenport was the bane of my existence. And had been over the last four dreadful months I'd been working for him. He was rude, condescending, and worst of all, dismissive. He made it clear with every sigh that my title of legal secretary made me less than in his eyes. Then again, as bad as he was as a boss, at least he always behaved appropriately. The same couldn't be said for the last partner for whom I'd worked.

God, I couldn't wait to quit this job. Hopefully, I could do just that in the next few months.

"Ms. Tate, I need you in here," came the sound of his way-too-sexy-for-being-an-asshole voice over the phone intercom. He didn't utter a *please*. No *if you have a moment*. And he never called me by my first name, even though I'd offered in the beginning, thinking perhaps if we weren't as formal it might break his icy demeanor.

I stood up, grabbing my notebook and pen, smoothing down my newest skirt, happy with the purchase. My thrift-store clothes were both fashionable and budget friendly. Since I worked for one of the most successful partners in one of the top law firms in Los Angeles, I was expected to dress well.

But no matter how well I dressed, walking into my boss's office always made me anxious. There wouldn't be one nice word coming out of his mouth. Nor would he indicate he was the slightest bit content with me as his legal secretary. Perhaps he had his own list of ways he'd like to see me reassigned to someone else.

Liam was one of the youngest to ever make equity partner at Lowry and Anderson LLP, and it seemed there was no stop to his trajectory. He certainly wasn't turning into one of those partners who rested on their laurels once achieving the milestone. Instead he seemed to be driven to keep doing more.

But the real reason I was always nervous walking into his office was because of how beautiful he was. It wasn't a word I would normally use for a man, but it suited him. He had the chiseled features of a Nordic Viking with the ice-blue eyes to match. His blondish hair was perfectly cut and styled without an inch of a receding hairline. But it was his eyelashes that often gave me pause. They were the long, sooty, lush type any girl would kill for. But none of his looks mattered the moment he opened his mouth.

"You don't knock?" he snapped, not bothering to glance up from his laptop.

My gaze flicked from him to the view out the windows. His office was one of the largest on the twelfth floor with a vantage point over downtown LA. I'd spent many a minute wishing I could be somewhere outside of the window rather than here, speaking with him.

"You were expecting me to come in, so no." I didn't often bother with a retort, but this morning I was feeling a bit feisty. It was the best way to combat the intimidation factor.

It earned me a rare quirked brow. A reminder that despite him acting like a robot most of the time, he was in fact human.

"Fine. How is the Hong Kong trip shaping up?"

"Let me grab your itinerary, and we'll go over it."

There it was. His unmistakable sigh.

I'd come in with a pen and pad in my hands trying to be prepared, but he expected I'd also know the subject for which he'd beckoned me. Considering he had three upcoming trips in the next eight weeks, how was I supposed to guess which one he'd want to talk about, if in fact I could mind read and know he wanted to discuss travel? Couldn't he have said, "I need you in here to discuss the Hong Kong trip"? Nope. It was almost as though he enjoyed setting me up to fail just so he could give me his trademark sigh of disapproval.

I was back in five seconds. Maybe six if you counted the one extra I took to roll my eyes before returning. "Yes, now about Hong Kong. You're set to leave next Saturday at five."

"In the evening?"

"Yes."

"First class?"

As if I'd dare book anything else for his pretentious ass. I could guarantee his suits cost more than a full month's worth of my pay. God forbid they touch a coach seat. Granted, I didn't actually know the difference between first class and coach myself. I'd been born and raised in Southern California and pretty much stayed here my entire twenty-four years. Sure, there was the one road trip to Vegas when I'd turned twenty-one where my friends and I had all piled into a room for one night, but I'd yet to fly on an airplane.

"Yes. Of course. You're in first class."

"At the Four Seasons hotel?"

If he'd read his damn itinerary which I had emailed him last week, he'd already have his answer. "No, it was full, but I booked the Ritz Carlton."

His full lips turned down into a frown. As if he was put out by the thought of having to rough it at the Ritz?

"You arrive the day before the deposition. I have a car and driver who will pick you up from the airport and take you to the hotel. Then another car will take you to the office building where the deposition will be held. The address of the office and the driver's number are all in your portfolio."

"I can't stress how important this deposition is."

Perhaps if he told me for a fiftieth time it would sink in. "I understand."

4

It was my key phrase whenever I wanted to tell him something like, *no shit*. Yep, just call me *Miss Understanding*.

The deposition he spoke of regarded a former government contractor employee who had evidence against the CEO of a security firm. This CEO had committed fraud and embezzled the employee pension funds. The key witness, who'd been the CEO's assistant, had fled to Asia to keep his whereabouts on the down low, but he had agreed to this deposition if we came to him in Hong Kong to do it. Considering the number of people who were suing, most being represented by this firm, his testimony was critical.

"Nothing can interrupt the preparation I have planned for the next two weeks. I'll need you full-time on this."

"I've cleared your schedule as requested. And I have no other priority but this deposition." Wasn't like I had another attorney I was working for. But I did dread the next couple of weeks. I'd learned Liam was the most stressed and the moodiest before a trial or deposition. Beyond that, preparation for this deposition would mean long days for me. At least I had a winter break next week in my night classes. If I had to work late, I wouldn't have to sacrifice school nights.

Suddenly his cell phone vibrated. He ignored it. I didn't think anything of it until his office phone rang a moment after.

He made brief eye contact with me but made no move to check the number.

Keeping myself from sighing aloud that he expected me to answer it, I stood up, stretched across his desk where the phone was inches from him, and picked up the receiver.

Dickhead's office who can't answer his own damn phone even when it's directly in front of him. How may I help you?

Lucky for me it came out, "Liam Davenport's office. How may I assist you?"

Hysterics from a woman greeted me. "Oh God, oh God, I need to talk to him."

What did I want to bet it was an ex-girlfriend who'd realized he'd ghosted her? Although I had some sympathy for her, I would keep him from having to deal with it. It was my job. To be the gatekeeper here at the office. To guard every billable minute Liam Davenport could be working for the firm. She'd have to deal with stalking him after hours. "Ma'am, please calm down. What is this regarding?"

My boss paused in his typing, looking over.

"This is his mother. His father died. I need to speak to him, please."

Oh, crap. Talk about instant guilt. Here I'd been thinking she was some jilted lover. "I'm terribly sorry. Of course. One moment."

I put the call on hold, mainly so I could take a deep breath. I may loathe this gorgeous, pompous ass I worked for, but I wasn't heartless. "Your mother needs to speak with you urgently."

"Tell her I'll call her later." Evidently, I was the only one in the room with a heart. His eyes were already back on the screen of his monitor, perusing his email as if he couldn't be bothered.

I refused to be the one to tell him his father had died. "You need to speak with her now."

He shook his head. "Actually, I don't. Take a message or tell her I'll call her back."

I lost it. It was the only explanation for my next words. "Pick up the fucking phone, Liam."

His shocked blue gaze met mine, and for a moment I thought his next words would be "you're fired." But he must've seen it in my eyes. The unmistakable seriousness of the moment.

He reached over, taking the receiver and pressing the button to take her off hold.

Figuring this was a private moment in which his world would be falling apart, I turned around and left the office.

Chapter Two

KENDALL

A s I sat back down at my desk, I realized I was shaking. Probably because a year ago I'd received a similar frantic call from my mother at the office. She'd been in hysterics, telling me my father had been taken by ambulance to the emergency room. It had been a heart attack. The two-hour cab ride south to Orange County had been the worst of my life. I hadn't known if he'd still be alive by the time I got there. Once I'd arrived at the hospital and found his room, I'd held his hand, cried my tears, and prayed harder than I ever had in my life for him to survive. Luckily, he had.

He'd listened to the doctors, changed his diet, and started taking better care of himself. He'd even lost thirty pounds. The only problem was he'd had to cut down on the hours he spent on the factory line. My mother, who was a school teacher, had taken a second job cleaning houses on the weekends. As their only child, I'd tried to help out where I could while also trying to finish school to get my bachelor's degree.

Now I took a deep breath, emotional over the feelings Liam's mother's call had evoked. Then the ramification of telling my boss to *pick up the fucking phone* started to sink in.

I'd also called him by his first name. He wouldn't care for that slip, either. By now, chances were he was beside himself learning about the death of his father, so perhaps he'd forgive the overstep of my cursing at him. God knows I couldn't afford to be fired.

Even if he did forget, I probably needed to apologize for my outburst. But walking in there right now wasn't an option. It would be selfish to make it about me and my need to ensure my job was safe. After the terrible news, he'd need a moment to absorb. He also needed time to speak with his mom. Knowing him, he'd probably take charge of making the funeral arrangements. I imagined he'd have to go home, wherever that was, in order to be with his family, and I'd offer to help with the travel logistics.

Oh, God. But what about the deposition? We'd have to postpone. Surely, they'd give an extension for a situation such as this.

As my mind wandered about what this next week would hold, the clipping of heels snapped me out of my thoughts. Looking over, I saw it was Tabitha Owings, another partner with the firm. I suspected she had the hots for my boss given the way she eye fucked him any time they shared a room.

"Tell Liam I'm here to see him." No please, no smile, no niceties. I bet she treated her shoes better than the staff.

She was a beautiful woman, probably in her late thirties, but her coldness toward anyone who wasn't a partner was legendary around this place. She and my boss were a match made in asshole heaven. Normally I wouldn't hesitate to buzz him, in order to get her out of my hair, but today I had to make an exception. I had to play the unhappy and underappreciated role of gatekeeper.

"Unfortunately, now isn't a good time."

Her newly injected lips made a weird duck-faced pout. "I

checked his calendar, and he has nothing booked for the next half hour."

"Something came up."

"Like what?"

"I'm not at liberty to discuss—"

Just then Liam's office door opened, and we both turned to see him standing in the frame.

"Hello, Tabitha," he said.

Her mouth curved into a seductive smile. "Liam. I came by to discuss the Maynard file, but your secretary tells me it's not a good time."

I hated the way she said *secretary*. Only in a law firm did they seem to keep this title. Outside the legal world, most other firms had evolved to calling the position an assistant. But Tabitha took it a step further. She used the word secretary as if to remind me I was in a law firm caste system where I should be executing a curtsey and emptying her bed pan. Yeah, so I had a very active imagination sometimes, but the point was she was condescending.

Forgetting about her for a moment, I studied my boss's face. He didn't look any different than before his mother's phone call. No red eyes, no ashen expression. No visible worries at all. It was as if his mother hadn't told him mere minutes ago that his father had died.

"Ms. Tate is mistaken. Now is fine. Come in, Tabitha." His ice-blue eyes only flickered to me briefly before he ushered her into his office.

Gatekeeping was such a thankless job.

She was in there thirty minutes before strutting out in her four-inch, red-bottomed shoes. She wore a smug look on her face. For all I knew, she'd just blown him in his office. Honestly, if it put him in a better mood, I wasn't sure I cared.

"Ms. Tate, my office," came the devil's voice from behind me.

Cue the dreadful music. My gently worn black flats were soundless on the carpeted floor as I walked into his office, wondering if it would be for the last time.

Chapter Three

LIAM

I'd sat there motionless for a full five minutes after I'd hung up the phone. My mother had cried, shrieked, and then finally calmed down enough to tell me how my father had died. Aneurysm. Quick and probably painless. Not the way I would've picked for him to go.

What should one feel for a father who'd abandoned him as a child? For a father who, before he'd done so, had been a raging alcoholic who liked to use his cruel words as well as his fists on his wife and children? The best thing he could've done was leave when I was eight years old. But then once he had, my mother had been forced to work two jobs while we relied on government assistance to help put food on the table.

For twenty-four years he was out of our lives without a word. Then, six months ago, he'd showed up on my mother's doorstep and begged forgiveness. Evidently, he'd found Jesus, been sober for over a year, and was looking for redemption. More like a roof over his head with a woman to cook his meals. My mom had happily fit the role despite strong advisement against it from her two adult children.

I didn't often entertain emotions, but repressed hatred

toward the man had bubbled up unexpectedly with the phone call. Now that he'd died, she expected me to come home and pay my respects—as if we'd been a happy family all along. I couldn't do it. Not for him. No matter how much she'd insisted he'd changed. Or how many times he'd called me over the last few months, wanting to make amends.

But I would travel home for her. Because despite the fact I now lived over two thousand miles away and had a very full plate at work, there wasn't anything I wouldn't do for the woman who'd sacrificed everything to raise me and my older sister. With one exception: forgiving the man whose actions were unforgivable.

I thunked my head down on my desk. This was not what I needed, now of all times. I should call Kendall back in to sort through logistics. But first I'd have to internalize everything as I often did, especially around her.

Although I suspected my assistant may want a friendlier work relationship, it couldn't happen. I didn't do emotional attachments at work. Hell, I hardly did them at all. This method had served me well; after all, I'd become the youngest equity partner in the history of Lowry and Anderson. Now with the goal of becoming a named partner for the firm, I couldn't afford to have anything get in the way.

It was easier to keep my distance, both emotionally and physically, if I simply treated her in a professional manner, possibly erring on the side of being cool toward her. I'd thought she might be just as indifferent to me as I was to her up until the point she had to go and tell me to pick up the fucking phone.

Jesus, seeing the fire in her eyes and hearing her curse had been like a shot to my cock. One I had to ignore. I was her boss. She was my assistant. End of story.

Hearing Tabitha's voice outside, I listened for a moment

before deciding to use her as a distraction. Moving to the door, I took a breath and schooled my features.

Tabitha was a smart, driven, and successful income partner specializing in tax law. She was also blatant about wanting to be more than coworkers. I could almost hear her biological clock ticking every time she walked by. But it would never happen. Especially not with a woman who would probably eat her own young if it meant she could trade up from an income partner to an equity partner and earn more money.

I invited her in, but after thirty minutes of barely listening to her drone on about her latest case, I glanced at my clock.

"Sorry, Tabitha, I have a call."

"I know the feeling. I need to get back to my packed schedule. I'll probably be here late. Drinks later?"

"Thanks, but no. I also have a busy schedule."

"If you want a break, you have my number."

Yes, I did. And I'd never use it. Although there wasn't a fraternization policy in place to preclude dating, in my mind there certainly should be. It was unprofessional and, worst of all, a threat to everything I'd ever accomplished. My rule applied to everyone with whom I worked. No exceptions based on title. A smart man did not sleep his way around the building he hoped to put his name on someday. "I do. Have a good night."

After Tabitha walked out, I sat at my desk unfocused. I needed to figure out what to do about next week and the funeral. And I required my assistant to help me do it, prompting me to ask her to come in.

She walked in slowly, her head held high, her shoulders back. I shouldn't have noticed how snugly her new skirt fit her hips or how her silk blouse, although demure, gaped enough at the top two buttons to allow a peek of golden skin at her collarbone. I wasn't sure of her heritage, but her skin appeared kissed by the sun in the most natural way. She was petite. Probably all of five foot two, but she had curves in all the right places. She was beautiful in such an unassuming, almost innocent way. And completely off-limits. Something I had to remind myself of several times a day.

"We need to talk about logistics for this next week."

She licked her lips, making me quickly take a seat behind my desk and focus on my computer. It was a strategy I often used when she was in my presence. I avoided all eye contact and pretended I wasn't attracted to her whatsoever.

"Of course. First I want to say I'm sorry."

"For my loss or for telling me to pick up the fucking phone?" Did I mention I was often a dick? I justified it by my need to ensure there were no personal lines crossed or blurred. I couldn't afford such a luxury in a place where my reputation and billable hours were everything.

She turned pink.

I shouldn't have glanced up at her to witness the pretty blush on her face.

She took a breath, brushing her brown hair back behind her ear. I noticed she did this gesture as a nervous habit. "For both. I needed you to take the call from your mother, but I'm sure there were better ways to accomplish it."

Probably, but seeing her stand up to me had been a very unexpected turn-on. Now it was time to reestablish our boundaries. "Yes, there were. Also you called me Liam." And I'd enjoyed the sound of my name on her lips way too much. Once, I'd seen her applying strawberry lip balm, and it had made me wonder if she'd taste like it. "Let's not make calling me by my first name a habit."

If she was irritated, she hid it well. I imagined she had

perfected this art since working for me. I wasn't easy to deal with.

"Understood, Mr. Davenport. You mentioned the upcoming week? What do you want to discuss?"

To the point. She was always to the point. I respected the fact she didn't waste time.

"I need to travel home."

"Okay. When and where?"

"We can fly into Roanoke, Virginia, or Beckley, West Virginia. Whatever is the easiest route from LAX. From there, we'll need a rental car."

She wrote into the notepad she always carried and looked up. "We. Is someone traveling with you?"

This was quite possibly the worst or best idea I'd ever had. "Yes. You."

I had the pleasure of watching her face flush again, this time with her big brown eyes going wide. Reason number ninety-two it was probably a bad idea to take her with me. But I had no other idea what else I could do if I hoped to get the deposition prep done while dealing with my family and the funeral. I had to have her assisting me.

"It's your personal travel, and no offense, but I don't think I should go with you to your father's funeral."

"For me it's personal, but for you it'll be all business. Are you not available to travel?"

She swallowed hard. "I'm available. But why would you want me there?"

"I'll need you there to help me with the deposition prep. To get the office set up at the hotel. I can't afford to lose time on this. As you're aware, the days leading up are crucial."

I realized talking nothing but business made me sound like a cold bastard in her opinion considering I'd only just learned about my father's death. I could easily dispel her opinion by telling her the truth about him. But I didn't. It wasn't necessary for her to know about my personal childhood demons.

At the same time, knowing she'd be traveling with me immediately eased the knot forming in my stomach. It was a foreign feeling to rely on someone, but I knew without a doubt she could handle anything I threw at her. She might not enjoy working for me, but she understood the importance of this deposition and its prep. She was damn good at her job.

"Right. Understood. What is the town we'll be staying in?"

"The town is Tazewell, Virginia." It was where I'd grown up, and I hadn't been back since I'd graduated high school fourteen years ago. Instead, I'd fly my mother out to see me. Or my sister and I would meet her in the larger city of Roanoke.

"Okay. When do we need to leave?"

"Tomorrow." My mother would need help with the arrangements. Since tomorrow would be Friday, I was hoping to get most of those tasks done over the weekend and then have the funeral soon after, making it possible for me to return to LA and have one uninterrupted prep week back here.

"So I'll be working over the weekend?"

It wouldn't surprise me to discover Kendall had a boyfriend and would have plans, but I definitely didn't want to know about it. "Yes. Don't worry. You'll be paid overtime for your hours."

There was temper in her eyes, but she tamped it down as always. Well, except for her earlier outburst over my mother's phone call. "Will we return in time for the following weekend?"

"Yes. We need to."

My answer eased the tension in her face.

Chapter Four

KENDALL

I think I would've preferred to have been fired rather than go with Mr. you-need-to-come-with-me-across-the-entire-country-and-do-my-shit-Liam Davenport. But the truth was I needed this job. I needed the paycheck. Even once I earned my bachelor's degree in business administration in a few months, there was no guarantee I would find a better paying job with the same great benefits. I'd been with this firm three years and made a decent salary even without my overtime hours.

My passion was to work as a chef or a caterer. But I didn't have the luxury of entertaining such an idea. As much as I loved the cooking classes I snuck in whenever I could, the truth was most culinary jobs paid less than what I was making now. I quite literally couldn't afford to follow my dreams when I had financial obligations.

Back at my desk outside Liam's office, I forced myself to stop thinking about my future and take a deep breath. I had to make travel plans—for a place I'd never heard of. And prepare myself to fly on a plane for the very first time.

My super strength was being organized. First things first,

I needed to book a flight. A half an hour later, however, I realized it was easier said than done. Flights were limited going into Roanoke and impossible from LAX to Beckley, West Virginia. But there was a bigger question. What client number did I charge this to? Most of Liam's travel was client billable, meaning the client was charged for it. But this was a personal trip. So was he paying? Maybe for himself, but what about my ticket?

When I thought of having to ask him any questions, my head thunked down against the smooth surface of my desk. I'd reached my max of wanting to converse with him.

"It won't help. Believe me, I've tried. We're still going to Virginia."

I sat up suddenly, startled by Liam's voice. I hadn't heard my boss come out of his office. And was that a spark of humor coming from him?

He reached a hand up to rub his temple, seemingly off from his usual cool demeanor. Perhaps he wasn't as unaffected by things as I'd unfairly judged.

"I have a question. How am I charging the travel?"

I waited. Waited for him to tell me to put it to non-billable or to a client which he'd then write off.

"Put it to my personal number, so I'm charged for it. Your travel, too."

I don't know why I was surprised. His integrity wasn't something I'd seen was an issue, but there was always a first time a partner would abuse the system by trying to charge the firm for their personal travel. I found the richer the man, the more he seemed to take liberties with spending other people's money.

"Roanoke is the only flight available from LAX tomorrow. There's one stop in Chicago."

"There's not a nonstop flight?"

"Afraid not."

"Are you sure?"

This. This was the reason I wanted a little doll of his likeness to jab pins into. Although I wasn't familiar with the art of voodoo, I could fucking learn to jab a doll dressed in a suit for this guy.

"I'm quite sure. Unless you'd prefer to charter a private jet." He'd done it before, but it had been for a client emergency and at their expense.

"No. It's fine. What time do we arrive?"

"After four o'clock in the afternoon."

"That late?"

Here is where I should've stayed quiet, but his obvious questions were grating on me. "There's a three-hour time difference and a connecting flight, so yes. That late."

"Fine, book it. And make sure to get an SUV for the rental car."

"Okay. As far as hotels go, there's not a lot to choose from. In Tazewell, there are two local inns and a bed-and-breakfast. The next town over has a Red Roof Inn?"

He simply stared at me. I imagined in his mind I'd just asked if he'd like to take a bed in hell. I wasn't sympathetic as I was already in hell, knowing I would be traveling with him.

"None of those options will do."

I figured he'd say as much. "There is a Hilton or Residence Inn in Blacksburg."

"Blacksburg is an hour and a half away. It won't do, either."

Evidently, he wanted me to pull a Four Seasons out of my ass along with a nonstop flight while I was at it.

He pinched the bridge of his nose. "You know what? Just figure it out."

Right. *Just figure it out.* I loved it when my boss took the luxury of uttering those words, thus absolving himself of the problem. I prided myself on being savvy, but what the hell did he expect me to do?

"Also, I need all of the case files for the deposition to come with us."

Although everything was available electronically, I knew my boss preferred paper copies he could hold in his hands. "I'll prepare to ship them now."

"No shipping. They are too confidential, and I'm not taking chances."

"All of the files?" There were at least three full boxes. He couldn't mean to take them all.

"The important ones."

Which were? I could feel the heat rising in my neck. Did he mean the red folders which were confidential, or did he want the other witness testimony files, too? And if I couldn't ship them, then what the hell did he expect me to do with them? I was about to ask him these questions, but he held up a hand.

"I'm done talking details, Ms. Tate. Just get it done. I'm heading home. Email me the itinerary, and I'll see you tomorrow at the airport."

With his departing words, he walked out. I had to keep myself from chucking my stapler at him. But then I remembered his father had died. Although he might not be displaying grief the way I would've expected, it didn't mean he wasn't upset. Plus, I liked my bright pink stapler too much to subject it to the abuse.

Chapter Five

KENDALL

*I*t would take three trips to get all of the boxes from the street up to my second-story garden apartment in Torrance. Since I had no idea which files were the important ones and Liam had taken shipping off the table, I'd had little choice but to bring every single one of them. I'd taken my normal bus from the office to class, then a Lyft car back to the office so I could load up all of the files into boxes, and grab another Lyft ride home, cursing my boss the entire way. Nothing like having to ask one of the janitorial guys to help me to the curb with three heavy boxes after nine o'clock on a Thursday night. I still couldn't believe I was having to facilitate my boss's unreasonable request.

At least the driver had been nice enough to unload the car and take the boxes to the bottom of my apartment steps. Too bad the complex didn't have an elevator to help schlep them up. Which meant I was on my own.

When I opened the door, my roommate, Chloe, was studying sprawled on her futon sofa—which doubled as her bed. Our studio apartment wasn't much, but it was in a safe area and seven hundred square feet. Since rent wasn't cheap, we'd both compromised on a small studio instead of paying twice the rent for a two bedroom. It made things cozy, but considering all we both did was work, go to school, and sleep, it worked for us.

She glanced up, frowning. "What's with the box?"

"Files I have to take with me tomorrow. I have two more boxes downstairs." I flung my bag off my shoulder and set the box down by the door.

"I'll help you."

That's what I loved about her. She was always offering to help. I'd met her through a Craigslist ad, and we'd instantly hit it off. Not that it was hard as the girl was the nicest person on the planet. I was convinced all Canadians must be. We had a lot in common given that she, too, was a working student, helping out her family where she could. "I'd appreciate it."

"Wait. Where are you going tomorrow?" she asked as we proceeded down the two flights.

"To some small town in Virginia with my boss."

"You mean your hot boss?"

She'd seen his bio picture when I'd first started working for him. Chloe had quickly given him a nickname.

"Doesn't make him less of a dick, but yes. I'm traveling with him."

We each took a box up the steps. Her with a lot more ease than me. Chloe was in amazing shape, having danced most of her life. I didn't have a sporty or dancing bone in my body.

"You can be both hot and a dick. But you can't be both cute and a dick. Like, no one says, 'what a cute dick.' They wouldn't say 'handsome dick,' either. Of course I think he could probably be a sexy dick."

I rolled my eyes at Chloe's rambling. "There's nothing sexy about being a dick."

She shrugged. "I don't know. Hearing, 'Ms. Tate, get in

here and suck my sexy dick' might in fact be both a dick thing to say and sexy all at once."

I burst out laughing. "It seems you've given this some thought."

Once we were back in the apartment with the boxes, she flopped down again on her sofa. Like me, Chloe was a student at night, a full-time employee by day in an office, and a weekend moonlighter. She was the only person who knew about my part-time job on Friday and Saturday nights—at the same hip dance club where she worked as a waitress. I preferred working behind the bar.

"Considering I'm a virgin at twenty-one, I'd say my imagination is all I have," Chloe said.

It had been over a year for me, but I still wasn't about to think about my boss in that way. "Liam Davenport is more than a dick. He's an ass, too."

Chloe huffed out a long sigh. "I bet he has a sexy ass." Her romantic notions were hard not to smile at. As beautiful as she was, looking like a Grace Kelly throwback, it wasn't as though she couldn't have her pick of men, but she was focused on working and obtaining her degree in the next year as a graphic designer.

I was shaking my head while taking off my shoes. "You have a one-track mind. Maybe you need a boyfriend?"

"After graduation maybe. Currently my only free night is Sunday, which means I don't have the time. Plus, the last guy I dated was completely freaked out about me being a virgin. I do not want to have another awkward conversation. Wait. So, you're leaving tomorrow, meaning you're out of town for the weekend?" She got up to make tea.

I sighed. "Yep. And I'm billing the bastard overtime for it." The last thing I could afford was to lose both Friday and Saturday night paychecks from the club. "I'm not sure what

I'll do about Nan. I was supposed to go down Sunday to spend the day with her."

My grandmother looked forward to my weekly visit where we'd watch an episode or two of *Little House on the Prairie* and talk about our weeks. Frankly, without knowing how much longer she'd be on this earth, I hated not being able to spend the time with her.

"I'll go there for you on Sunday," Chloe said. "I like your grandmother."

"I can't ask you to give up your free time." As generous as it was for her to offer, Sundays truly were our only days off.

"You're not asking. I'm offering, so long as I can borrow your car. You'd do the same for me. I'll miss seeing your face at the club this weekend, though. It's not the same when one of us is gone."

No, it wasn't. I liked having a friend at the club. "Of course you can borrow my car. Use it for work, too." I didn't like the idea of her taking the bus at that hour. "You'll make sure to have Mikey walk you out to the garage?" I always worried when we got off and took up the bouncer's offers to see us out. But Chloe could be naive. What could I say? She was from Canada which meant she was way too trusting when it came to other people and their motives.

"Yes, Mom," she joked.

"Thank you. And thank you for spending time with my nan. You know you'll have to suffer through *Little House*."

She smiled. "I don't mind so long as it isn't the blind school fire episode. That episode scarred me."

I laughed because she was right. "I'm hoping this funeral is over by Thursday, so I'll be back by next weekend."

Her big blue eyes widened. "What funeral?"

After I filled her in on the details about my boss's father, she sat there with her mouth open. "You actually told him to pick up the fucking phone?"

"I did. I apologized later. He reminded me not to make a habit of calling him by his first name." I rolled my eyes at the memory. "At least he didn't fire me. By the way, can I borrow your large suitcase?"

"Yeah, of course. Wait. You have to take all of these files with you?"

I didn't see any other option. "Yeah. He didn't give me a choice considering he told me to deal with it." Again, it irked me. Most of the files had already been scanned in electronically.

She sighed. "At least tell me you're staying in a posh hotel for the week?"

"Hardly. Although it should be interesting to see my boss's face when he discovers what I booked."

NOT ONLY WAS Liam Davenport messing with my weekend plans by insisting I go on this trip with him, but he was also causing me some serious back pain. I had to lug my medium suitcase with my clothes plus the large suitcase borrowed from Chloe, full of about fifty pounds of case files. Of course, that didn't include my carry-on suitcase which had the most confidential files in it along with a change of clothes. While I was pulling my bags inch by inch through the hour-long check-in line for economy, I had no doubt my boss was probably in the first-class lounge enjoying a cocktail.

Bastard.

I winced at the internal thought. Maybe he was sad in his own robotic, icy, dickish way. Who wouldn't be after losing a parent?

Finally, after dropping off my two bags at the check-in counter and paying the extra bag fee, which I needed to remember to expense back to him, I got in the security line. Once through that, I put my shoes back on and glanced at the time. I was cutting it close. Frowning at my phone, I read the text message from Liam. He was formal even now.

"Ms. Tate. Where are you?"

"Coming up on the gate now."

Since he was tall, standing over six foot, it wasn't difficult to spot him. Of course he looked devastatingly handsome in his charcoal gray suit with a soft blue dress shirt. Damn, I hated when he wore the blue shirt. It only served to highlight his eyes of the same color. Not fair since the devil should really have black, beady eyes.

"Cutting it close, aren't you?" Those were his first words which he coupled with a frown of disapproval.

If I ever wondered if I could be attracted to my boss, he only needed to open his mouth to assure me that would never happen. "Yes, well, I had a load of bags to check, and it took a while." I blew my bangs out of my face, feeling as if I'd already sweat through my navy jersey knit dress. I regretted not wearing pants.

"How much stuff could you possibly need for a few days?"

"Most of it are the files you wanted to come with us."

Both his brows shot up. Then his face did this thing I could only describe as between a twitch and a cramp. Yep. Definitely a face cramp.

He reached up and pinched the bridge of his nose. "Please tell me you didn't put confidential case files in your suitcase, which is now being tossed around before getting shoved into the baggage compartment?"

I was tempted to say: *Fine. I won't tell you I indeed put*

the case files in a large suitcase to be gently handled and put safely in the belly of the plane.

I didn't often get defensive, but what did he expect? "Yes. I did. You didn't give me a lot of options when you said not to ship them."

"I'm sure if we looked at the statistics, we'd see airplane luggage is lost more often than FedEx packages. Jesus."

Huh. The vein on the side of his cheek was throbbing. Evidently, he was really pissed off about my choice to put the files in a suitcase. Hoping it might mitigate his annoyance, I offered up, "I have the red, confidential files in my carry-on."

"With you?" He glanced down at my small pink suitcase.

It would be what carry-on means. "Yes. In my carry-on."

"Then, what's in your other suitcase?"

"All the rest of the files."

This time there was no mistaking his throbbing temple. "You brought all of the files?"

"You said to bring the important ones. I had no idea which ones those were."

"You couldn't have simply asked me?"

Was he serious? Forget paper cuts or voodoo dolls, I was bound to snap. I only hoped the documentary on the Oxygen channel showed all of the compelling reasons why a nice girl from Orange County had absolutely lost it at LAX.

I was saved from my murderous thoughts when the loud-speaker announced first class was now boarding. It meant he could finally leave me alone.

"Fine. All the files are better than none. Let's hope they arrive without an issue. Let's go."

"Go where? They asked for first-class passengers to board."

"Yes, and that's us."

Was he high? "No, it's you."

His handsome face seemed to be in a perpetual state of confusion this morning. But now it showed complete shock. "You didn't book yourself in first class?"

"Of course I didn't." Why would I ever presume to do so on his dime?

His exasperated sigh was the response.

By now you'd think I'd be used to his sighs, but it still rubbed me the wrong way.

However, he shocked me with his next words. "Then, let's upgrade you."

"What? No." Frankly, I didn't want to sit next to him during the flight. Wasn't even worth the free cocktails and extra leg room. Besides that, it was way too expensive.

"Why the hell not?"

"Because there was a three-thousand-dollar difference between the tickets. I'm fine in coach."

Again with the vein-throbbing thing. It was telling how much he didn't care about the money when he walked up to the counter and asked the woman there, "Excuse me, do you have any room in first class, so I can move my assistant's seat assignment?"

The redhead took a look at him and smiled. I was sure a lot of women reacted similarly before they got a load of his non-charming personality. Or maybe it was just me who was lucky enough to evoke it.

"Sorry, sir. First class has checked in full. Do you wish to board now?"

"Yes. Fine." He sighed fully, pointing at my carry-on. "Make sure it doesn't leave your sight. I don't need to worry about another suitcase not arriving."

With his departing criticism, he turned and boarded.

Mentally I was flipping him off with both middle fingers.

Chapter Six

LIAM

orking hard was something on which I prided myself. I'd been doing it since I was old enough to have a paper route at age eleven. Therefore, now that I had the money, I rewarded myself with certain things like flying first class. But I wasn't a complete asshole to expect my assistant to fly coach on the same flight. The fact she'd assumed I was didn't sit well. Not well at all. Neither did the guilt I was experiencing. I briefly entertained the thought of insisting on switching seats with her, but I didn't think it would send the right message about who was the boss. Besides, I was still irritated about her checking her suitcase with an entire year's worth of work in it. Here was hoping they made it all the way to Virginia.

Who did that? Of course, I had to admit I hadn't given her a hell of a lot of other options when I cut her off as she'd been asking questions yesterday afternoon. I should've been more clear about only needing the red folders. Or I could've been more reasonable and let her simply ship them. The thought of her having lugged all of those files from the office made me feel like a complete ass. I should've been the one lugging them, not her with her small frame.

I smiled at the pretty blond flight attendant. She offered to take my jacket and then came back with a hot coffee and a Wall Street Journal. Although I might be tempted to drink a bourbon, I had to remember it was only seven o'clock in the morning. Something told me there would be plenty of liquid numbness in my near future in order to get through this next week. No need to start now, especially if I hoped to get some work done while in the air. Having the confidential files in Kendall's carry-on would help.

So I waited for her to board. And waited. And waited some more while the plane filled up, and she was not amongst the passengers walking in. I had a flicker of panic, thinking she might have changed her mind. Quit on the spot. I could swear sometimes she wanted to. I wouldn't blame her. No way I could constantly try to keep another human being organized the way she did.

Finally, her shiny brown hair came into sight. When she'd arrived at the gate, her long hair had been disheveled, but now it was back in a sleek ponytail. As soon as she caught my eye, her entire body stiffened. Not a smile. Not a word. Simply an awareness as if she braced herself for what I might say. It wasn't a reaction I prided myself on causing.

Deciding to stand up, I reached for her carry-on, thinking I was being helpful to find it a space up here with me and not make her handle it a moment longer. "I can put this up here with me."

She tugged it out of my grasp. "No. I have it. I'll keep an eye out for it."

I pulled it back. "No. I insist. They're my files, and I may need them during the flight."

"Fine." Her smile was tight, but she let me take the suit-

31

case, hurrying by to get to her seat, which appeared to be all the way in the back of the large plane.

Great. Even while trying to be a gentleman in putting the heavy suitcase above in my carry-on bin, I'd managed to be a dick.

———

ONCE WE REACHED CRUISING altitude and the fasten seatbelt sign went off, I used the lavatory and then came back to my seat. Time to get some work done. Opening up the overhead bin, I took out her small pink suitcase.

My window seat companion couldn't help commenting. "Nice color," the older man said with a comical smirk.

I didn't bother with a reply, not needing to give him an explanation. I simply unzipped the hard case and flipped open the lid. What greeted me had me completely freeze.

A low whistle came from the same man beside me. "Damn."

Damn, indeed. In the case were two thongs. One lacy bloodred. The other lacy black. Along with a black demi cup bra. There was also a small bag of toiletries in clear plastic and slacks and a blouse. An extra change of clothes. Made sense. However, they were on top of the folders I needed. And I was at a loss as to how to move my assistant's unmentionables without touching them.

"Now that's something I don't see much of at my age," the nosey old man offered up.

I could feel my face heating as I touched the fabric and tried in vain not to think about how it would look against Kendall's skin. I prayed I didn't do something worse like hold them up and sniff them. Jesus. How old was I? I'd seen women's underwear before. Plenty of it. But none tied to someone I didn't want to associate with sex. I moved the lingerie to the side and took out the labeled folder I needed.

After zipping up the offensive suitcase and putting it back up where it belonged, I took my seat again and tried to concentrate on work. But I couldn't. I was distracted. By lacy thongs and a sexy bra.

My irritation grew at the fact she'd put these items in here with my folders. I shifted in my seat, thinking about her conservative, yet designer, attire in the office—and what I now knew she wore beneath it.

Something told me it would be a long trip.

Chapter Seven

KENDALL

reat. I'd just handed my boss all the personal stuff in my carry-on. I'd been tempted to tug it back, but I knew the action would not only hold up the rest of the line, but it also would've made me look like a six-year-old. Here was hoping he didn't open it during the flight. Wasn't my fault I'd been obliged to stow his confidential files along with my extra change of clothes.

I still couldn't believe he'd had the audacity to be annoyed about me bringing all the paperwork with me. What the hell was I supposed to do with it if he wouldn't allow shipping? And he hadn't told me which files he'd need. Ugh. Infuriating man.

"You okay?" the guy next to me asked.

I imagined cursing under my breath was getting me some funny looks. "Yeah. Sorry. It's my first time flying."

My mind had been so wrapped up with my asshole boss, I'd forgotten this was my first time up—until those words came out of my mouth. But now I was focusing on the issue and starting to get anxious at the sound of the engines firing up. I was in the aisle seat, and the stranger talking to me was seated in the middle. The girl in the window seat was already asleep. I wished I could be as relaxed.

He was cute with an easy smile. A bit unkempt with his fuzzy beard and longer, curly hair, but probably in his early twenties like me.

"Don't worry. I fly a lot. And nothing has ever happened. Flying in a plane is safer than riding in cars on the highway."

"So I've heard," I murmured, changing my curses to a small prayer when the plane started moving.

"Except of course when a plane does crash, it's normally during takeoff or landing."

I side-eyed him for that bit of information, taking a deep breath when the pilot told the flight attendants to take their seats.

"Your final destination Chicago?"

"No. A layover on my way to Roanoke, Virginia."

"Good thing. I heard the windchill is minus twenty in the windy city."

"Degrees?" It was a stupid question, but when you lived your entire life in Southern California, the idea of negative numbers didn't compute.

He chuckled. "Yep. That's why I have my heavy parka and gloves."

Shit. I didn't own such things. "It's warmer in Virginia, though, right?"

"Oh, I'm sure it is."

I relaxed until his next words.

"Probably at least double digits. Although it is January, so the nights get colder."

Crap. I'd only brought the sweater I was wearing on the plane and packed a fleecy type light jacket, but I didn't own anything warmer. Between class and making last-minute travel plans, I hadn't focused on the fact it was going to be cold. In my defense, late January near the beach meant chilly mornings in the forties, warming up to the sixties most days.

"But no snow?"

He shrugged. "Never know this time of year. You heading into the mountains or near DC?"

"Mountains I think." I really wished I'd done more research on the town.

"Then, I hope you have some snow boots."

I doubted my secondhand three-inch-heel soft leather booties were what he meant.

THE CHILL of the air was evident the moment I deboarded the plane and walked along the sky ramp in Chicago. Holy crap. It almost took my breath, it was so dry and cold. I was in serious trouble. I'd have to figure out something when it came to getting warmer clothes, but for now I only had a short layover with barely enough time to get to the next flight.

I was surprised to see my boss waiting for me outside of the gate with my suitcase in hand.

"Have a good rest of your trip," my row mate said, touching my arm and giving me a smile as he walked past. He was cute in a backpacking-across-Europe-without-a-care-or-a-shower type of way.

"Thanks. You, too."

Liam was frowning. "We need to hurry. Our gate is some distance from here." He acted as if I was at the back of the plane just to irritate him.

I took my rolling carry-on from his hand and noticed he didn't argue this time.

He seemed to know his way around O'Hare, only pausing

a moment in front of the monitor screen, reading it quickly, before striding away.

I had trouble keeping up even in my flats. I'd have to add an entry to my notepad document.

Him tripping over his own feet and sprawling in the middle of the terminal floor. Yep. I wouldn't mind that scenario at all. But with my luck, he'd probably fall gracefully or get hurt and make me feel horrible.

We didn't stop until we were at the gate. Thankfully, they weren't boarding yet which gave me a few minutes. "I'll be back."

"Where are you going?"

"The ladies' room, and then to grab something to eat."

"They didn't feed you on the plane?"

"No, not in coach. I'll be back." I turned to go only to have him stop me with his words.

"While you're in the ladies' room, please remove your personal items from your suitcase."

"What?" I pivoted around so I could face him.

"Your clothes. Especially your, you know, underthings. They're on top of my folders."

Underthings? The term reminded me of something someone would say in *Little House on the Prairie*. I deadpanned him with a look that said *you can't be serious.* "Yes. They're on top of *your* folders in *my* suitcase. I have nowhere else to put my stuff even if I wanted to."

I had a small purse into which I wasn't shoving my clothes.

Annoyance was obvious in his expression. "Can you at least put them in a bag, so I don't have to touch them again?"

He'd touched my underwear? The thought sent a shiver down my body and heat straight to parts that had no business taking notice of such a thing. "You could always put the files in your carry-on." It didn't look big, but if he was so adamant not to see my personal belongings, he could simply take them.

"I don't have the room."

"Fine. I'll see what I can do." Frankly, I had to pee, and I didn't want to stand there discussing the thongs he'd touched. I wanted to point out that if I'd known about his insistence in keeping my suitcase with him, I would've put them in a bag to begin with.

I quickly went to the ladies' room before stopping at Hudson News. No down parkas here. Or snow boots. The store only sold snacks and souvenirs. And the Chicago Bears sweatshirts were way too expensive to consider buying. I'd have to see about buying a coat once we got to Virginia. I settled on a protein bar and a bottle of water. At least the purchase gave me a small plastic bag in which to put my underwear. Then I walked back to where the passengers were starting to line up at our gate for the flight to Roanoke.

Setting my suitcase down on an empty seat in the waiting area, I moved my water bottle and protein bar into my purse and unzipped the pink case.

"You're not doing that here, are you?" came the sexy voice of Satan.

Did he walk over here with the singular goal of criticizing me? "You asked me to put my stuff in a bag."

"Yes. In the ladies' room where it's private."

I glanced up in time to witness his neck turning red. I could only imagine what he'd think to see me bartending at the racy dance club every weekend. Had the man never been around a thong? I pitied the woman who had the disappoint-ment of such a prude in the bedroom.

"It isn't as if I intended to hold them up and announce it."

"Thank God for small favors."

The fact his tone was so snobby was the only explanation for what I did next. I slowly removed my red thong and leisurely took the time to fold it before putting it into the plastic bag. I did the same thing for the black one. Lastly came my bra, which I took the time to fold in two before carefully placing it in the bag next to the other two items, and into my carry-on.

"You can't just keep the bag with you?"

If there was ever a look for *what the actual fuck*, I was giving it to him now.

"I'm not carrying a plastic bag of my underwear on the plane. It won't fit in my purse, and here, I'll even put it under the files."

"Fine. You can just get the folders for me once we're on the plane. We'll be seated next to each other."

"What do you mean we're seated next to each other?"

"I upgraded you to first class. You're sitting next to me."

Oh, fucking goodie.

Chapter Eight

LIAM

"**How** can the SUV you rented not have four-wheel drive?" I posed this question to Kendall at the rental car counter. I couldn't believe she hadn't rented a four-wheel drive.

"I didn't know to ask the question about it being four-wheel drive. Not like you told me it was winter here."

My mouth almost fell open. "It's the end of January. Do I need to educate you on the seasons?"

She crossed her arms, hugging herself. "I've never traveled outside of Southern California."

"Never?"

"Well, technically I drove to Vegas one time, but it was warm there, too."

A thought kicked in. "Was this your first time on an airplane?"

Her chin went up a notch. "Yes."

I'd just assumed she was a nervous flier and tried not to notice her gripping the armrest or closing her eyes when we took off and landed on the second leg from Chicago. Hell, during the entire flight I'd tried to ignore her—to no avail. I was way too tuned into her movements, soft sighs, and the damn smell of strawberry gloss.

I turned toward the guy at the counter. "Do you have any four-wheel drive vehicles available?" Although there was no snow currently, it didn't mean there wouldn't be. Especially two hours away, further into the mountains.

"Unfortunately, we're running low on inventory, but we do have a pickup truck. You may want to put some weight back in the bed, though. Sand bags or wood normally works for when you don't have it in four-wheel drive."

The rules of snow driving in a truck were all coming back to me. I pinched the bridge of my nose. "We'll take it. Does it have a club cab at least?" Frankly, I didn't want to put the suitcases with all of my precious files in the back of a truck exposed to the elements.

"Sure does. And heated seats for the lady." The guy smiled at Kendall, and I noticed she returned it.

Having never been on the receiving end of one of her genuine smiles, I felt an unexpected pang of jealousy. Weird.

As we got into the Dodge Ram four-wheel drive pickup truck, me in the driver's seat while her in the passenger, I noticed for the second time she was shivering. "Do you have a jacket in your suitcase I can grab you?" I'd already taken my winter coat out of my luggage. I put on the heat, but even so, it was below freezing outside, and the temperature would only drop overnight.

"No."

"No, you don't want me to get it for you, or no, you don't have one?" If she hadn't thought of a four-wheel drive or what winter was like outside of Southern California, she might not be prepared with her clothing.

"I'll go by a store tomorrow to get a warmer one."

"Unless you're planning to get it at the Dollar Store or Food Lion, you're out of luck once we get to town."

She blew out a breath. "Could I trouble you to stop at a Walmart or Target, then, while we're here in Roanoke?"

"You're okay with shopping at Walmart?"

"What's wrong with Walmart?" Her tone was defensive.

"I didn't say anything was wrong with it, but you're sitting there in designer clothes and shoes, so you'll have to excuse me if I'm surprised you're okay with shopping at Target or Walmart."

Her lips flattened into a scowl as if she was biting her tongue.

"It's none of my business." I typed into the GPS app on my phone, hating to admit I'd noticed her clothing. "Looks like Walmart is closest."

"Fine. Thank you."

PATIENCE WAS NOT one of my better traits. So waiting on my assistant in the parking lot of Walmart, knowing we still had a two-hour drive to go, put me in a mood. I felt annoyed even though she'd only been gone twenty minutes so far, and I'd been busy part of that time myself—purchasing several bundles of wood to weigh down the back of the truck. There was nothing worse than a pickup with no weight in the back on a slippery road.

I was perusing the email on my phone when Kendall came out. She looked as though she'd been swallowed by the ugliest, puffiest coat known to man.

I climbed out to come around and take her shopping bags. "What the hell is that?" I was sure even the Army would reject this particular shade of green.

She opened her door while I put her bags in the back. "It's the only winter coat they had in my size."

"Being your size is debatable." It was way too big. "Did you get boots, too?"

"Yeah, they're in the bag. Don't worry. Those are a wonderful lavender color with sparkles."

I couldn't help the chuckle. And when she attempted to climb into the truck in her cocoon of a coat, I nearly doubled over with laughter. Because she couldn't bend her body in order to do it. It was a big puffy straitjacket. And she was like a green caterpillar trying to bend and wiggle her way in. I wiped my eyes as I watched her attempt it twice.

Finally, she unsnapped the front and jumped in with a huff. She sat there with her hands on her lap. "If you're quite through laughing at me, we can go now. Thank you."

I was still grinning when I got back into the driver's side. God, I'd needed that. Humor had been in short supply lately for sure.

"Did you get gloves?"

"Yes, and a scarf and some ear thingies. All are basic black, thank God."

We got on the freeway in silence until I asked the question: "You really brought all of the case files?"

"Yep. All fifty pounds of them."

The suitcase had seemed rather heavy when I'd lifted it up into the truck. Once again I kicked myself for not communicating better about which folders I'd needed. "What about a scanner and printer? The hotel has one?"

"It says it does. Also wireless internet."

"Good. I realize it's been a long day, but I have a document I need some edits done on once we arrive."

"Tonight?"

"You'll get the overtime." I fought the guilt about making

her work as soon as we arrived. But in my defense, it was in fact a workday, and we'd spent most of it traveling. I had at least a dozen more documents to go through. Every minute counted. That was one of the reasons I'd brought her with me.

If I wasn't mistaken, she was rolling her eyes in the darkened cab of the truck. "I figured you'd want to go over to your mother's house once we arrived."

"You figured wrong. Tomorrow is soon enough."

She gave me a side-eye full of judgment. Again, I could've explained how I wasn't affected by my father's death the way most sons would be, but I chose to stay quiet. It wasn't her business.

"Are there any restaurants in your town?"

She'd barely touched her lunch on the plane. Now I wondered if it was because she'd been anxious about flying. "Why? Are you hungry?"

"I'm okay for now, but I will be."

I would be, too. "I think there's a McDonald's and Hardees if you want fast food. But I'm not sure. It's been awhile since I've been home." Like over a decade.

"When was the last time?"

"Why does it matter?" I regretted my harsh tone as soon as the words left my mouth.

She simply sighed and gazed out the window, deciding to ignore me.

I didn't like speaking about my past. And I sure as hell didn't want to do so with my assistant, a girl I had already vowed not to get involved with. The fact I'd already touched her panties, was taking her to my hometown, and was therefore involving her in my personal business wasn't sitting well. Perhaps it had been a mistake to bring her after all.

Two hours later as she guided me to our lodging, I absolutely knew it had been a mistake.

Chapter Nine

KENDALL

···········

My temper was simmering. I'd asked an innocent question about the last time he'd been home and he'd reminded me there was no off duty for his asshole-ness. And to think we'd established some sort of human interaction when he'd helped me with my bags and laughed out loud at my ridiculous coat. Foolishly, I'd thought I was witnessing a glimmer of a different side to him. Let it be a lesson. Once a dick, always a dick. No matter how cute of a package it was part of.

I'd be lucky if I didn't murder my boss by the end of the week. Then again, I looked terrible in orange and was certain I wouldn't like prison. Such a shame.

The navigation on my phone took us into town, four blocks off of Main Street to the two-story house I'd rented through Airbnb. I'd texted the owner we were on our way, so she was there on the front porch to greet us.

"What is this?" Liam asked, once we pulled into the narrow driveway in front of the house.

"Where we'll be staying. Let me jump out and get the

keys from Shirley." Easier said than done because my coat restricted my movement, even when unsnapped. But I managed to somewhat roll out. The moment I was outside of the warm truck, the cold took my breath away. Jesus. How did people live in this type of weather?

"Hey there. I'm Shirley. You must be Kendall," the older woman greeted. She was about my mom's age, completely bundled up in a cute black coat with a matching hat and boots. Evidently cold weather could produce fashion. Just not for me.

"I am. Thanks for meeting us. We ran a bit later than we thought we would."

"It's no problem. I hope you and your boyfriend will be comfortable here for the week."

"He's not my boyfriend," I said at the same time the dick-head said, "I'm not her boyfriend."

Shirley tugged on her ear. "All righty. Well, let me show you the place."

I was about to step inside to follow her when my elbow was tugged back, and Liam's hot breath was in my ear. "Please tell me this is not what you booked. A house?"

I was in no mood to deal with his dissatisfaction. Especially in front of Shirley. "Yes. It is."

"Um, y'all still with me?" Shirley asked from inside.

"Yep, we're here." I quickly went inside, not waiting to see if he followed.

Thankfully, the online pictures had done the house justice. It was both modern and clean.

"Here is the living room. Woodstove will keep you plenty warm at night in this main room—wood is out back, but feel free to use the electric heat in the bedrooms. Kitchen is fully functioning. Go ahead and use anything left behind. There's a cabinet full of spices, as well as condiments in the fridge. Down this hall is the master bedroom with the master bath. Has a nice new soaking tub put in with the renovation last year."

I couldn't wait to sink into it. We followed her silently through the small but cozy home. "Up these stairs are two more bedrooms. One with a queen bed, the other with a twin which doubles as the office."

"With internet, a scanner, and a printer?" Liam inquired.

"Yes, indeedy. There's also a full bathroom up here. Linens are in the closets, but I did take the liberty of making up the beds. You'll wanna go by the Food Lion to get groceries, I imagine. Also, we may be getting snow later this week, so best to stock up before then. But remember it closes at nine every night but Sunday, when it closes at eight."

We certainly weren't in LA any longer with those early hours. "Thank you, Shirley."

As soon as the tour was completed and the front door closed with Shirley's departure, Liam rounded on me. "We are not staying here."

"Fine. I'll get my things from the truck, and you can go stay wherever you want." I'd reached max capacity in trying to accommodate his unrealistic expectations.

"What?" He was looking at me like I was crazy.

"If you're so displeased with the house, then you can leave me here and find a different place to stay." Although I couldn't believe the words were coming out of my mouth, I realized there was no stopping this runaway train. I was not *Miss Understanding* at this point. Instead I was *Miss Over It*.

"But it's your job."

"Correction. It *was* my job. But I was off the clock hours ago. So unless you want a two-star motel with less-than-favorable reviews, four of which included stories of bedbugs, or you'd rather stay at a bed-and-breakfast which only had one room available with a twin bed, or you'd prefer to stay ninety minutes away in Blacksburg, this is your only option. I'm cold. I'm hungry, and I'm tired, not to mention sore from lugging your stupid files in my suitcase. And if I don't get dinner soon, I'm likely to lose my shit. I don't do well when I'm hungry. Not well at all. So either take me to the Food Lion so I can get something to cook, or help me get my luggage out of the truck, so you can go find someplace else to stay."

His jaw ticked, but he must've realized it was not wise to argue with a hangry woman.

"How will you get to the store if I leave you here?"

I shrugged. "I don't know. Lyft. Uber."

He shook his head. "You aren't likely to find either in this small town."

I took out my phone as if making a point in bringing up the Uber app. "You haven't been home in how long? Oh, right, you won't tell me. Anyhow, here we go. I'm booking one now. Let me type in the Food Lion and boom. See, he'll be here in, er, twenty-seven minutes." Crap.

A smirk played on his lips. The type that made me want to strangle him with my ugly green puffy coat. We were in a standoff, neither one of us moving. Finally, he relented.

"Let's go to the grocery store, Kendall. We'll stay here at least for tonight and talk about other options in the morning."

Huh, it was the very first time he'd called me by my first name. Progress, maybe?

LIAM OPTED to take a call from the truck while I got a cart

and started shopping. Since he'd given me his Visa card, an unexpected boon, I fully intended to use it. I absolutely loved to cook. Unfortunately, the options were somewhat limited in the small store, but thirty minutes later I'd found everything I needed for dinner tonight and meals for tomorrow. Guaranteed, though, he'd have something to say once he saw how many groceries I'd bought. But he hadn't fired me so far. What was one more strike against me?

"How many people did you shop for?" he asked, getting out of the truck to help me with the bags.

"Shirley said it may snow. So I had to get more than I planned just in case."

"In case of what?"

"I have no clue. But I once remember watching the national news about a big snowstorm where people were stocking up on bread, water, milk, and toilet paper. Since I've never been in snow, I wasn't sure what to do."

Hell, I'd even bought things for baking. I hoped I'd have some time over the weekend at least.

He simply sighed, taking the groceries and putting them into the back. "I should probably grab some things."

"Like what?"

"Coffee. Food stuff."

"Have you finally realized the house is the best option in town?"

Jaw tick. "It's fine."

Probably as close to a yes as I would get. "I bought you coffee. I also got you eggs for your omelets along with veggies to put in them." He always ordered the same thing every morning, making it easy to know what he wanted.

"You do realize those things are already cooked from the downstairs cafeteria when you get them for me at the office, don't you?"

Although I had no issue cooking an omelet for him, I wasn't at a point where I was willing to tell him that. "I also bought you protein bars, yogurts, energy drinks, and different kinds of nuts."

I could only hope at least one of those things would put him in a better mood.

Chapter Ten

LIAM

$\mathcal{A}$ good assistant knew all of the things Kendall had rattled off. After all, she brought me breakfast and lunch most days from upstairs in the on-site cafeteria. I rarely ate anywhere but at my desk because I was constantly working. Yet hearing her recite all of my food preferences left me feeling unnerved. But not any more than the thought of us sharing a house.

There was something very intimate about doing so, and I didn't like it. Not one bit. But once again, she'd raised the point of me not giving her many options. Honestly, I'd resigned myself to having to stay in one of the cheap motels in town, but she'd surprised me with her resourcefulness. Even more, she'd shocked me by basically telling me I could go to hell if I didn't choose to stay here. Her little outburst was way too much of a turn-on to be comfortable.

Once we were both inside the truck, I started it up and pulled out of the parking lot onto the main road. The house wasn't too bad, I thought, pulling into the driveway. It was only a few miles from my mother's home, and if it had a functioning office, that would be better than working in a hotel room. I had to give Kendall credit.

"You sure you don't want to head over to your mom's tonight? I can unload everything and get your office ready."

Considering her irritation with me earlier, I was humbled she'd offer. "I'm sure." Although guilt gnawed at me for not driving over there right away, I fought it. I needed another night before I could see my mother and talk about my father.

"Okay. So I'll start unpacking the groceries, move my stuff upstairs to the bedroom, and set up the office equipment."

"No. I'll take the room upstairs. It will be easier for me with the office up there. You can have the master." Perhaps ceding her the bigger bedroom would alleviate some of my guilt for being a dick to her. Unfortunately, I could already picture her soaking in the tub. It was not a good professional image to have in my mind.

I decided to make myself useful and finish bringing everything in.

While Kendall took her things into the master bedroom, I started taking the folders out of the large suitcase in order to organize them. Although there were electronic copies of everything, having the actual copies here made me feel better. I was old-fashioned when it came to using paper and a reliable highlighter. Even if I only needed the folders she'd brought in her carry-on, I was more comfortable having everything here at my fingertips.

"I could've done that."

I glanced up from where I was kneeling on the floor putting the files into boxes.

She'd changed her clothing. Now in yoga pants and a sweatshirt, she'd put her hair up.

I was speechless. I'd never seen her outside of the office

or so casual and was taken aback by how naturally beautiful she was.

"It's fine," I told her. Unloading the files was the least I could do after making her haul them here. "At least there was no underwear on top of these files."

She rolled her eyes. "Oh, yeah, I'm sure it traumatized you to see a woman's thongs."

While Kendall bustled around the house, I busied myself upstairs in the office. I got my laptop signed on to the Wi-Fi and managed to hook it up to the printer. Luckily, there were simple directions for doing both tasks. I'd just finished marking up a document I needed her to make edits to when she popped her head in.

"Dinner is ready."

"You didn't have to cook." She might be my assistant, and her presence here was part of a work trip, as far as she was concerned, but she didn't have to be my cook and house-keeper, too. Even I wasn't ass enough to assume that.

"I wanted to. Oh, you have the edits ready. My laptop is set up downstairs, so bring them down."

It was after nine. I should tell her she could leave them until morning. But I couldn't because I needed to work tonight. Needed to get back the balance tipped by yesterday's phone call from my mother. Work is what soothed me. Work is what reminded me what my priority was. What I was good at. I'd busted my ass to get out of town, go to college, and achieve what I had.

When I got downstairs, I expected pizza or maybe a frozen entrée heated in the oven. I hadn't expected a gourmet meal. "You cooked this?" There was salmon, beans, and a green salad on the small, round dining table. She'd set the table with plates and silverware.

"Yep. It's pesto salmon, sautéed green beans with a bit of

onion and bacon, and a salad with ranch dressing. I went low carb as it seems to be what you do most often."

Panic suddenly seized me. The house. The dinner. Her underwear on top of my files. Her knowledge of everything about me. Was she trying to catch herself a husband by playing house? Unfortunately, she wouldn't be the first young woman in a law firm with the idea of landing a rich husband. "I think we need to talk."

She quirked her head to the side. "About what?"

How could I possibly say this without sounding like a complete asshole? For all I knew, she had a legitimate crush on me and wasn't trying to be manipulative. "Look. This week I needed you here to help me be able to work while balancing my personal shit. But the house and dinner— I don't want to give you the wrong idea. I mean you're my assistant. I'm your boss."

She stood there with her brown eyes wide, before understanding seemed to settle in. "Are you trying to let me down easy because you think"—she motioned between us—"I'm pursuing some sort of relationship with you?"

"It certainly appears that way." But maybe putting her on the spot was causing her to backtrack. Oh shit, what if there were tears? I didn't do well with crying women. Not well at all.

But much to my shock, she simply started laughing. We're talking the kind of laughter that caused her to brace herself against the table and grab her side. "Oh my God. You thought— Wow. Oh, Jesus. It's too much." She was shaking her head and went to grab a drink out of the refrigerator.

If ever my ego had taken a hit, this was a direct one. "Okay. Fine, you've made your point. But in my defense, you got this house, and the underwear, and freaked me out with this meal."

She was still grinning. "I got this house because you are impossible to please with your *just figure it out, Ms. Tate* when I told you about the motel options."

I didn't care for the way she did my impression. I sounded like a real jerk.

"As for dinner, I grew up cooking, and I take classes whenever I can. And you gave me your Visa, which was basically a free pass to buy and cook what I wanted. And I'm not going to talk about the thongs in the suitcase. My embarrassment equaled yours, I'm sure. But rest assured and believe me when I say you are soooo not my type."

There were a lot of o's in so. "That's a relief, then."

With my irrational panic attack having subsided, and my embarrassment maxed out, I took a seat and started eating my food. "So, you go to culinary school?"

"No. I'm studying for my bachelor's degree in business administration and take cooking classes when I can."

Damn, the green beans were the best thing ever. And the salmon divine. I couldn't remember the last time I'd had a home-cooked meal. "When do you go to school?"

"At night."

"After work?"

"Yep. Monday through Thursday."

Which meant she was missing class in addition to everything else. Great. Add it to the list of how I'd been a selfish prick in dragging her here.

"Next week is winter break, so it was good timing for travel, I suppose."

What a relief. "Business administration is what you hope to do?"

"I wouldn't go that far, but it looks good on a resumé."

I studied her. "And the cooking classes are for fun?"

"Yeah. If I had my way, I'd do cooking classes full-time."

"Why don't you?"

She gave me a small smile. "Maybe someday, but for now I need to get a bachelor's degree."

I wanted to ask if she intended to search for another job since her true passion was cooking. But I tamped down on the urge. I'd already found out more about her in the last few hours than I'd known in the four months she'd worked for me.

"Are you truly okay with staying here at the house? Or do I need to make a reservation at the two-and-one-half-star motel with the reputation for bedbugs?" she asked.

Taking a look around the house, I realized it was clean, homey, and spacious. "I guess this will do. But I don't want the wrong impression to get around the office because we shared a house."

Again with the eye roll. "Yeah, because nothing improper could possibly happen in a hotel."

She had a point.

"I have no intention of advertising our accommodations if you're worried about that part. And if you're still concerned about the other, as previously established, you're not my type."

If I heard those words one more time, I was likely to ask something stupid like what was her type.

"Given the limited options in town, this place looked the cleanest," she said. "And it had an office. Did you get on the Wi-Fi?"

"I did. And the printer seems to be working." I finished up my dinner, washed it down with water, before standing up. I should offer to do the dishes since she went to the trouble of cooking.

As if she read my mind, she spoke first. "Leave them. I'll do the edits real quick and do the dishes later."

"I can do them later."

"You're billing on a case. And I'm charging overtime, don't you worry."

Chapter Eleven

KENDALL

My muscles relaxed the moment I eased into the hot water. My apartment only had a shower, so soaking in a bubble bath was a luxury I hadn't enjoyed in quite a while. With a couple drops of the lavender bubble bath I'd found under the sink left from the last occupant, I was finally winding down from the weirdest day in the history of strange days.

I chuckled as I remembered the expression on my boss's face when he'd thought I was turning into Suzie Homemaker in the hopes of catching myself a husband. I don't think I'd ever laughed so hard. If only he knew how many times over the last four months I'd written in my notepad document of ways to have him suffer. He hadn't a clue. Instead, his expression when I'd said he wasn't my type had been almost offended. To be honest, he was my type in all ways physical —I couldn't deny how handsome he was. But everything else was a deal-breaker. He was too uptight, too controlling, and way too much of an ass.

But today, I had to admit that in addition to his normal dickish behavior, I'd also seen glimpses of a gentleman. He'd taken my luggage to load it up into the truck. He'd gotten out of the truck to take the grocery bags and brought them in the house. He'd even offered to do the dishes. Well, sort of. He'd offered to have them sit until later. But one thing I couldn't stand was a dirty kitchen. It was a pet peeve of mine, so I'd taken on the task myself.

God, I was tired. And as soon as I stepped out of the bathroom, I was also a bit chilly. I should've purchased a pair of flannel pajamas while at Walmart tonight. But I'd already spent enough money on winter gear I wouldn't need after this week. I opted to dress in my long-sleeved UCLA shirt along with my yoga pants.

I decided to go through the house in order to ensure it was locked up before I went to sleep. I didn't expect to see Liam at the kitchen table.

His head was in his hands. His laptop to the side, obviously not something he was looking at. Shit. He almost appeared vulnerable.

Enough for me to make a mistake in asking, "Are you okay?"

He instantly stiffened and sat up. "Fine. Go to bed, Ms. Tate. Tomorrow will be a long day."

We were back to Ms. Tate and his dismissive tone. It was just as well, I supposed. It was becoming apparent we weren't meant to be on friendly terms. I turned without saying another word and went back to my bedroom.

The next morning, my alarm went off way too early. I think my body was still on California time and hadn't yet adjusted to the three-hour time difference. But it was seven o'clock Virginia time, which meant I should probably start the day. Especially since I didn't know what it held. As I hopped out of bed, I realized how cold it was even with the bedroom heater on.

I made quick work out of washing my face, brushing my teeth, and dressing. I wasn't quite sure what attire was called for on a working weekend, so I settled on slacks and a blouse, covered by my cashmere sweater. Looking at myself in the full-length mirror, I realized I managed to appear fashionable. I even had my boss thinking I never shopped at places like Walmart or Target. But the fact was most of my clothing was secondhand. It's what I needed to do in order to get my wardrobe to an acceptable level for my corporate job.

As I walked out to the kitchen, I didn't see anything out of place. Maybe Liam wasn't up yet. Picturing him asleep upstairs was unsettling. Guess he was right about the house having a different vibe than a hotel where we'd be in distinctly separate rooms. But damn if I'd admit it to him. I went about starting the coffee first. Then, as I was whisking up eggs with some milk, I heard the front door shut.

Because of the open layout from the kitchen to the living room, I was able to see him there in the foyer, bent at the waist. He was wearing basketball shorts, a sweatshirt, and running shoes. He appeared to be catching his breath before standing up and lifting his sweatshirt to wipe the perspiration from his forehead.

Holy shit.

My boss had a six-pack.

And I was staring at it.

I tore my hungry gaze away just as he realized I was there.

"Good morning," I greeted, busying myself with the eggs and trying to calm my pulse from the peek of his delicious body. Damn. I would've preferred if he'd been soft around the middle. It would've been karma for being a dick. But no. He had to have a hot body, too.

"Morning."

"I have coffee if you want it. But I'll let you pour it so you don't think I'm penning little hearts next to your name in my head." Could I help it if I messed with him a little? What could I say? He was starting to bring out my sassy side.

"I think you made the point of me not being your type very clear last night," he retorted before walking over to take a mug and pour his coffee.

"Cream is in the fridge and sugar is next to the pot." Yeah, so I knew how the man liked his coffee. Most assistants did.

"I grabbed a protein bar, so no need to make me eggs."

Damn. I'd already mixed six of them. Twice as many as I'd eat. "Okay." I'd make an extra omelet and put it in the fridge for later. Maybe I'd eat it for lunch.

Putting the mushrooms, onions, and peppers in the pan with some butter, I sautéed them slightly. I then added the egg mixture, letting it firm up on all sides before flipping it over with a flip of my wrist.

"I always wondered how people do that. With pancakes and omelets." The fact he'd stayed, standing there to observe me, was curious.

"It's all in the wrist. Of course, it took many ruined versions which turned into scrambled eggs before I perfected it."

He didn't respond. Only watched while I put the cheese in it and folded it over before then sliding it onto a plate.

I went about making a repeat.

"I said I don't want one."

"I heard you, but I'd already made enough for two. So I'll make the extra and keep it for later."

He sighed. "If it'll go to waste, I guess I'll eat it."

I tried not to roll my eyes this time around. Whatever. As much as I sought approval with my food creations, expecting to get such from this man was a losing battle. "Help yourself, then."

We ate in silence at the kitchen table. He didn't offer a word. Not about how good the food was. Not what we were doing for the day. Nothing. It was beyond awkward. Finally, I'd had enough of the silent treatment.

"What's on the agenda today?"

"I have five pages of a briefing for you to edit. Then I need to get the Myers bill out the door. Also, I need you to set up a call with Mr. Lambert over at Johnson and Johnson for next week." He suddenly paused while I was taking a bite. "Do you need to get your notepad to write these things down?"

It was a good thing my omelet was so good; otherwise, I'd be flinging my eggs at him for thinking I couldn't keep a mental list. "Nope. I got it."

His brow arched as if he was skeptical. Forget the eggs. I wanted to fork him. And I meant it in the most unsexual way possible.

He sipped his coffee with practiced manners. I bet the guy didn't slurp anything. I bet sex with him was clinical and boring.

Jesus. Where had that thought come from? Luckily, he snapped it with his next words.

"I need to take the truck for the morning but will return this afternoon."

At least he was finally seeing his mother. "Take your time."

"I will." Suddenly he was up rinsing his plate and then up the stairs. No offers to wash the dishes today.

Chapter Twelve

LIAM

*D*espite knowing I'd be overdressed for seeing my mother, I donned my suit and tie. Perhaps it was a sort of armor, reminding me I was a successful partner in a firm at which most lawyers would give their right arm to be hired. I made more money a quarter than most houses cost here in my hometown.

I'd made something of myself in leaving this town. The fact I'd returned didn't mean anything other than I'd chosen to be here in order to support my mother. The suit also reminded me that this house situation with Kendall needed to remain purely professional. I'd meant to skip her breakfast this morning in order to gain some equilibrium in dealing with her, but the moment I'd eyed the omelet she'd been making, my mouth had started to water.

I left the house without saying goodbye. Another dick move to add to the list when it came to my assistant. Hell, I cringed now to think of my reaction last night when she'd asked if I was all right. I'd been way too vulnerable to talk to her about any of it. It wasn't a side I wanted anyone to see, least of all someone who worked for me.

My plan this morning had been to run, shower, change, and be out of the house without seeing her. Instead, I'd sat down to breakfast with her, eating the best omelet I'd ever tasted and thinking about her in a way that left me very uncomfortable. There was a reason I'd worked so hard to put up barriers between us. The last thing I needed was for this one week to unravel it all.

Being behind the wheel of a pickup truck made me nostalgic for my youth. Every boy in town had driven one. Including me. Of course mine had been a beat-up Chevy my grandfather had passed down, but it had been all mine. He'd been the only positive male influence in my life growing up. Which reminded me. I needed to be sure to go by his and my grandmother's gravesites in the local cemetery while in town.

Pulling up in my mother's driveway was bittersweet. My childhood brick, two-story home appeared unchanged. I smiled the moment my sister came out of the front door. She had one kid on her hip and the other tugging on her leg. Shit. The girls were how old again?

"Hi, Allison," I greeted, getting out of the truck and walking up to the door.

She was in jeans and a sweater, her blond hair up in a messy bun. "Hi yourself, little brother. Don't you look over-dressed."

Leave it to her to bust my chops. "I live in suits almost daily."

"Are they dry-cleanable?"

"Yes. Of course. Why?"

She thrust the toddler girl to me. "Good. You remember little Mavis. She's two now, but last you saw her she was only a year old. And, Chelsea, say hello to your uncle Liam. She's four now, by the way."

Right. I could feel my blush at not being able to

remember any of this. Both girls had my sister's genes with their big blue eyes and warm smiles.

"Hi, Uncle Liam. Did you know that Grandpa died?" Chelsea asked.

"Yes, I did. But I wasn't aware you called him Grandpa." Given that my sister was two years older, she remembered the horrible times from our childhood even more than I did. So I was surprised she'd given our deadbeat dad the honor of being called Grandpa.

She sighed long and loud. "It's Mom's doing. Not mine. What do I say at this point when she tells the girls to call him that?"

Nothing, most likely. My mother had a tendency to worry more about how things appeared than the reality. Nothing like rewriting history one *Grandpa* at a time.

"Sorry, I shouldn't have said anything." They were kids, and it wasn't my business. I smiled at my youngest niece. "I think Uncle Liam already needs a drink."

My sister snorted. "You and me both. Come on in. Hoping we can go today and meet with the funeral home."

It was fine by me. The sooner we got the arrangements settled, the better.

Stepping into the house was like traveling back in time. The same pillows on the floral sofa, the familiar pictures on the mantle of my sister and me as kids, the same smell bringing back all the memories of my childhood. Hell, even the same outdated wallpaper; it was faded but still intact.

Once I'd made partner, I'd offered to move my mom into a new house and out of this town, but she'd insisted on staying. Part of me wondered if it had been so my father would know exactly where to find her. As if she'd decided to stay in this house, waiting on him this entire time.

My mother came out of the kitchen, immediately smiling

when she saw me. "Oh, my darling boy. You're home." She hurried toward me and hugged me tight, her five-foot-five frame only coming up to my chest. It was in this moment I knew I'd done the right thing in being here.

Until her sobs started. If ever I was at a loss, it was with tears. I tried to comfort her the best I could, with my sister slinking out of the room to keep from getting nominated to step in.

"It's okay, Mom." What else could I say? I didn't share her grief, and I certainly didn't know how to fake it, either.

Finally, the crying abated. "Why don't we sit on the sofa?"

The first thing I noticed, despite her reddened, puffy eyes, was how much better she looked than a year ago when I'd last seen her. Her brown hair was newly highlighted. Her nails were done. I insisted on paying her taxes and any other large bills, but it was like pulling teeth to get her to spend anything on herself. Evidently, that had changed recently.

"Thank you for coming home, Liam. I know this isn't easy."

It was the understatement of the century. "I'm here for you, Mom."

She smiled, straightening my tie. "And so overdressed."

"It's what I wear most days."

"I know, and you look so handsome. Do you want some breakfast?"

"No, thanks. I already ate." Once again, my mind flipped back to Kendall. But I forced it back to my mom and what we needed to accomplish today.

By NOON I had a raging headache. It was made worse by the fact the funeral couldn't be held until Thursday. It was only five days away, but I'd hoped for something sooner that would enable me to fly back earlier. Spending almost a week here would be torture.

"Where are you staying?" my sister asked me when I helped her carry the girls out to her SUV to get them loaded up. They'd been troopers today, but it was clear they were ready for their naps by the way they kept rubbing their eyes.

"At a house in town. It's an Airbnb rental."

She quirked a brow. "Anything is better than the motels, I suppose. You're welcome to stay with us. I promise I won't put you on diaper duty."

Staying with two kids under the age of four sounded like a fresh hell. "No, thanks. We're comfortable at the house."

I realized my mistake as soon as her brows shot up. "We? Did you bring someone with you?"

"Shhh." I had to shush her before my mother heard. She was standing on the front porch smiling at us. "I had to bring my assistant."

Allison scoffed. "You dragged your assistant all the way to your hometown from LA? You expect me to buy that?"

"I don't care what you buy. It's the truth. I have a deposition in two weeks, and I need her help."

"Fine. Fine. What's the address?"

"Why, so you can show up out of the blue? Nope. Not happening."

She didn't bother to deny her nosiness. "You got me. Is it at least nice? It isn't too run-down, is it?"

Considering a lot of the houses in town had seen better days, I didn't blame her for asking. "It's fine. Newly remodeled with a fully functioning office. That's all I care about."

"Good. So, I guess I'll meet you at Mom's house tomorrow, and we'll go do the headstone thing."

"Yep." I'd rather stab myself in the eye with a dull butter knife, but again, my mother had asked me to go. I'd have to find a way to suck it up.

"It's nice of you to offer to pay for everything."

"It's not a problem." My mother was on a fixed retirement and social security income. And my sister was a stay-at-home mom with two children and a husband who worked hard in middle management. I knew money was tight. The last thing either of them needed was a twelve-thousand-dollar funeral expense. Although I hated the idea of paying for a man who hadn't given one dime toward child support, I supposed in a way it was the ultimate fuck you.

I'd never been one to take a nap, yet the thought of doing so sounded amazing as I pulled out of my mother's driveway. Especially with my head still feeling as if it would explode. Deciding I wouldn't make it through the evening without some sort of alcoholic beverage, I stopped at the liquor store and bought a bottle of bourbon.

Then, because I was feeling so down, I next went by the Food Lion to grab flowers. I was thankful no one had yet recognized me in my small town.

The cemetery was only a couple miles outside of town and completely void of people on this freezing Saturday afternoon. I made my way to the unfamiliar graves of my grandparents and laid the flowers down. The gray sky and chill in the air was reflective of my mood while I paid my respects. I'd been lucky to have them both in my life when my father had left. They'd made sure my mom had kept it together for us kids and had gone out of their way to spend time with me and my sister. They'd both passed away when I was in law school, only months apart. At the time, I hadn't been able to afford to come home for their funerals. Guilt still gnawed at me for not being there.

Finally, unable to stand the cold any longer, I walked back to the truck and drove the few miles to the Airbnb.

As I walked through the front door of the rental, I wasn't sure what to expect, but seeing my assistant's sexy ass hadn't been on the list of possibilities.

She was bent over getting something out of the stove, shaking it to the beat of whatever pop music was playing on her phone. She'd changed back into those infuriating yoga pants, showing me just how shapely her bottom half was.

I went over to the phone playing the music and pressed pause.

She stopped and smiled at me. "Hello."

My temper snapped. "I'm not paying you to bake cookies. You had a list of things to do today."

She stopped, putting the pan on the stove and shutting the oven door before turning back around. "Actually, you're not paying me. The firm is. Second, it's Saturday, which means I'm not officially on the clock. Third, I've accomplished all of those things you did ask for. The draft bill for Myers is there on the table for you to sign off on. The call with Johnson and Johnson is set for Monday morning because, like me, their assistant is also working on a Saturday. All of your edits are in the document that was emailed to you an hour ago. And for the record, these aren't cookies. They're scones."

They smelled delicious, making my stomach rumble. Not eating them would be my penance for jumping down her throat simply because I was in a shit mood. "Fine. I'll be upstairs in my office. Finish up your scones or whatever and meet me up there in ten minutes. I have another list of things for you to do."

"Fine. Did you eat lunch?"

The last thing I wanted was her offering to make me some. "I'm not hungry. Ten minutes."

I could swear I heard her curse under her breath.

Chapter Thirteen

KENDALL

I watched Liam go up the stairs while I mentally calmed myself. I liked to think of myself as a good person. Aside from my secret document listing ways for my boss to suffer, I was normally even tempered. And to be fair, wishing for suffering via papercut or an ugly cold sore wasn't all that bad. Okay, maybe the entry imagining him getting explosive diarrhea during a trial went too far. But in my defense, I'd written that one after he'd told me I was too chatty in the office and needed to remember I was there for one reason.

Little did he know. The one reason was to collect my paycheck. Oh, I was also taking advantage of the education benefit, and as soon as I was done with that, I wanted to quit. Hopefully I could find a job which paid more and allowed me to pursue my passion for cooking. Beyond that, I wasn't sure. Someday meet someone. Have kids. Host family parties like my mother did with all of my cousins, aunts, uncles, and of course, my nan. She might be in her eighties, but it didn't keep me from hoping she'd live forever.

Meanwhile, I was working for Liam. He was an asshole,

but he sure as hell beat the last partner I'd worked for. That guy had stared at my chest and legs. After he made an inappropriate ass grab at the office holiday party, they'd reassigned me to Liam. Of course, my former boss had merely received a slap on the wrist and was probably on to harassing the next legal secretary.

I couldn't wait to be done working for attorneys. Although I didn't mind learning about the law and keeping someone organized, it was stressful to live around the billable hour. Even if I wasn't the one charging for my time, I could feel the tension in every ten-minute increment Liam billed. I wondered if they'd add another partner to my work load soon, but it had yet to happen. Considering he was more than enough to keep me busy, I wasn't anxious to start working for anyone else in addition.

Eleven minutes after Liam had gone upstairs, I followed. The extra minute was my way of rebelling. Oh, yeah, I was a real wild one. Then again, I had no doubt he'd noticed.

Just like back in LA, he didn't glance up when I came to stand on the other side of the desk. And just like before, he started talking without any chitchat or niceties.

"The Myers bill can go out. I have one change." He handed it over.

"All right."

"I see the call on my calendar for Monday, but is it Pacific time or East Coast? There's the three-hour time difference."

Is there now? It was on the tip of my tongue. "It's all East Coast time; I adjusted for the time change in the same way for the other appointments on your calendar."

"Fine."

God, how I loathed the F-word. It sounded as if he wasn't happy but would deal with it.

"The funeral won't be until Thursday. When did you schedule our return flights?"

"They are for Friday." I'd anticipated a week, thinking I could always change it if we'd be able to leave earlier.

"And the house rental?"

"Also rented through Friday."

"I don't want you to feel as if you need to cook for me. It's uncomfortable enough as it is."

Funny for him to use the word *uncomfortable*. For me it was a bit strange. Weird. But uncomfortable? Meh. Not really. He was the same condescending asshole here as he was in the office. "How about you see it a different way? You bought the food. I'm cooking meals for myself and may have more left over for you to eat? Frankly I don't get a lot of people I have time to cook for. You can be my guinea pig."

He didn't crack a smile. I mean how could you not at the words *guinea pig*? Picturing their cute little faces didn't even inspire a twitching lip? Nope. Not for Mr. Personality.

"Fine. But don't take offense if I don't like something."

"I never do." The words left my mouth before I could think about it. Needing a change of subject, I pivoted quickly. "Is there anything I can do for the funeral? Order flowers. Food? Anything?" Although Liam was usually self-sufficient when it came to managing his personal affairs, this was something for which I actually hoped he'd ask for help.

His face softened a smidge. "If you could arrange the food catering for the reception after the funeral, it would be helpful. Unfortunately, there aren't a lot of options in Tazewell, but I'm sure there are some possibilities in the neighboring towns."

"How many people?"

He pinched the bridge of his nose. "I don't know. Maybe fifty. I guess to be safe, figure seventy-five."

"What time is the funeral? And what are the arrangements?"

"It's at eleven o'clock, so I guess lunch-type food. Maybe heavy appetizers. What do you mean by arrangements?"

"I mean is there a gravesite gathering after the service and then the reception? Or would the reception be straight after? It gives me an idea of timing."

"It'll be straight after. He'll be cremated."

"Do you have a specific food in mind?"

"I couldn't care less what is served. Anyhow, I could use some time. I'll have the next round of edits to you in a couple of hours."

I was being dismissed. Liam was back to rubbing his temples. I conjured up some sympathy and reminded myself not everyone dealt with grief the same way.

"I'M TAKING the truck to the store. Need anything?" I called up the stairs two hours later.

No answer. So I climbed up and peeked into the office.

Liam was sound asleep with his head on his desk. God, he almost looked human and way nicer in slumber. And way more handsome with his features softened.

I shook my head at the thought and backed out of the room quietly to descend the stairs. I left a note, then grabbed the keys and went out the door.

The Food Lion was a hopping place. Probably because of the impending weather alert calling for snow. I only had a few things to get there, which included wine, wine, and another bottle of wine. Considering it was Saturday night and I was stuck with my boss, well, I needed it. I also needed some recommendations regarding catering. Where better to get them than at the local supermarket? I asked Peggy, the same checkout lady I'd chatted with the last time I'd been here. She seemed to know everyone in town.

"Catering in this immediate area isn't great. I recommend getting someone from Blacksburg. It's ninety minutes away, but most will deliver for an extra fee."

"Thanks, Peggy." I guess I knew what I'd be doing the rest of the afternoon. Searching online for reputable caterers. The last thing I wanted was to screw up the food for my boss's father's funeral.

I returned to the house in a little over an hour and was unlocking the front door when it was yanked open. I almost lost my balance at the unexpected action. Looking up, I saw Liam's pinched face.

"Where the hell were you?"

"Uh, at the store."

"You don't get paid to go to the store. I needed you here, and you weren't."

"Really? Did you need me while you were napping? Because last time I saw you, you were facedown on the desk."

His entire neck turned red. "I was only out for a moment."

"Sure. Sure. What did you need?"

His face softened as though he'd realized he'd been over-reacting. "I need you to make these edits and send the document back to me."

After putting my two bags down on the table, I took the paper from his hands. "Okay."

"What did you get at the store?"

"Not nearly enough wine."

ALTHOUGH IT WAS NEARING eight o'clock in the evening, we were both still working. This time in the living room with files spread out everywhere. Up until this point, I would've argued everything I needed to do for him could've been done while I remained in the LA office. But as I went through documents to highlight name references, I knew this case was better served with us both working late and together. I also recognized it was easier to go through papers than to try to stay organized with electronic copies. Again, not something I would admit.

Dinner had consisted of Parmesan-crusted pork chops and wilted spinach. I didn't think I'd ever seen a man hoover down his meal as quickly as Liam had. But again, he hardly said anything. Definitely no compliments.

I shivered at the chill in the room. I was still wearing my yoga pants and sweatshirt, and he'd changed over into jeans and a sweater. I'd never seen the man in denim before, and it was quite the different look for him. Made him appear younger. Sort of like he had when he'd been sleeping earlier.

Getting up to stretch my legs, I eyed the wood stove. I had no clue how to start a fire, but how hard could it be? That being said, the wood was outside, and it was already dark. Perhaps it would be a task for tomorrow. "Need anything?"

"No." He didn't look up but just sighed, making it clear I annoyed him one hundred percent of the time.

First, I finished putting the food away and gathered the dishes.

"I said I'd get to those later," he grumbled from the couch.

"It's fine. I'm only soaking them." Even that pained me because I'd rather get them done and out of the sink. But on the other hand, I wasn't opposed to him pitching in.

Deciding what the hell, I reached for a wine glass and

poured the red. It had been calling to me all night. One glass certainly wouldn't hinder my ability to word search. As I took my seat again, I sipped some of the rich Malbec and set down my glass. I found his gaze resting on me.

"What are you doing?"

"Having a glass of wine and going back to work."

His disapproval was obvious. So what? If he was going to be annoyed anyway, I'd give him a reason this time around. I wasn't going so far as to throw back shots and party, but he had hijacked my Saturday night. And frankly, I needed a glass of wine in order to deal with him.

"Can you scan these three pages of my notes and email them to me?" he asked, holding up the papers.

"Sure." I was getting up to take the pages and climb the steps when the doorbell rang.

Our gazes locked in surprise.

"Maybe it's Shirley to check on the house?" I posed.

But he'd apparently decided he wasn't curious, after all. He simply went back to his laptop and ignored the summons.

Guess it was up to me to answer the door. I did so to see a stranger on the doorstep.

She was pretty with blond hair and a bright smile. "Hi. I'm Allison. Liam's sister."

"Oh, hello. I'm Kendall. Nice to meet you. Uh, come in."

"Thank you. Smells like snow out there for sure."

As soon as she walked in, Liam stood up from the couch. He looked none too pleased at the intrusion. "Allison, what are you doing here?"

"Oh, you know. I was in the neighborhood. Wanted to check out the digs."

He scrubbed a hand over his face. "I thought I was clear how I felt about drop-ins."

"Tough. I'm your big sister. Like I've ever listened to your suggestions."

Too funny. Her gaze scanned the room briefly before landing on me. "So, Kendall. You're adorable. How long have you worked for my brother?"

Awkward, yet she had an instant likeability about her. "Um. Almost four months now. But I've been with the firm over three years."

"What did you guys do for dinner?" She walked into the kitchen, taking off her jacket as she did so. Clearly, she wasn't in a hurry to leave.

"Oh, I cooked."

"He has you making his meals?" I could tell it hit a nerve, especially by the way she was glaring at him.

"She cooks whether I want her to or not. I'll probably end up gaining five pounds by the end of the week."

Asshole. "I enjoy cooking, and since your brother was nice enough to pay for the food, I've made the meals."

"Mm. I'd say he got the better end of the deal."

I was tempted to fist-bump her.

"Ms. Tate. Can you get those documents scanned for me?"

In other words, I was dismissed. "Sure. Um, nice to meet you, Allison." Because I was sure she wouldn't be here once I returned.

*W*hat the hell was my sister doing here? Never mind, scratch the question. I knew exactly what she was doing here. She was nosey as hell.

"Allison, as you can see, we're working."

Her roaming gaze landed on Kendall's blanket and glass of wine. Of course she did a fake cough while muttering, "Sure, she's just your assistant."

"Maybe she's an alcoholic who has poor circulation for all I know."

"I heard that," came Kendall's voice from up the stairs. Evidently sound carried in this house.

I pinched the bridge of my nose and watched my assistant come back down, all smiles for my sister. "Would you care for a glass of wine, Allison?"

"No, she can't stay," came my reply at the same time as my sister's: "I'd love one. Thank you."

"I see why you drink now, Kendall. Tell me. How is my little brother to work for?"

I witnessed my assistant's blush. "Jesus, Allison. You're putting her on the spot."

"Yeah, I mean it's not like I could tell you if your brother was a dick," came Kendall's retort.

Now it was my turn to go red in the face. I had no doubt there was a healthy measure of truth in her words.

My sister found it hilarious. "True. But seriously, is he a dick?"

I held my breath, bracing for her response. I knew for a fact she had every reason to say yes.

But she surprised me. "Your brother is professional and hard working. I respect his work ethic. Also, he's not big on sharing his personal life, which is why I can guess he's so unbelievably uncomfortable right now."

Allison laughed. "I can only imagine he is. But I'm nosey, so I couldn't not take the opportunity to meet you."

She took the glass of wine Kendall offered. Taking a sip, she commented, "Mm. Good wine. Plus, I don't get out of the house much or see my brother very often."

Guilt welled up. It had been a year since I'd seen her or her family.

"Yeah. You work at home?" Kendall asked.

"You could say that. I have two girls. One four, the other just turned two. What did you cook for dinner?"

"Oh, tonight was Parmesan-crusted pork chops and wilted spinach. I have leftovers if you're hungry?"

"Yeah? Sure. I had a couple of my daughter's chicken nuggets and cold spaghetti noodles, so grown-up food sounds divine."

It had been divine. Once again, she'd knocked it out of the park. I tried to ignore them both as they got along like long-lost friends at the kitchen table. I think my sister complimented Kendall on the food at least a dozen times. I'm not sure I'd remembered to even do so once.

I was about ready to call it a night, when Allison posed a question I hadn't been expecting.

"How about you come over tomorrow night, Kendall? We're having a Sunday night family dinner at my place with my mom. She'd love to meet you."

Fuck. Kendall's uncertain gaze met mine.

"I'm sure she has other things she'd rather do," I offered.

Allison laughed. "Oh, yeah, it's a real happening nightlife in Tazewell on a Sunday evening. Or you know what? We could go bowling tomorrow after dinner. Chelsea has been bugging me to go for weeks, and she'd love to go with her uncle Liam."

Double fuck.

"I don't want to make anyone uncomfortable," Kendall started to say, but my sister was never used to hearing the word no.

"Nope. You won't. Matter of fact, you can help me decide what to make tomorrow night for dinner. I'm not a great cook."

"I thought we could order pizza," I interrupted, not wanting my assistant to go to any more trouble than she already had when it came to preparing meals.

Both women frowned. "I was hoping for something better. Maybe Mexican food," Allison suggested.

Kendall's beautiful face lit up. "I could make enchiladas if you want to get all the fixings?"

The word enchilada made my sister practically drool. "Oh my God. Are you sure? I mean I love enchiladas, and since there isn't a decent Mexican food place for miles, it would be amazing."

"Yeah? Great. I'll go by the store tomorrow and pick up the ingredients."

Jesus. She was becoming a frequent shopper at the Food Lion in town. "Isn't it supposed to snow?"

My sister dismissed it. "Only a couple of inches. Enough to prove you haven't become a completely useless driver by living in LA. I'll be sure to pick up the sides. Tequila goes at the top of the list."

They were fast at work on items for tomorrow night's dinner while I stewed about the intersection of professional and personal.

By the time my sister left, I swear she and my assistant were BFFs. The front door was barely closed before I started pouring a glass of bourbon. All hope of my working longer had gone out the window.

"I don't have to go tomorrow," Kendall said from behind me.

"It's fine." I took a long, burning swallow.

"I don't think it is. You seem upset."

"If you don't show up, my sister will make my night hell."

"Way to make me feel welcome."

My annoyance got the best of me, and I turned to face her. "It's not supposed to make you feel welcome. You're here to work. Nothing else."

The hurt was obvious in her expression.

"Maybe I should've revised my answer and been truthful to your sister when she asked if you were a dick to work for. Don't worry. I won't go tomorrow night. What time did you need me to start tomorrow?"

We stood there staring at each other. "Eight o'clock."

"Fine. Good night." She turned on her heel and walked away.

Not even the taste of my whiskey could erase my self-loathing.

I WASN'T a man who drank to excess. Having an alcoholic father had always made me cautious of becoming too dependent on the stuff. Thus the three glasses of whiskey I'd downed the night before had me nursing a hangover this morning. It was freezing in the house. Probably time to start a fire in the woodstove. Or to have remembered to put on the heat in the bedroom when I'd gone to bed last night.

I was a jackass who owed Kendall an apology. Frankly, if she had much-needed coffee ready for me this morning, I'd pledge my undying devotion.

After a hot shower, I dressed in jeans and a sweater. Looking out the window, I saw there was a good inch of snow already covering the surfaces. It reminded me of my childhood when we'd pray for a snow day so we could go sledding down the neighborhood hill instead of school. A movement shifted my gaze to the corner of the back yard. I saw a figure in olive green on the ground.

Holy shit. Kendall had fallen. I rushed down the stairs, pausing only to frantically yank on my boots before running out the back door and down the steps toward where I saw her on the ground.

I found her laughing. Was she delirious from the cold? A bump on the head?

"What the hell are you doing?" I asked.

She looked up with rosy cheeks, bright eyes, and the biggest smile I'd ever seen on her face. "Making a snow angel."

"Why?" It was truly baffling to me.

"Because this is my first time seeing snow."

Her purple sparkly boots peeked out from the giant parka,

making me shake my head. She looked like a toddler poorly dressed for the weather in hand-me-downs.

"You'd best get up before the snow seeps through all of your clothes."

She stuck her tongue out in response. "Go away. I'm not on the clock yet, and you're ruining my fun."

"I came racing down here because I thought you'd fallen."

"Oh, yeah? Did you come out to rescue me? Or hope you could quickly hide the body?" she asked, holding out her gloved hand.

I pulled her up without much effort. I'd be surprised if her petite stature weighed more than a hundred pounds. Her grin was infectious despite my hangover. "Depends. Did you make coffee?"

Her lips twitched in a smile. "I did. I'll even give you some. Just as soon as you help me make a snowman."

She was adorable. And not in the toddler kind of way. The type of way that made me want her to hook her legs around my waist so I could take her against a wall. "You can't make a snowman with an inch of snow."

She frowned. "Bummer. But maybe it'll snow some more."

She trudged up the back porch steps, knocking her boots against the house before turning around. "Oh, I forgot the original reason I came out here. I need to get wood for the fireplace."

"I'll take care of it. After coffee."

She smiled, forever a morning person and thankfully not holding a grudge about last night. "You got it."

Chapter Fifteen

KENDALL

I refused to let Liam ruin my good mood over seeing snow for the very first time. But he had been right about the snow seeping through to my clothes. Once I went inside, I could feel the wet and the cold. "Coffee is in the pot. I've gotta go change."

He grunted something sounding like "fine" and proceeded into the kitchen while I went into my bedroom. I'd already showered, so I made quick work of exchanging my yoga pants for jeans and my fleece for a light sweater. Too bad I didn't have a warmer one like the one Liam had been wearing. Then again, when would I wear it in LA?

Liam was standing in the kitchen staring at the French toast I'd made earlier this morning.

"If you don't want any, you don't have to eat it. Don't want to cause you to gain too much weight." His comment still stung from yesterday. Then again, it was one of many that had stung.

"Look, I—" He turned to face me, his intense eyes on me. "Jesus, you're going to freeze."

My arms wrapped around my waist. "My hoodie and jacket are both wet. I have this sweater."

"Not warm enough. Hold on." He was up the stairs before I could ask what he was doing. He came back down with a heavy, navy blue wool pullover sweater. "Here, put this on."

It looked way too warm to bother to protest. I slid it over my head and relished the instant heat.

"It swallows you whole, but it'll keep you warm." He was already rolling up the sleeves for me like I was a child.

The kind gesture made me stand there like a deer in the headlights. My heart started beating faster. Weird. Then he sent it into overdrive.

"I owe you an apology for yesterday."

What the hell was happening? Who was this man? Maybe I had bumped my head. Was it possible to get hypothermia from five minutes outside? Perhaps I was hallucinating.

"I dragged you here and have been less than appreciative of your time. And since my sister really liked you and invited you over, I want to say I'm sorry for getting annoyed. I'd like it if you came tonight."

I simply stared. Seeing this human side of him while wrapped up in the warm sweater that smelled of him was doing funny things to my insides. I should still say no. Hell, I never should've accepted the invite to begin with. But his sister was so friendly, and I was in serious need of company outside of the Grinch who stole any sense of humor. Not to mention I had a burning curiosity to learn more about his family. Considering Allison was the complete opposite of her brother, who could blame me for wanting to discover more about his home life?

"Say something."

"I don't know what to say. I think it's the first time you've ever apologized."

"I'm sure it's not the first time it was owed. I don't properly appreciate all you do. I realize I don't always make it easy."

Holy. Fucking. Shit.

Maybe this whole grief thing and being home was making him sappy. Or perhaps he was the one who'd hit his head. "I, um, appreciate you saying that. Sorry for calling you a dick." It wasn't my best career move for sure.

He cracked a smile. "I'm sure I've been thought of as worse. Thanks for cooking the meals. I'm afraid I'm horrible in the kitchen, and French toast sounds way too good to pass up. Let me get the fire started, then I'll eat."

Taking a tally, there were two *thank yous* and an *I'm sorry*. And even a compliment. As I watched him start a fire with practiced ease, I wondered for the very first time if perhaps I didn't know the real Liam Davenport at all.

AFTER THREE HOURS of going through paperwork and highlighting important details, I was ready for a break. Unfortunately, the snow had stopped with only a couple inches on the ground, which meant no snowman today, but on the other hand, it wouldn't make driving terrible. At least that's what logic told me. But apparently I had absolutely no reference point.

"Do you mind if I take the truck to the store?"

He gave me a side-eye. "Yes, I do mind. You can't drive in the snow."

"How do you know?" I was mildly offended despite realizing he was probably right.

"You're a Southern California driver. A drop of rain causes people to freak out there."

This was true. We did freak out. Still I didn't want to admit it.

"Do you know what to do if you skid?"

Had no clue. "Um, push on the brakes?"

My guess earned me a shake of the head. "Stepping on the brakes is definitely what you don't want to do. You have to turn into the skid. Give me ten minutes, and I'll take you to the store. I want to be sure I pay anyhow."

Fifteen minutes later Liam was pushing the cart down the aisles for me while I got the ingredients for enchiladas. There was something very strange about the situation. It was almost domestic. Like we were a couple. Of course, smelling him on the sweater I was wearing wasn't helping such weird thoughts. I probably should take it off, but I hadn't yet.

"Where is the medicine aisle?" he queried.

"Normally in the middle. You okay?"

"Just a headache."

"Oh, you should've said something. I have Motrin in my purse."

"It's fine. I'll get some for myself."

We were walking toward the center of the store when he stopped suddenly. "Aw. Hell."

"What?" I scanned the aisle, spotting a busty redhead coming right for us.

"Oh my God. Liam Davenport," she yelled from ten feet away, rapidly approaching in her stilettos.

"Do you think running away would be too obvious?" he asked quickly.

The fear etched on his face was comical. "Probably. You need a rescue?"

"Yes. Anything to keep this impending conversation as short as humanly possible."

"Oh, yeah. Anything?"

"Anything."

He seemed desperate. Desperate enough to tempt me to walk off and leave him alone. But my next thought was to mess with him a bit. He wanted a favor. He'd get it. But with a price. After all, he'd thought I was trying to catch myself a husband by cooking for him. "You got it, babe. Now put your arm around me and pretend to like me."

"What?" He simply stared at me as if I'd grown a second head, so I took the initiative and put my arm around him.

The fiery redhead, in a cheetah-print dress with heavy makeup, squealed, causing my fake boyfriend to cringe.

"It is you. I wondered if you'd be back in town for your daddy's funeral. How are you, handsome?"

"Uh, good, Tonya. How are you?"

"Great. You know, I got divorced a few months back." Her gaze traveled down his body like she had every intention of making him husband number two.

"I wasn't aware."

She then seemed to notice me. "Who's this?"

I stuck out my hand. "I'm his girlfriend, Kendall."

She frowned, popping her gum several times instead of taking my hand. Okay. Miss Manners she was not.

"I ran into your mom last week at the post office, and she didn't say you had a girlfriend."

"Yeah, well. It's all very new," he stuttered.

So much for being any good at this game. Frankly, he sucked at it.

"You know Liam and I dated in high school. Went to prom together. Had quite the night, remember?"

I could practically feel the repulsive shiver go through him. I had to stifle my laughter at his expense. But then I realized if I was actually his girlfriend, her words would be offensive. "He never talks about high school since it was so long ago. Anyhoo, nice to meet you, Tonya. Have a good night."

"Oh. Yeah. I mean sure. You, too." She seemed put out when we were ready to move on.

Liam was already two steps ahead, moving quickly toward the drug aisle while I asked, "What's your poison? Tylenol, Motrin, Advil?"

"Advil is fine." Once we were stopped and alone, he asked, "What was that back there?"

I quirked my head to the side. "You said, and I quote, you would do anything to keep the conversation short. You're welcome, by the way." I quickly shut up because approaching was none other than Tonya again.

She gave him a seductive smile. "I realized I left without giving you my card. It has my new contact information on it."

My boss stiffened but stood still while she gave him the card. I noticed her hand lingered on his as if she wanted to be sure to put that little added touch in there. Then she walked off with an extra shake to her hips.

"Her card?"

He flipped it over and sighed, showing me the back.

"If you get bored and want a real woman, call me."

Jealousy and a healthy dose of rage hit me all of a sudden. I had to remind myself that I wasn't in fact his girlfriend.

Chapter Sixteen

LIAM

One minute Kendall was standing there, her face getting red while reading Tonya's not-so-subtle note, then the next she proceeded to push the cart as if this was a normal everyday occurrence.

I didn't bring up the whole fake girlfriend thing again while in the store. Probably wise as it was in fact a small town and the checkout clerk knew about everyone, evidently including my assistant.

"You're back, honey. Whatcha making tonight?"

"Hi, Peggy. Enchiladas. Black beans and rice."

"Sounds good. Hi, Liam. Nice to see you again."

I couldn't place her, even after reading her nametag. "Nice to see you, too, Peggy," I offered, wanting nothing more than to down my Advil and go lie down. But I had to drive over to help my mom pick out a headstone.

Once the bags were in the truck and we were settled inside, I turned to Kendall. "Do you mind telling me what the hell that was all about in the store with Tonya?"

She sighed. "I could say the same to you. For wanting me to rescue you, you did a lousy job of acting. And I can't believe the nerve of her. Giving you her card implying I'm not a real woman."

My gaze floated to Kendall's purple sparkly boots. They could be part of the reason. She looked like she could be my kid sister.

"Gotta say, I'm not a fan of high school Liam's taste in women."

Yeah, that made two of us. I certainly hadn't dated Tonya for her personality.

"Where did you get the idea to be my fake girlfriend to begin with?" This was a small town, and news of her being my girlfriend was bound to reach my mother. My sister was already suspicious, so this wasn't what I needed.

"How the hell else did you intend for me to rescue you?"

"I don't know—something else."

She simply blinked three times. "Like what?"

I didn't have a clue. Matter of fact, her idea probably was the best one. But I didn't like how it was making me feel. "Look, this is a small town. The last thing I need are for people to think I'm in a relationship with my assistant."

A pretty blush crept up on her face. "Right, I mean with all the times you come back to Tazewell, I'm sure it'll really affect your reputation. You wanted a rescue. I went with the path of least resistance, not that it seemed to deter her. Must've been some prom night."

I had to keep myself from an awful shudder. "Point taken."

One had to admit I hadn't given Kendall a lot of choices. But she'd been clever. Now I needed to ignore the fantasy of me ripping off her green puffy coat and having her naked beneath me. I was all out of sorts and blamed the fact on my apology this morning. From there on out, it had become weird all the way around. Having her in my sweater.

Spending time with her in the house. Having her be my fake girlfriend for a half a minute. Now having her come to my sister's house tonight. I could practically feel the lines blurring.

"Sorry if I made you uncomfortable."

I shook my head, chuckling despite wanting to pretend I was annoyed. "No, you're not."

She flashed me a smile—the type that hit me square in my solar plexus. The kind I'd never been lucky enough to have been on the receiving end of.

"You're right. I'm not sorry. Consider it retribution for thinking I was trying to play house with you the first day."

I wasn't sure when we'd crossed the line into this easy teasing banter, or her giving me special smiles, but I found myself preferring it to the icy coldness we'd previously established. Which was a problem. A big problem judging by the way I was having a hard time breathing without smelling her strawberry lip gloss.

Suddenly, I needed space. Space to figure out how to get back into a professional balance and routine. I reasoned it was the circumstances of the week making me feel off-kilter.

"I'm dropping you off at the house. Then I have some errands to run."

"'Kay." She either didn't notice my panic or was simply too laid-back to care. Either way, I was relieved once we pulled up in the driveway.

I stepped out of the truck to help her with the grocery bags, then was out the front door and back on the road in minutes, already breathing easier with each mile I put between us. I had no destination in mind as I was too early to meet my mom and sister, but I found myself back at the cemetery my grandparents were buried in.

I didn't get out of the truck. Just sat there gazing out the window, taking in the peaceful landscape the freshly fallen snow had made. My father's ashes would be buried here. Eventually, so would my mother.

My sister had told me she planned to buy a plot for her family here, too. She'd asked if I wanted to be included, but I'd declined. I wasn't ready to think about it. Nor did I want to face the fact I led a lonely existence. How depressing to think at the end of my circle, I'd probably end up buried in the same small town I'd avoided for my entire adult life.

This town and all of the painful memories were the reasons I hadn't been able to wait to get out. Start over. Become a new version of Liam Davenport where everyone didn't know about the verbal abuse, bruises, and the abandonment. Where people didn't whisper with looks of sympathy when they saw my mother using food stamps at the local grocery store. Those days might be long over, but the scars still ran deep.

Finally deciding to make my way to the funeral home for our appointment, I braced myself for the task of picking out the headstone. But I wasn't prepared enough.

"I want it to say loving husband, father, and grandfather on the stone," my mother announced to the director.

Wearing a tasteful suit, he sat in a comfortable room with the three of us.

I shared a look with my sister. Thankfully, both her girls were with her husband and wouldn't be here for the tension-filled afternoon. I decided to voice my opinion first.

"Mom. I know you'd like to think of him that way, but Allison and I didn't have a relationship with him."

She sighed. "You would've if you'd answered his calls over the last few months. It's my one regret that he wasn't able to make amends to you."

My gaze landed on the director. "Can you give us a moment, please?"

He was more than happy to excuse himself. Once he was gone, I took a deep breath, hating the fact I had to be the one to burst my mom's imaginative recollection of things. "He wasn't a loving husband, father, or grandfather."

My mother was a religious woman who believed in forgiveness. And who hadn't wanted to move on despite her husband being gone for years. Her religion was probably why she never divorced him, despite my urging once I'd become a lawyer. She hadn't wanted to break her vows even after he'd shattered every single one.

"He was a good husband, father, and grandfather in the end."

I stood up and went to the window. "Not when it counted." My last word broke in my throat. This was too much. I wanted to rage about not paying for it, but I wasn't dick enough to threaten something so petty.

Luckily, my sister backed me, her words causing me to turn. "Mom. It's too much to ask of us. Instead, it could say loving husband if you want. But not the father part. Or we could simply have it say rest in peace—or something else. Please."

My mother glanced between us and seemed to deflate under the weight of the truth. "Okay. If it's what you both want."

Allison and I both let out a breath of relief.

As I WALKED in the front door of the rental, the aroma hit me. It smelled delicious. Of course, I'd skipped lunch which had me starving.

In the kitchen, Kendall was slicing and dicing peppers with the precision of a proper chef. She had her iPad on the counter, watching some show, and was dressed casually. The way she worked was fascinating. She was so quick and efficient with her movements in the kitchen. Almost like a dancer who was expertly choreographed.

Suddenly she turned her head and startled at seeing me standing there. A yelp quickly followed.

"Oh, shit. Did you cut yourself?"

She was holding her finger and walking over to the sink. "Yeah. You startled me. Sorry."

I was over in a flash to take her hand and inspect the damage. "Just a nick luckily."

Her doe eyes locked on me. "Yeah, good thing they weren't the sharp knives I'm used to."

"Let me get you a Band-Aid." Only I didn't move. I simply stayed there with her hand in mine, staring at her.

"I think I have one in my purse. It's on the kitchen table stool. Look in the side pocket."

There was something strangely intimate about going into a woman's purse. But with her bleeding over the sink and me to blame, who was I to argue? I tried not to focus on the cute little spotted change purse, the pack of cinnamon gum, or the strawberry lip gloss I'd already spent too many hours obsessing about. After pulling the adhesive strip out, I opened it for her.

She was over at the table, having put her finger in a paper towel, and reached for it. "Thanks."

"I'll do it. Hold your finger out." It was always easier to have someone else do it.

"At least it was my left hand. Wouldn't want it to ruin my bowling game tonight." She gave me another genuine smile, making my stomach do this weird little flip.

We both jumped at the voice on the iPad. "Honey, you still there?"

Kendall giggled. "Oops. I'm, um, FaceTiming my nan," she whispered, going over to the iPad. "Sorry, Nan. I was distracted by cutting some veggies while watching."

"It's okay, honey. Let's get back to the show."

Her nan turned the iPad back to her television, which appeared to be playing some Western-type show.

Kendall muted it quickly and turned back to me. "I'll be done in about twenty minutes. We, um, our thing is to watch *Little House on the Prairie* together every Sunday." A blush stained her cheeks with the admission.

I recalled the title as something my sister may have read when she was younger, but I'd never seen the TV shows. Guilt crept up. Kendall had to FaceTime her nan instead of being there with her. It also made me miss my grandmother and all of the time I used to spend with her as a kid. "There's nothing on the agenda. Take your time."

Chapter Seventeen

KENDALL

Nerves struck me once we pulled into Liam's sister's driveway. I looked forward to satisfying a burning curiosity about my boss's family, but I needed to remember they'd just experienced a loss. Although his sister was nice and friendly, I wasn't here for a party. I was here as part of a family dinner occurring three days after they'd lost their father. It was just difficult to remember that since Liam didn't seem to want to talk about it nor did he act overly upset. Hell, neither had his sister, come to think of it.

Allison let us in with a smile. She hugged her brother to the side since each of us were carrying trays of food, and much to my surprise, took a turn to hug me, too.

"Oh my goodness, I can smell the enchiladas already. They smell delicious. Thank you so much for cooking, Kendall."

"It's my pleasure." I absolutely loved being able to share my food with everyone.

We went into the large, two-story house, and I was immediately greeted by an adorable four-year-old who took exception to my jacket.

"Your coat is ugly," she said without warning.

"Chelsea, don't be rude," Allison admonished her daughter and turned a deep shade of red.

I unzipped the offensive garment and knelt down to her level, loving her curly hair and freckled face. "It is rather hideous, I know, but I live in California where it's warmer, so I didn't have a winter coat. This was the very last one they had at the store here in Virginia."

She gave me a smile. "You live in California with my uncle?"

"Uh, the same state, yes." Didn't need to perpetuate the girlfriend rumor which was probably already running through town.

The girlfriend ruse had been more fun than I probably should've had at his expense. To be honest, I'd liked putting him out of his comfort zone. Probably wasn't the best career move, but it had been an icebreaker of sorts. We'd been able to laugh about it in the truck later. And what could I say? Having his arm around me hadn't been the worst feeling in the world, either.

"I like your boots," the little girl said shyly, rocking back and forth in that adorable toddler fashion that either meant she had to pee or was nervous upon meeting someone new.

"Thank you. I definitely lucked out with those."

"I have pink ones. You wanna see?"

"You bet."

Within no time I was introduced to Allison's husband, Warren, and Liam's mother, Clara. While her children and grandchildren seemed to be dealing with grief in a very non-grief way, I could tell with one glance that Clara was struggling. Her smile didn't quite reach her red eyes. I'd seen the same expression on my nan when she'd buried my grandfather.

"Hello, my dear. Allison tells me you're quite a chef."

"Oh. Well, I certainly enjoy cooking."

"And you work at the same law firm as my son?"

"Yes."

Her pride was evident in her expression. "He's such a hard worker."

"He definitely is." At least it was something we could agree on.

As we all dished up and sat at the dining room table, it soon became obvious there was something off in the dynamic. After grace, Clara remarked, "Freddie's favorite food was Mexican. He loved it when I made him tacos for dinner."

Liam's jaw tick clued me in that I was missing something.

But I was always one to mind my manners, so I forged ahead. "I was very sorry to hear of your loss, Mrs. Davenport."

"Oh, thank you, dear. Please call me Clara. It was just so unexpected. He would've loved this meal. He wasn't a bad cook himself."

"You don't say?" I gave her a smile, but when I glanced over toward her son, he seemed tense and uneasy. I didn't get it. And evidently I wasn't to be enlightened anytime soon.

"You know anything about making a good margarita, Kendall?" Allison asked straight after dinner. She looked as though she needed a drink.

"I do. You in the mood for frozen or on the rocks?"

She grinned. "Frozen would be divine. I bought tequila and lime juice. I also have a mix, but it's kind of nasty."

She led me into her kitchen.

"Tequila and lime juice are good," I said. "Do you have triple sec? And some sugar?"

She fished through the cabinet and came out with a bottle. "Yes. I have it."

"Great. I only need a small sauce pan and sugar to make the simple syrup." Margaritas always tasted better to me with a balance of sweet and sour.

"How do you know all this?"

"I bartend on the weekends."

"You do?" came Liam's voice as he entered the kitchen with plates from the table.

Shit. I hadn't meant for him to overhear me. Not that my moonlighting was against the firm rules, but I didn't want him asking questions. "Yeah. On Friday and Saturday nights."

"Where?"

"Um, at a dance club. Do you have a blender?" I inquired toward Allison, hoping to change the subject.

"So, you work full-time, go to school, and work part-time on the weekends?" she asked.

"I like to stay busy." I stole a glance at Liam and saw his scowl and a throb in his jaw. Did it piss him off to hear I had a life outside of him? The only thing missing was his sigh of disapproval, and it would have been like old times in the office. Deciding to ignore him, I went about making the best possible margaritas.

An hour later, I noticed my boss hadn't indulged in anything alcoholic. Too bad. It probably would have improved his mood.

After the dishes were done, we all piled in the cars to head to bowling. I chanced a glance at my driver, whose mood seemed to be worsening by the moment. "Everything okay?" I asked.

"Fine."

The word almost made me snap. I started to second-guess

my decision to come tonight. Or to get in the car alone with him while everyone else had ridden in the minivan. At least I could be grateful the bowling alley was only five minutes away.

Once we arrived and got situated with our rental shoes, we decided on two lanes and were put on the far side. Bumpers were put up for the kids which meant no gutter balls. Probably a good thing since I hadn't bowled in years.

Allison came over with a pitcher of beer and some cups. "My bowling game gets better with beer," she joked.

I winced a bit since it seemed everyone was into this little family outing except for their mother, who'd been quiet so far. She'd decided not to bowl and was only helping her granddaughters with their shoes. But who was I to point this out? Perhaps this was the way her children hoped to put a smile on her face.

Finding a yellow six-pound ball, I was relieved to find it would fit my small hands and wasn't a weight that would embarrass me.

"You realize your ball is a child's ball?" Liam smirked.

I simply shrugged, returning his smirk. "Great, then Chelsea and I can share."

We were about to start when Allison shouted toward us. "You two should bet something on the game." Her cheeks were rosy from the alcohol.

Warren, her husband, had already pronounced her a light-weight and had fetched her a glass of water to try to offset the effects. Clearly, this hadn't done much yet to settle her down.

But the idea of a bet made my boss smile. "You any good?" he challenged.

Nope. Not at all. Much to his amusement, I changed my selection to the eight-pound pink ball. I might need the extra two pounds. "Go big or go home, Mr. Davenport. Now, what shall we bet?"

"What do you have in mind?"

Oh, damn. The way his husky voice hit me conjured up thoughts completely inappropriate for family time or a boss.

As if he could read my mind, his brow quirked.

Think fast, think fast. "If I win, you cook with me tomorrow."

"What?"

"I teach you how to cook a meal. You give me your undivided attention."

"Deal." He turned to walk away.

"Wait. What's your side of the bet?"

His eyes sparkled. "To be determined."

TBD was an option? What did that mean? With my luck, I'd probably be tasked to work extra hours.

He was up first, affording me an unobstructed view of his great ass. Which I must say looked incredible encased in denim. Jesus, he even bowled like he was in control. And when his first shot was a strike, I knew I was in trouble.

Three frames later, I wasn't just losing; I was being annihilated.

But right now, his four-year-old niece was up, with her tongue between her lips and a look of fierce concentration. And when her second throw knocked down all of the pins after taking an excruciatingly long time to go down the lane, we all cheered. Even Liam, who hadn't been drinking and wasn't overly relaxed, was all smiles for his niece.

At the tenth frame, I took my stance and glanced back at his smug face. I so wanted to stick out my tongue at him, but I refrained. Barely. Then I focused. Point the ball in the middle. Little extra umph. Nope, went left. Shit. It hit the bumper but then it bounced into the middle and—holy shit. Strike.

I did a little dance and squealed. Turning around, I saw him shaking his head.

"Good thing for the bumpers."

Leave it to Liam to rain on my parade. Never good enough in his eyes. At least everyone else seemed happy with my small success.

They decided to play another game, but my boss couldn't be bothered. Nope, he was too good for it.

"I have a quick call to make, but you guys go ahead and play without me."

Disappointment was obvious on everyone's face. It only fueled my annoyance with him. I took a seat next to his mother while the kids took a quick bathroom break before the next game.

"I should've warned you not to bet against my son. He's an athlete like his father was."

"Oh, yeah? What other sports did Liam play?" Call me forever curious about someone I shouldn't be.

"Baseball was his sport of choice. I used to love watching him play catch in our front yard with his father. They'd do it for hours."

Shit. I had a prick of conscience. Perhaps my boss was coping in the only way he knew how.

We were four frames into the second game when Liam returned from his call. His mother patted the seat beside her. "I was telling Kendall about the times your father used to throw the baseball around with you out in the yard. Remember?"

His entire body stiffened up. "Yeah. Do you want anything to drink, Mom? Soda? Iced tea?"

"No, thank you. He'd take you to your practices, too. And

watch your games. Do you remember?" Her expression seemed hopeful for her son to give her the slightest crumb.

He shot to his feet. "I remember. I'm getting something to drink. Anyone else want something?"

What the hell? He couldn't even be nice to his own mother who wanted to reminisce about his father?

"I just want to talk about the good times, Liam. Can't you do it for me?" Her tears were welling up, but he was downright icy.

"I'll be out in the truck." He leaned down to kiss her cheek and whispered something into her ear before stalking out.

If I'd thought my boss was a dick before, this took it to an entirely new level.

Chapter Eighteen

LIAM

I whispered to my mother that I loved her more than anything, but I still wasn't over all the bad times that had followed the good ones. And I was sorry.

God, was I sorry. I wished I could fake it. I knew she wanted me to. Feeling like a class A prick for hurting her, I went out to the truck to wait. I was tempted to ask if my sister could drive Kendall home, but it would only add to my level of asshole. I turned up the heat and tried to calm myself from the resentment brought on by my mother's skewed recollection.

Yes, I remembered him throwing the ball with me. I'd been five or maybe six and would do almost anything for his attention. But the moment I wasn't perfect, he'd get irrationally angry. I was never good enough. And yes, I'd remembered the T-ball practices and games when he was sober. They'd been amazing. But they'd been few and far between. Instead, my memories were of fighting tears at the constant critical comments. My mother wanted to paint the picture differently, rewrite history, yet I couldn't forget the bruises, the screaming, or the sound of the front paned window breaking the night he left us for good.

He'd been livid because social services was investigating my black eye from the week before. I'd stepped in the way of his fist when it had been directed at my mother and had received the brunt of the blow on my face. There'd been no way to hide it this time around. I believe it had been that investigation which had saved us all. Sometimes I wondered if my mother would've ever had the courage to tell him to leave.

I tamped down on the resentment that threatened to bubble up. I couldn't go there. She'd been an abused and battered wife and mother without the self-esteem to recognize she could do better. Afterward, she'd done the best she could. Growing stronger. Working hard for us kids.

I'd finally calmed myself down by the time Kendall hugged my family and got into the truck. I gave my sister a small wave, knowing she understood more than anyone else why I'd needed the space.

We were silent on the way back to the house. I could only imagine what my assistant was thinking, but I wasn't about to dump my family history on her.

The house was cold when we went inside. It was after nine o'clock, and all I wanted was some peace and quiet along with a glass of whiskey.

I noticed Kendall's agitation as she took off her coat. She didn't bother to make eye contact with me. Instead, she went out the back door and came in with an armful of wood.

"I can do that."

"Don't bother."

"What's with the attitude?"

She turned and glared.

"If you're somehow pissed that I needed to leave the

bowling alley, it's none of your business." Her obvious judgment made me defensive as hell.

"You're right. It's not my business. But I'm also not surprised by it."

Her assessment stung more than I'd like to admit. "You know nothing about it." I should have walked away before things escalated, but instead, I stood there clenching my fists.

"No, I don't know anything about it because you don't share anything."

"Do I need to remind you? You're my legal secretary. We work together." Maybe I was the one who needed the reminder. "Anything personal is off-limits."

She grabbed the matches and lit the paper under the kindling. "Then, why did you bring me here?"

"I brought you here to work. Nothing else. Yet somehow you've managed to become entwined in my personal shit."

"Obviously with an agenda, right? I'm forcing myself into people's lives and cooking them meals. What a dick move of me to be nice to people who have only been nice to me."

Smoke started to come out of the stove, interrupting our conversation and prompting me to ask, "Did you open the flue?"

"The what?"

"Never mind. Clearly, you didn't." I moved past her to open the lever that allowed smoke to go up the chimney.

"God, you are such an asshole. I never do anything good enough. Ever. Not all of the files I brought in a suitcase instead of shipping them, not the house because you didn't want the motel, not the non-four-wheel drive I didn't know to reserve. Hell, I couldn't so much as get a fist bump for my very first strike tonight because it wasn't good enough, either, since there were bumpers. But I can handle your perpetual disappointment. After all, you're just my boss, and I'm just your secretary. And this is just a fucking job until I can afford to quit it. But watching you make your mother cry tonight three days after your father died— That was a new low. Even for you."

I stood there in shock, absorbing her words like a punch to the gut while she turned and strode down the hall to her bedroom.

She shut the door and effectively shut me out.

Did I really make her feel that way? The way my father had made me feel? Like she was never good enough?

KENDALL STAYED in her room while I got the fire to the point where the heat was finally warming up the house. I sipped my whiskey, sitting at the dining room table, feeling lost as to what to do next. When I heard her door open, I stood up from the chair.

But she walked straight to the kitchen, keeping her eyes averted, and simply went for the refrigerator for a bottle of water.

"My father abandoned us when I was eight. He'd given me a black eye while in a drunken rage toward my mother, and social services was investigating. He broke the picture window in our living room with a lamp and just took off."

She turned quickly, her eyes wide. Her voice was small. "He hit you?"

"Mostly it was directed toward my mother after he'd get drunk, but I'd get in the way of his fists sometimes trying to protect her. This was one of those times."

Her arms hugged her waist.

Since I was in for a penny, I might as well go for the full pound. "He only came back six months ago. Said he found

Jesus and had been sober for a year. He moved back in with my mother. She forgave him after twenty-five years of desertion."

"But you didn't?"

I shook my head. "Not even a little."

She let out a broken sigh. "I'm so sorry."

I held up a hand. I wasn't sure what I was more afraid of: her sympathy or the fact we'd just obliterated a thick line between professional and personal. "Don't. Don't apologize. You didn't know."

Shit. I could see the tears run down her face. I stepped closer, having to put my hands in my pockets to keep from wiping the moisture from her pretty face. The instinct to touch her was incredibly strong. "Don't cry for me, Kendall. It was a long time ago. I struggle when my mom wants to only remember the good times. Because there weren't nearly enough of those."

"Still, I went and called you an asshole and said those terrible things to you. I'm sorry."

"I deserved them especially if I caused you to feel that way. I don't mean to."

If I was making her feel less than, then I was probably a lot more like my father than I'd ever want to admit. Maybe the apple didn't fall far enough away from the tree. The thought left me chilled to my very core.

"In all honesty, I don't know what I'd do without you this week—or any day, for that matter. I realize I'm not easy to work for or, hell, even be around, but I do appreciate your efforts even when it doesn't seem like I do." Matter of fact, I was still reeling from her outburst about wanting to quit her job.

"Thank you," she said and suddenly hugged me.

I was stunned but soon relaxed, tightening my arms

around her. Her head came up to my chest, and her petite frame fit into my body almost as though it had been made to. Suddenly, I felt I had to break the connection and stepped back. I instantly missed the warmth when I did so.

Ironic that the reason I had never let her close was the fear of letting her too close.

"Sorry. I didn't mean to hug you."

Yet she had. When was the last time someone had tried to give me comfort? Her gesture was so unrehearsed. So authentic. "It's okay."

Despite the dim light, I witnessed her face flush. Then she was quickly changing the subject. "Are you hungry at all?"

"No. I'm still full from dinner. It was really good, by the way." Compliments. I could be better at giving them. Judging by the way her face lit up, she appreciated it. Driving the point home that I should be a lot freer with giving them.

"Thanks. You want wine?"

"No, thanks, I have whiskey."

She poured herself a glass of red and joined me in the living room where I took a seat in the reclining chair.

She was quiet for a moment, then biting her lip as if she wanted to ask something.

"I can practically hear your brain humming. What is it?"

She sighed and was out with it. "Why did you come home, Liam? If it would be this painful?"

It was a question I often asked myself. And now that the hard stuff was out in the open, it was easier to give her more of the details. Hell, it felt good to have someone in whom to confide. "I didn't want to, but ultimately I came for my mother. After my dad left, my mom worked two jobs and did everything for us kids."

"It's why you don't come home. Because of the bad memories?"

"Yeah. It's not easy. Especially since my mom lives in the same house from our childhood. I tried to get her to move, but she loves it."

"Must mean there were some good memories there, too, then."

Probably. But I'd never focused on those.

Needing to change the subject, I asked something I was curious about. "What club are you bartending for?"

She gulped more of her wine. "Um, it's in LA."

There was something she wasn't telling me. "And? What's the name?"

Again with another gulp. "I'd rather not tell you."

Now she had to. "In that case, I'm calling in my bet chip."

She sucked in a breath. "You're calling in what?"

"The bet from bowling. You owe me something, and I choose the truth. Spill it."

She drained her glass and got up to pour more. "I don't believe it when they say there are four glasses to each bottle. More like two and a half."

Her stall technique was only making me curious. It also made me forget about the melancholy part of the evening. "Tell me."

"No. Pick another bet chip to cash in."

"I argue for a living. Do you really think I'm letting this drop? What is the name of the club? Not like I intend to go there."

"No, I don't imagine you would." She took a deep breath and drank more of her wine. "But if I tell you, you have to promise not to judge."

"All right."

"Fine. It's the Cheetah Club."

Why did the name sound familiar? Then it hit me. I'd previously done business with the owner. "The dance club?"

My voice had gone up an octave. If I remembered correctly, the place had a number of scantily clad women dancing in cages above the floor, not to mention a private club on the upper floors which catered to gambling and private stripping. I could only hope she wasn't involved in that side of the club.

"Yeah. But I don't dance. I only bartend."

I was silent.

"You said you wouldn't judge." Her hands fidgeted with her hair.

"I'm not. I'm simply processing. It can't be safe." I could only imagine how many men hit on her on a nightly basis. Thinking about it, I didn't like the idea of her working late every Friday and Saturday night with a crowd of drunks.

"It's perfectly safe. At least if I get groped there, then someone is getting tossed on their ass out the door, never to return. Can't say the same for my other work place."

"What are you talking about?" She'd been groped at the firm?

"It's the wine talking. Anyhow, the club is safe. My room-mate and I have a bodyguard who walks us out to our car each night."

Unlike me, she had a life outside of the job. "Let's get back to the groping in the office. Who?"

She didn't say a word. I tried a new tactic. "I've just spilled my guts to you, Kendall. You know you can trust me."

"I know."

I jogged my memory for the partner she'd been assigned to before me. "Mike Octavus?"

Her face said everything before her words. "The secretaries call him Octopus. Eight arms all trying to touch you. Anyhow, it only happened once at the office holiday party."

My temper instantly reached a boiling point. Especially since he was still with the firm. "Did you report it to HR?"

"Yes. Afterwards, I was reassigned to you."

"And you don't have any contact with him?"

"No. I mean sometimes I'll see him in the cafeteria, but I keep my distance."

The Executive Committee would definitely be hearing from me on this. Mike might be a longtime partner, but frankly, his billings were down, and he didn't have nearly the client power that I did. I would never work to put my name on a firm condoning that type of behavior. Ever. It made me question the integrity of the firm in general if they were covering up an issue like sexual harassment.

"You look angry."

"I'm not angry."

"Mm, I might disagree. Your jaw sort of does this thing."

I had to let it go for now. The last thing I wanted was for her to think any of my anger was directed toward her. "Not at you. At him. For touching you when he had no right."

We were silent for a few minutes before I vocalized my thoughts. "I think you should go home tomorrow. I can drive you to the airport, or we can find a car service to take you."

"Why? Tomorrow is Monday, and your schedule is packed."

"I know. But this is more than a simple business trip, and I'm sure my mood will only get worse the closer we get to the funeral."

"It's only four days away, and I want to be sure I'm here to oversee the catering. Make sure everything goes smoothly. And if working helps ease your stress, then I'll help you with that, too."

Although I'd been sincere in offering to let her get the hell out, I was instantly relieved she was willing to stay. "Who did you end up going with for the food?"

"A catering place out of Blacksburg. They have great reviews and were willing to travel here."

"Good. Thanks for taking care of it."

Her wide eyes met mine; she was clearly surprised by my appreciation. It only drove home how shitty I'd been for withholding it for so long.

"You're welcome."

Chapter Nineteen

KENDALL

*A*s I lay in bed, unable to sleep hours after our conversation, my head was spinning. And it wasn't the wine. My heart broke for what Liam and his family had endured. I could only imagine how difficult it was for both Liam and Allison to be there for their mother despite their feelings about their father. Did I believe in second chances? Absolutely. But I wasn't sure beating on your kids and wife was redeemable. Even two decades later.

I also couldn't believe I'd hugged the man for whom I'd made a list of ways he could suffer. My, how times had changed. I'd gone from loathing to sympathizing. And now that I'd managed a peek behind the curtain, I could understand a lot more about what drove him. I could also see his absolute sincerity when he'd apologized for his behavior.

Although he'd said I could trust in him, I wondered if it had been a good idea to confide that I worked for the Cheetah Club. Or to have told him about my former boss groping me. I blamed my loose lips on the alcohol I'd consumed tonight. Yet despite having revealed those things, I sensed we were in a much better place. It was almost like learning about one another had opened up the door for—well, a sort of connection. Maybe friendship?

Yet the little voice in my brain asked if I thought of my other friends naked.

Nope. I sure didn't.

Nor would I think of my boss that way. Not pressing me into the mattress with his body weight. Not his delicious abs I'd practically drooled over when he'd come back from his run. Not his piercing eyes locked on mine. Not the feel of his warm lips against my skin. Shit.

Ugh. What I needed was sex. The good kind. I'd had a high school boyfriend during my final two years, and then there was a guy I'd dated about a year ago, but the sex had left a lot to be desired.

Although I had plenty of offers every working weekend at the club, I wasn't a girl who did sex without feelings. Someday, perhaps when I had more time to meet quality guys, I hoped to have a relationship. Meet a man with whom I could plan a future with and eventually have children. But for now, I had the responsibility for my grandmother's care and was busy trying to finish my degree.

The next morning while I was making breakfast, Liam came into the kitchen dressed casually in jeans and a dark gray sweater.

"What are these?" he asked, watching me flip the pancakes.

He seemed more relaxed than I'd seen him all week. Perhaps our talk last night had helped break the ice of the previous formality.

"Snowman pancakes." I'd done three circles in the batter, then was fixing bacon as a scarf and blueberries and chocolate chips for eyes and buttons.

"How many are you making?" He was staring at the large pile accumulating on the plate.

"A few. Your sister texted this morning and sort of invited herself and the girls over for breakfast. Hope you don't mind?"

He only smiled. "No, I don't mind at all. She likes you."

"I like her. And your nieces are adorable."

"Agreed. They'll love these pancakes."

Ten minutes later, both girls were at the table squealing at my snowmen.

"These pancakes are so cute. Will you teach me how to make them?" Allison asked.

"Of course." We did a quick lesson in which I showed her snowmen and Mickey Mouse shapes.

"These are amazing. So, Kendall, I'm curious. You want kids?"

I wasn't sure why I found myself blushing. It was an easy answer. "Yeah. At least three or four of them someday." What could I say? Being an only child had made me always wish for siblings.

We both looked over toward Liam, who was holding the baby on his lap and choking on his OJ. Weird.

She gave him a smile. "You okay, little brother?"

"Yes. But stop matchmaking." His handsome face was a shade of pink while his sister was the picture of innocence.

I was confused. "Matchmaking who? Me?"

Allison smiled. "I just thought maybe you and my brother."

My mouth hung open. No wonder her brother was choking on his drink. "No. We're not. I mean we don't." Shit, I couldn't seem to form complete sentences. Maybe because I'd had quite the vivid dream last night of him in my bed.

"I'm not her type," he offered up.

What the hell? "Yeah, and he's my boss." Did he forget about that part?

"What's your type?" Allison inquired.

I peered at Liam, holding the youngest girl on his lap. My ovaries wanted to revolt and shout he was my type, after all. My mind wouldn't let them.

He fixed his narrowed gaze on her. "Stop teasing, sis. We're only coworkers."

She sighed. "Alas, one can hope. But I don't believe my brother would ever slow down enough to have kids."

From what I'd seen, I believed it.

Liam stayed quiet despite smiling at his baby niece.

"Do you have a boyfriend?"

The question earned Allison a glare from her brother. "Give it up, Ally. You're making her uncomfortable."

"No, it's okay. To answer your question, I don't have a boyfriend at the moment."

"With working two jobs and school, I'm sure you don't have the time."

"No. Not really."

"Does your firm not pay enough, brother dear?"

"Are you sure you're the only litigator in the family? I feel cross-examined," I teased, not wanting to get into my reasons for needing a second job.

Thankfully, Liam laughed at my joke and got up with the baby. "You're nosey, Ally, and I think this one needs a diaper change."

"Nice segue. Fine. Come here, you." She took her daughter in her arms.

"You can use the master bedroom at the end of the hall."

"Thanks, and sorry if I made you uncomfortable."

"It's fine. Really." The only thing making me uncomfortable was thinking way too much about her brother.

LIAM and I spent the afternoon knee deep in files. Then, when I got an hour break from organizing key information, I finished a couple of his invoices and put his billable time into the system. I also submitted my overtime.

"Why are your overtime hours so low?" he asked two minutes after I hit the submit button for his approval.

"What do you mean?"

"I mean you've been working more hours than what you put in. Travel time, et cetera."

"I wasn't sure about the travel time. And I'm only putting in hours above the eight normal hours I work in a day."

"You're about twenty short by my estimation. I'm sending it back for you to correct."

Twenty more hours was being generous. It would also more than make up for missing the two nights at the club.

"Also make sure you put the house rental to my personal number. And let me know how much I owe you for the coat and boots and other winter stuff."

"You can't pay for my clothes."

His brows drew together. "Yes, I can. You wouldn't have needed them if I hadn't insisted you come with me. It's the least I can do."

I hesitated, but logic and the fact every dollar counted won out. "Okay. I will. So, I realize you won the bet, but any chance you still want to learn to make fettucine Alfredo tonight?"

His hesitation made me immediately regret the offer. He was busy with much more important stuff. I don't know what I was thinking in asking.

"It's okay. Forget I asked."

"I'll do it. I love chicken Alfredo."

"Yeah?" I wasn't sure why I was so excited to share my love of cooking with him, but I couldn't help my smile at the thought of him in the kitchen with me.

"Sure. But please tell me we don't have to return to the grocery store."

"Don't worry. I have everything we'll need."

By six o'clock I was starving and started taking out all of the ingredients, prepping my work station on the counter. I was pleased when I didn't need to remind Liam, who came in with his sleeves rolled up.

"Okay, I'm washing my hands, then I'm ready to help."

"Great. We'll start with making the pasta."

His brow furrowed. "What do you mean *make* the pasta? Don't you get it from a box?"

I laughed. "You can, but I promise this is so much better."

I poured the flour on the countertop and made a volcano-type mound of it into which to crack the eggs.

"Won't it take a lot of time?"

I shrugged. "Yep, and it'll be worth it. I promise. Okay, crack four eggs into the center of the flour well."

He did as I asked, his big hands fully capable of the task. I tried not to stare at his muscled forearms. Never would I have guessed cooking with him would be quite so sexy.

"Next, use this fork like you're scrambling the eggs, pulling in more flour as you go."

"Like this?" he asked, stirring them.

I scooted in front of him. "No, more like this. Then, when it gets too thick, we'll switch to you using your hands."

He let out a long sigh.

"What, too slow for you?"

"A bit. I guess you could say I like to do most things as quickly as possible."

"Why?" Didn't he ever want to slow down and enjoy the process?

"I'm a man who likes to be efficient and not waste time. The quicker the better."

I felt my face heat as his words instantly sent my mind to the gutter.

Chapter Twenty

LIAM

*H*eat creeped up my neck when Kendall blushed, and I realized the way my words had sounded. "I didn't mean— You know what I meant."

She cleared her throat. "Of course."

Neither of us was admitting we'd slipped into dangerous territory. The thought of my assistant hinting at sex made me all sorts of uneasy.

Damn. I blamed the fact it had been months since I'd last had a woman in my bed. With as many hours as I clocked, it simply wasn't the priority. Perhaps I would call Gina once I returned. She was down for a no-strings commitment when she was in town. She worked in PR for one of the movie studios in LA. I'd met her through friends. She was beautiful, successful, and driven. Yet she didn't hold a candle to the natural beauty standing beside me.

Frankly, aside from Gina, who was always up for a good time, I didn't stay in touch with anyone I'd slept with. I'd never sought anything serious. Hell, I barely had time for my family across the country, let alone a girlfriend. And although my sister had been nosey to ask Kendall the questions she had, I'd learned an important fact about my assistant. She was undoubtedly a relationship girl.

She broke my train of thought. "Time for you to knead the dough."

I found myself fascinated by how much effort went into making something I'd only ever bought from a box. That way, it could have been boiled by now. But I was also completely enthralled by how her eyes lit up with the task. It was clear this was her passion.

"Really get in there. Don't be afraid to get your hands dirty."

My cock felt her statement. Little did I imagine cooking with Kendall would be seductive, but here I was trying to think of things to calm down the start of an erection.

"What's next?" I asked, my voice huskier than intended.

"Ah, this is where we improvise a bit since I couldn't find a rolling pin, and we don't have a pasta maker."

She uncorked her bottle of red wine and chugged down the remainder. Christ. The action was so unexpected, I started to laugh. She grinned in return. "Classy, I know. Okay. Let me wash the bottle quickly."

"For what reason?"

"To roll the dough. First, let's cut the first blob into eight pieces." She handed me a knife while I did as she instructed.

"Okay. We have to keep the pasta we're not working with moist." She took a dampened towel and laid it over the pile of seven. "Now we roll as thin as we can."

It was very clear I sucked at it, but she was patient, showing me how to get the dough to the right consistency. I'd be lying if I said having the excuse of being this close to her wasn't both heaven and hell. She smelled the way I imagined sunshine in a bottle would. Her long, brown hair was tied up in a messy bun. Her beautiful face was devoid of makeup except for her gloss. I could practically taste the strawberries from it.

"Good. Now we slice it. It'll puff up a bit, so we want thin strips." She showed me, then let me have a try. This took a long time, yet the motions were weirdly soothing.

"What's next?" I asked after cutting all of it.

"Seven more times with the remaining blobs."

I must've made a face.

"It's okay. I'll do it. Can you get the large pot out of the drawer over there?" She pointed. "And fill it with water for me. Also, I need the large saucepan."

That I could do. I noticed how quickly she went about rolling out the remaining dough and deftly slicing up the noodles. It was weirdly arousing.

I finished the tasks she'd requested. "What's next? You want me to boil the water?"

"Not yet. It'll only take a couple minutes to boil fresh pasta, so we'll wait until the sauce, chicken, and bread are done."

It sounded like quite the production. One I wasn't sure I had time for.

She flashed me an understanding smile. "You've more than humored me. I'll finish if you want to get some more work done."

"You sure?" I didn't want to hurt her feelings, but I did have a couple more hours' worth of review to do.

"Yes. Of course."

I went back to my laptop but moved it to the kitchen table to be closer to her. I didn't know why. But it seemed natural to do so. However, I soon found myself distracted. Watching her again. "What are you doing with the chicken?"

"Slicing it into strips. Then I'll use salt and pepper and brown it in a pan with a bit of olive oil. To be honest, I don't do a lot to the chicken. I sort of let the sauce and the noodles be the stars."

I could hear the sizzle and smell the meat. While it cooked, she poured something into the pan. "What is the sauce made from?" Forget it. Working wasn't happening. Instead, I was absolutely fascinated with the woman in front of me and what she was doing.

"Cream and butter. You melt them together, then add in the Parmesan. Salt and pepper. I also like a dash of nutmeg."

"Alfredo sauce is only made from those ingredients?"

She smiled. "Yep. Sure is."

"Tell me what you do with the bread."

She smiled widely. "You back in?"

"Yeah. I guess my stomach is curious to see this through."

"Think of it this way. After this lesson, you'll have your perfect date-night meal to impress someone."

Not that I took much time for dating, let alone making homemade meals. "My dates would probably prefer to be taken out to an expensive restaurant."

She opened her mouth as if to say something but then stopped.

"What?"

"Nothing."

"Haven't we passed the point of you holding back? You're aware of my painful childhood. I know you moonlight at a rowdy nightclub."

Her blush was worth the teasing. "I just think most women would appreciate the time spent on them rather than the money."

I met her gaze. "I think you're probably not like most women, then."

She stepped back and got something out of the refrigerator. "What's your mom doing tonight?"

"She's having dinner with some of her church friends. I'm going over there tomorrow."

"You're welcome to invite her over here tomorrow night instead. I'm guessing it probably isn't easy for you to go to the house."

The fact she understood my struggle took me off guard. So did her offer. "I appreciate it. Maybe she can come over. But please don't feel like you need to cook. I think you've fed enough of my family."

"We can order pizzas. I can go check out the Tazewell night life to leave you some time alone."

"No. I meant I'd rather you stay. If it's not too uncomfortable for you."

"It's not uncomfortable. Your mom reminds me of my nan. She likes to relive the good old days, too. Some of it I'm sure has been altered with rose-colored glasses."

"Where does your nan live?"

"Orange County. Near Anaheim. She's in an assisted living facility. Unfortunately, in addition to her diabetes, she has trouble remembering some things. It's not a great combination regarding taking her medication."

"No, I don't suppose it is. Your parents live nearby?"

"Yep. Only a few miles away from the center. I go to visit every Sunday."

Guilt hit me. "I'm sorry you missed seeing your family yesterday."

She regarded me curiously. "It's okay. I FaceTimed her, and we watched an episode of *Little House on the Prairie*. My roommate went by to see her, too. And I'll see her next Sunday, and we'll have the whole day. She's who I got the love of cooking from. I remember countless hours she would teach me when I was little."

I could almost picture her in pigtails up on a step stool absorbing every word. "You seem close with your family."

"I am. Probably why I only moved, like, twenty-five miles north of them."

I couldn't imagine living so close. Even as much as I loved my sister and mother. Guess I'd been gone too long to want to be part of everyday family activities.

The questions kept coming up in my mind. Now that I was getting to know her better, I found I didn't want to stop.

"You're an only child?"

"I am."

"And you're going to school for business administration, but your true passion is cooking?"

She shrugged. "The firm agreed to help with tuition if I chose a degree in line with their purposes. Business administration fit the bill. Culinary school did not."

"Then what is your goal after school?"

"I don't know yet."

"You should have a goal." The very thought of her not having one baffled me. I'd always focused on goals. Even now, I had my next goal in mind. The next rung on the ladder was always something to strive for.

"I'll get there eventually, but for now, I don't have a plan."

"But you mentioned quitting in a few months."

Her face turned red. She removed the sauce from the burner, then turned it on high for the water. She also moved the chicken onto a cutting board. "That was my anger talking. Truthfully, I don't know when I'll leave. The law firm is steady and has good benefits. Why? Were you hoping it would be sooner?"

Yes, because the lines were getting blurred. And no, because I liked how good she was at her job. Not to mention,

I already knew I'd miss her. "No. The last thing I want is to have someone new."

"There's still a possibility I might have to support another partner. At least it's what I was told after my transfer from Mike's team."

Most of the partners shared their secretary with at least one other partner, but so far I'd made the case for having mine support me full-time.

"I know. But if he does anything inappropriate like the last one, you need to come to me."

I already had a call with the managing partner scheduled for tomorrow to discuss my issue with Mike.

"Yeah. I will. Thank you."

This. This was reason one hundred eighty-nine I could not possibly entertain the idea of getting involved with her. Forget my hard line about being involved with someone I worked with. She'd been harassed by her last boss. She didn't need her new one entertaining inappropriate thoughts.

"What do you need the extra money for? Working week-ends at the club?"

Kendall made a good salary at the firm, and given she had a roommate, I wondered why she needed another job.

"School and stuff."

She averted her eyes as she answered. Something wasn't adding up. The firm helped her with school tuition. I was getting the hum I got when I started asking questions and discovered there was something I wanted to dig into.

Chapter Twenty-One

KENDALL

hy did I feel like I was at trial being cross-examined? Probably because I had one of the best in the business asking me questions. I didn't mind sharing some personal details with Liam, as I was glad he was interested, but I certainly wasn't about to spill all my secrets.

"So once school is over in a few months, you'll be able to quit your job bartending?"

Definitely not, but I didn't want to get into the reasons. "Uh. No. I actually enjoy it. Gets me out of my apartment. Otherwise, I think I'd be a homebody all the time."

"What do your parents do?"

"Oh." I was surprised he cared to know. "My dad works part-time on a factory line. He had a heart attack a couple years ago, so he's slowed down a bit. My mom is a teacher." She also cleaned houses on weekends, but I kept the news to myself.

"And your grandmother. What did she used to do?"

"She was a stay-at-home mom. My grandfather was a police officer. He passed away about five years ago."

"And the facility your grandmother lives in is called?"

"It's a Sunrise Living Facility. It's nice. Convenient to where my parents live."

I busied myself with melting the butter in the microwave and grabbing the French bread.

"Are you helping to pay for her care?" His voice was soft and knowing.

I simply stared at him. "I feel like you may have led the witness."

He smiled. "Sorry. It's a bad habit when I think someone is hiding something."

My shoulders drooped. "Not even my parents know."

His forehead crinkled. "How is that possible?"

"I pay the facility directly, and the administrator bills the difference to my parents. I only pitch in two thousand a month."

"How much is the care?"

"Five thousand a month. My grandfather's pension and social security pays some. My parents pay the rest."

"Why lie to them about it?"

"I don't like to think of it as a lie. But I do it because my parents would never dream of having me help. Pride and all that. And I couldn't stand having my nan in a cheaper facility, further away from us."

"Why didn't you simply tell me?"

"Because talking about money makes me feel weird. If someone is complaining about it, then it feels to me like they're asking for some. I make a fair salary at the law firm." The only other person who knew I paid for my grandmother's care was my roommate, Chloe. If anyone understood having to help out with the family, it was her. She, too, had to supplement her family's finances.

He gave me a quick glance, stirring the sauce. As if he

knew how important my admission was, he reassured me. "I won't tell anyone, just like I trust anything I've confided in you won't be repeated."

"No. Never." I knew how the gossip mills worked at the firm. I'd take it to my grave. "The water is boiling. Let's put in our homemade pasta."

After everything was cooked, we sat down at the table in silence. I held my breath and watched Liam's expression when he took his first bite.

He closed his eyes and made a humming sound in his throat. "Jesus, this is good."

My grin was the stupid, silly kind. "You helped. So thank you." I took my own bite and was immediately assaulted with the rich flavors. "Nothing beats homemade pasta. I especially love making ravioli or gnocchi."

"If you ever decide to be a personal chef, please let me be your first client. I may have to up my gym routine, but I think it would be worth it."

He had no idea how much his words meant to me. "Thank you."

He let out a sigh and changed the subject back to his favorite: work. "Tomorrow I need to focus on billing. I can't put it off any longer this month."

He did have a number of clients for whom we needed to get bills out the door. "What if I take a crack at it? Since they're Word documents, I'll do everything in Track Changes, and you can accept or not. Then you can focus fully on the deposition."

"Sure. I'd appreciate it. Also I have four calls tomorrow."

"Yes, I saw that on your calendar. Do you need anything for them?"

"No. Thank you. I think I'm good."

My mind was having trouble catching up with the turn of

events. He was acting reasonable, and I was no longer thinking of ways for him to suffer.

The only problem was that now I was no longer thinking of him as an asshole, I was just left thinking about him period.

I WAS EXHAUSTED by Tuesday night. It had been another fourteen-hour workday. But at least it had been productive. For once I was glad not to be cooking. Instead Liam went out to pick up pizza in preparation for his mom coming over. I quickly vacuumed, only stopping when he came in holding two pizzas and a bag.

He was frowning.

"Everything okay?"

"You don't need to clean."

I rolled my eyes. "Sure, I do. Your mom is coming over, and there was some dirt on the carpet from us getting wood." I flipped the on switch on the ancient upright only to be shocked when he took it from me.

"Then, let me do it. You're off the clock."

The vacuuming really seemed to bother him. I went to get the pizzas he'd put on the table only to have him frown again. "Leave them. I can heat a pizza."

"Okay, then." I decided to go back to my bedroom and change into jeans. The knock came just as I'd buttoned them up.

"Come in," I called out.

Liam opened the door but stood in the frame. "I didn't mean you needed to leave. But it bothered me to see you cleaning."

"Why?"

"Because you do enough for me. You don't need to go and clean for my mother coming over."

My lips parted in surprise.

"Anyhow, you're welcome to join us for dinner. I bought more wine."

My lips curved up into a smile. "Red?"

"One Pinot Noir and another Malbec."

"My hero." We exchanged grins which made my stomach flutter. With us getting along, that sort of thing was happening more often.

An hour later once his mother arrived, we sat down to a pizza dinner. "You took care of the catering for the funeral reception?" she asked him.

"Yes. Kendall found a place out of Blacksburg to cater it."

"Good. But I hope the snow doesn't interfere."

"Snow?" we both said at the same time.

"Yes. But it'll probably only be a couple of inches like the last one."

Thank goodness.

"Liam, I'd like you to go down to the mortuary tomorrow morning to at least see your father one last time before the body is released."

His entire body stiffened with her words. His voice was flat and monotone when he spoke. "I thought he was being cremated."

"He is. But I think you should at least make peace with him before that happens."

"I've made my peace, Mother."

"Please. For me."

"I'll think about it."

She clasped her son's hand. "It would make me happy. So very happy."

After his mother left, Liam cleaned up the kitchen without a word.

I decided to leave him to his thoughts despite the urge to comfort him. I'd already made the mistake of asking him if he was okay and been snapped at in return. It wouldn't be worth risking our truce to ask a second time.

I heard the sound of his footsteps climbing the stairs around ten while I lay in my bed. Deciding to grab some water then, I puttered out to the living room in my LA Ram's jersey. Considering it hung to my knees, it was more than modest. Still, I wasn't prepared to face Liam. But when I opened the refrigerator, its light showed him sitting at the table. He had a tumbler of whiskey in his hand.

"Oh, God, you startled me. I thought you'd gone to bed."

"It was warmer down here with the woodstove." His eyes roamed over my jersey and bare legs.

"Yeah, I guess it is. Do you, uh, want to talk about it?"

"Not with you dressed like that I don't."

I sucked in a breath. "I'll go put on pants." Rushing down the hall, I could feel my skin heat at the way he'd responded. Not like he was offended but almost like he was tempted.

When I returned to the kitchen, I noticed he'd moved to the couch in the living room. I took the chair and folded up my feet beneath me. I knew exactly what had to be weighing on his mind. And since he didn't seem to be shutting me down this time, I went for it. "You don't have to see him."

"You saw how happy it made my mother when I simply said I would think about it."

"Then, lie."

His head snapped up. "I won't lie to my mom."

It was clear there was some judgment about my hiding from my parents the payments for my grandmother. "Right, the way you don't lie to her that you're too busy to come home."

"I am busy. You see me. I spend every minute trying to turn it into billable dollars."

"Agreed, but you could also reprioritize if you wanted to. You simply don't want to. Not that I blame you, but you're not only lying to her, but to yourself if you say being busy is the only reason you haven't been home in years."

"Fourteen."

"What?"

"It's been fourteen years since I've been home. The day after I graduated from high school I didn't look back. Went off to UVA, then Stanford Law School, then moved to Los Angeles. While I was in law school, my grandparents died. I couldn't even afford to come home for their funerals."

At the age of thirty, he'd become the youngest income partner with the firm. Now at thirty-two, he was one of the highest paid equity partners. A feat I was sure many were envious of. A feat I was starting to understand he'd been driven to attain. Rumor was he was gunning for named partner. It would be unprecedented to have someone other than the founding two partners up on the letterhead. Yet it wouldn't surprise me if Liam made it happen.

"Do you enjoy the law?" I found myself wondering now if all his hard work and ambition was more about proving himself than about doing something he liked.

"It was always my goal to make partner. To allow my mother to live comfortably without a worry for once. We were on food stamps growing up. Scraping every penny. It was the only way my mom could hold it together."

I could imagine he'd been eager to get out of the small town and away from everyone who'd known. "It's incredible how she made it work. How hard you worked to make something of yourself."

His somber eyes met mine. "It's not the town's fault my father was an alcoholic who left us, but I hate it just the same."

"No, you don't. You hate the memories. It's the real reason you don't want to come home."

He lifted his glass in a mock salute. "I sometimes worry about becoming like him."

"You wouldn't."

"You don't know that."

Chapter Twenty-Two

LIAM

*M*y eyes stayed glued on Kendall's face after expressing my last words. The fear of becoming my father was what would prevent me from ever having a family of my own someday. Hell, hadn't I already made her feel less than? Like she couldn't do anything right? Those weren't the actions of an honorable man. I could argue all I wanted that my unpleasant behavior had been self-preservation in not allowing her to get too close, but the truth was too hard to ignore. Perhaps it was in my DNA to be an asshole.

"You didn't answer my question," she said.

No, I hadn't. Instead, I was busy trying to rein in my erection from the sight of her in nothing but a jersey a few minutes ago.

"What question is that?"

"Do you enjoy the law? Or being a lawyer? You told me the reasons you went into it. And I can see your drive. But do you love it?"

"I love certain aspects. I guess you could say I enjoy

being good at my job. Being respected for something which seems to come fairly naturally."

"And the hours?"

"They're part of the job."

"No work-life balance?"

I supposed I'd need a personal life in order to want to balance it. "It's where it needs to be for the moment."

"Are you hoping to make named partner?"

I took a sip of my whiskey, not at all surprised the rumor mill had gotten wind of my aspiration. "What partner wouldn't want the distinction?" Of course few were actively killing themselves for the goal, but that was fine by me. Less competition in the way. In my mind, I was one large client away from sealing the deal. But time would tell.

"Well, my ex-boss was one of the laziest partners, so not him."

No, he was too busy groping his staff. "Speaking of which, Mike Octavus is leaving the firm."

Her eyes went wide as saucers. "What? Since when?"

"I received the news today."

"Did something else happen?"

Something had happened, all right. I'd spoken to the managing partner. He'd admitted the incident with Kendall hadn't been Mike's first transgression in sexually harassing women. Obviously, the guy was a major problem. I'd made it clear I wanted him out. It was an easy decision for them to make, considering I was the top biller in the firm, and Mike had struggled the last few years.

"Upper management realized what a liability he was."

"You said something? After I spoke about him?"

I didn't bother to deny it. "Of course I did. His behavior was unacceptable."

Her glare was quick. "I told you what happened in confidence."

"Why wouldn't you be happy? Now he can't inflict any more unwanted advances on women at the firm."

"How would you feel if I'd told your mom how much it bothers you to go see your father? Something you told me in confidence. The intention can be good, but I can guarantee my meddling would upset you."

She had a point. One I was sure I could argue ten different ways, especially since I absolutely didn't regret getting someone fired who sexually harassed women, but ultimately it came down to how I'd made her feel. "I'm sorry. You're right. I should've run it by you first."

She seemed to settle down with my apology. "I honestly didn't know it would bother you that much."

"Of course it did. You weren't the only woman, by the way, who Mike had harassed. I think of his dismissal as preventative. No future female will have to put up with him."

"I suppose that's true."

Deciding I'd reached my limit on personal baggage, I stood up. "We have a busy day tomorrow. I'm going to turn in."

"Okay. Good night. And thank you. Although I was initially upset, I appreciate you for caring enough about what I said to do something about it."

Later that night, as I lay in bed, I thought of Kendall. I absolutely wouldn't get involved with someone I worked with at a firm of which I hoped to be in charge someday, but I had to admit our newfound friendship meant a lot to me.

Of course, I didn't typically think of my friends naked.

THE NEXT MORNING, I sat in front of the funeral home in the truck, trying to figure out what I was going to do. I was tempted to do as Kendall had suggested. Lie to my mother. But it didn't sit well. Of course, neither did the fact that I'd been lying to her all along about why I didn't come home. Kendall had hit the nail on the head with that one.

Finally, I got out of the cab of the truck and looked up at the cloudy sky. With the cool temperature, it wouldn't surprise me to see some flakes soon. Once inside, I was immediately greeted by the director, Larry White.

"You must be Liam. Right this way. We were expecting you. Your sister is already here."

It was unexpected for Allison to be here. Yet not in a bad way. Considering she and I had shared our childhood, it was comforting to have her here. I walked into the room slowly and spotted her sitting in a chair, her head in her hands, weeping. Ah, crap.

I sat down beside her and put my arm around her. "Shhhh, let it all out. I've got you."

After a few minutes of crying, she took a deep breath and met my gaze. "You always did. God, you were two years younger, yet you were such a little man. I was terrified the night he left, but you told me to go hide in my room. That it would be okay. I could hear the sound of shattered glass. Hear Mom crying and begging him not to go. All I could think of was *please go*. Please leave and never come back."

I swallowed past the lump in my throat. In all these years, we'd never talked about it. Never spoken about the night forever etched on my brain. "I prayed for the same. Then felt guilty when Mom had to pick up the pieces." Both literally and figuratively.

"I'm so angry with her for forgiving him. It makes me

think if he'd come back at any time, she would've forgiven him then, too. There could've been more violence. It could've been a cycle we never would've escaped from."

For the very first time, I appreciated the fact he hadn't come back. The thought struck me so profoundly. "You're right. She probably would've. I was angry, too. But I think, as a victim, she didn't know what else to do. I can forgive her for it, but I'm not sure I can ever forgive him."

"Me, neither. Mom ambushed me with him at the house. Brought him over to try to talk to me. I wanted to tell him to get the hell out, but I couldn't do that with the girls there. Which meant I had to listen. Listen to all of the apologies. Mom sat there like she was so proud of him for changing. Told me the Christian thing to do was to forgive him."

I scoffed. "Just because she did doesn't mean we have to, but I think we can make peace with it. Be grateful we both turned out somewhat normal despite what happened."

She nudged me with her elbow. "You mean I'm halfway normal after loads of counseling. You have workaholic issues."

I laughed. "Yeah, I suppose I do."

"I've missed you, brother. I understand why you don't like to come home, but I've missed you."

"I've missed you, too. And I need to make an effort to come home more often. Make new memories to cancel out the old ones."

"Make sure you bring Kendall. I really like her."

I let out a long sigh. "She's my assistant."

"So you keep saying, but don't think I don't notice how you look at her."

My wide eyes met her knowing ones. "She's all of twenty-four, Ally, and did I mention she works for me? She's employed by the firm I hope to put my name on. I need to be untarnished by even a whisper of a rumor if I ever hope to make named partner."

"But she only works there until she gets her degree, right? Then she's probably leaving, and you'll both be free to date who you want."

Kendall had mentioned quitting during the next year. My heart started beating harder with the thought. Could I pursue her after she quit? But to what end? It wasn't as if I had time for a relationship. And she wasn't the type who seemed to want anything less than the real deal. "I don't think she'll be ready to leave the firm for a while. And I don't have the room in my life for anything serious."

She sighed. "You don't have room because you don't make room. Are you planning to talk to him?" She gestured to the body up in the front of the room.

"I don't know."

"I did. It wasn't very nice, but I think I needed to say it. I have to get back to the girls, but I'll see you tomorrow for the funeral. We'll get through it, little brother. I promise."

I stood up with her and hugged her tightly. "Yes, we will. See you tomorrow."

As soon as she left, I forced myself to walk closer to see him. He looked so different. Older, though that was to expected. As much as my mother would've liked for me to make peace, I found my fists clenching and painful, suppressed memories coming to the surface. Damn. I'd never been good enough for him. How many times had I hoped if maybe I hit a homerun, or got an A on a test, he'd finally say it was enough? Finally be proud of me. Finally love me.

Why did he have to come back? We'd all been better off forgetting about him.

Turning around and stalking out, I was already counting the hours until the man could be officially out of my life forever.

As SOON AS I'd pulled into the driveway of the rental, Kendall was out the front door in her ridiculously ugly coat and lavender boots. It had started to snow, so I thought at first she was outside to try another snow angel. Then I saw the absolute panic on her face.

I jumped out of the truck immediately. "What's wrong?"

"The caterer just called to cancel. They said the woman who was supposed to drive is petrified of the snow. I offered to pick it up instead, but she said the cook won't be coming in, either, with the ice storm they're getting today. Evidently, the weather is worse in Blacksburg. I called all around, and it's too short notice to hire anyone else. I need to go to the grocery store."

"Do they have deli platters there or something?" My mom would have to understand.

"I'm not sure. But I'll think of something. Can you drive me? I might be awhile, so you can come back and wait for my call when I'm checking out. I know you have a lot of work to do."

I did have some pressing items. "I'll drive you, then make the calls I need from the truck. Are you attempting to cook something?"

"Yeah. I'm going to try."

"This isn't the end of the world. We'll get cookies and brownies or something."

She was already shaking her head. "No. We can't. Your mother will be disappointed. I can fix this. I can cook."

"I don't want you stressing over this." Not over a man who didn't deserve it. "Not for him."

She took my hand in her gloved one. "It's for her. I promise."

Chapter Twenty-Three

KENDALL

*M*y hand was shaking as I wrote out a list of the things I needed from the store while Liam drove us the few miles. He turned to me once we parked.

"Kendall, I mean it. I don't want you going to any trouble."

I knew he meant it, but it didn't matter. I wanted to make sure this was done right.

"We can get some meats and cheese and bread and people can fix sandwiches."

That was true. I'd probably do sandwiches. But there needed to be more. His mother was just saying last night how the entire church was coming. How she'd told everyone about the food. "Yes. We can." I looked across the parking lot to see the Dollar Store. "I need to go there first for serveware."

"Okay. You want me to go in with you? My call doesn't start for twenty minutes."

"Nope. Twenty minutes is almost three hundred dollars' worth of billable hours." Frankly I didn't need the pressure of him waiting on me.

"Here's my credit card. Text me if you have any trouble using it, and I can come in."

"Okay. Thank you."

Think, Kendall. Think. What did I need? I was pleased to see they had a variety of foil pans, paper plates, cups, and serveware. But the last thing I needed was to start shoving stuff into the cart without an idea of what would go with what. I took a deep breath, picturing the menu I had in mind. Then I went to work. Fifty-eight dollars later I had a cart full.

Liam got out of the truck and helped me with the bags, holding a finger to his Bluetooth to indicate he was still on a call. "Yes, I understand what you're saying. However, you hired me to give you advice. If you don't choose to follow it, then I can't be responsible for the result."

Damn. I'd heard him plenty of times on the phone, so why was his authoritative voice turning me on now?

"Good, I'm glad we agree, then. I'll be sure to get the paperwork to you tonight."

He hung up, giving me a smile. "You buy out the store?"

"Not quite. At least everything was only a dollar, and it only came to fifty-eight. Okay, now the grocery store."

"Do you mind if I do another call?"

I was shocked he asked. "Nope. Not at all."

It took me an hour. I went back and forth with many menu possibilities in mind. I had to settle on some because the place was a zoo given the threat of snow. Jesus, weren't people just here a couple days ago? Then again, wasn't I?

Once we got back to the house, Liam helped me bring stuff inside, but then he had to disappear upstairs for a video call. I knew he would need me to do some work, so I put away what needed to be frozen and refrigerated and then went upstairs once I heard his call end.

"Okay. What do we have?"

He looked torn, so I reassured him. "It's okay. I have plenty of time for the cooking later."

"I want to make sure I pay you for it. Whatever we were paying the caterer."

It was a generous offer considering it was near a thousand dollars, but I wouldn't take it. Hell, he'd paid for all of the food already. "We can discuss it later."

It was ten o'clock before we were done working. It was the disadvantage of being on the East Coast while most of our clients were in the LA time zone. It made me wish I'd picked up a Red Bull. Coffee would have to do.

"Shit," he cursed, reading his email. "They're asking if I can do a call with Hong Kong in ten minutes, but I wanted to help you with the food."

"It's okay." I'd probably do it faster without him in the kitchen distracting me with sexy forearms.

Two hours later at the stroke of midnight, I'd hit a wall. I'd done meatballs, mini quiche, and prepared two trays of mini sandwiches cut in triangles. There was a veggie tray to go with that. But I still had four more dishes to make plus desserts. I decided I needed a nap, so I cleaned up what I had done so far and went to lie down for ninety minutes. It sounded like Liam was still on the phone, so I didn't bother to tell him.

AT ONE THIRTY in the morning, I dragged myself out of bed and started to prepare my next dishes. A fruit salad, stuffed mushrooms, French piped potatoes, and salmon croquettes. By the time the sun was coming up, I was taking the last of the chocolate-chip cookies out of the oven to join the fudge brownies, snickerdoodles, and blondies.

The kitchen was a mess, with pots and pans in the sink and crumbs all over the counter. I was sure I looked worse.

"You're up already?" came Liam's voice as he walked down the stairs.

"Yeah. I think I'm finished." I rattled off the menu and watched his mouth gape.

"You stayed up all night, didn't you? I came down to check on you and didn't see you. I thought you'd gone to bed."

"I took a power nap. It's fine."

"No, it's not. You're exhausted. Come on. You need to sleep."

My eyes were heavy and my head muddled. It felt as though I'd had more than my fair share of alcohol instead of staying up all night. "I need to clean up the kitchen. I don't like dirty dishes."

"I'll do it."

"No, no. I'll get my second wind. You have the funeral today."

"That's not until eleven, and it's only seven now. My sister is driving my mom while we bring the food to the church."

"'Kay." My mind was already shutting down. Man, I really didn't do well without sleep.

"Go to bed, Kendall."

"Uh-huh. I will. Just need a little rest first." I intended to sit on the couch for a minute. But instead, strong arms lifted me up.

Chapter Twenty-Four

LIAM

*S*he was dead on her feet. If I'd known she would be up all night, I wouldn't have gone to bed. I would've helped. Now, seeing her sit on the sofa as if she was too tired to make it into the bedroom, I did the only thing I could. I picked her up.

She was so small. So warm. So snuggling into my chest. I had to take a deep breath to calm my rapid heartbeat, but breathing in her scent had been a mistake. Strawberry lip gloss tickled my nose.

"This isn't the way I imagined you taking me to bed," she murmured once I got into her room.

My breath caught at her admission.

I set her down gently, pulling the covers up over her to effectively tuck her in. "How did you picture it?" Despite realizing we were in dangerous territory, I had to know.

She was so beautiful despite her exhaustion. I found my hand couldn't help but reach out and move her hair to the side, stroking her cheek.

Her eyes went wide. "I shouldn't have said that out loud."

Which meant she was definitely thinking it. "It's okay. I know you're tired. Get some sleep."

"You'll wake me up in time?"

"Yes. I sure will."

I DIDN'T WANT to wake her. Her face was relaxed in slumber. Her body curled up on her side as she cuddled a pillow. I was tempted to leave her here while I delivered the food to the church, but I knew with all of the work she'd done, she should at least be there to take the credit. Selfishly, it also took my mind off of the funeral to know she'd be there with me.

Without even trying, she calmed me. Eased my tension and anxiety about today. This was ironic since merely a week ago I'd been intensely uncomfortable around her. But I realized in dropping my barrier with her, I'd been given a gift. A gift of getting to know her. But it came with a responsibility. A responsibility to keep the professional lines intact. She was my assistant. I was her boss. Despite the temptation, I couldn't risk a physical relationship with her.

I tapped her shoulder gently. "Time to wake up."

Her eyes blinked open slowly. The way she looked at me made my heartbeat double. As if we were frozen in this moment. As if she'd love nothing more than for me to climb into bed with her and gather her close.

The thought was so enticing I had to step back. "It's nine thirty. We should leave in a half hour."

"'Kay."

I left to give her privacy and heard the sound of the shower start. Jesus. Maybe I needed another one. A cold one.

A half hour later we loaded up the truck and headed to the church.

"You doing okay?" she asked.

I glanced over in her direction where she sat in the passenger seat. "Yeah. Thanks." And because it felt right to share, I said, "I saw him yesterday."

"How did it go?"

"Rough, as expected. But at least I can tell her I did it. I'm looking forward to getting back to reality tomorrow."

"If it helps, I checked on our flights, and they're still on schedule despite the snow."

"Good. I'm guessing you're working tomorrow night?" At the club.

"Yeah. Both Friday and Saturday nights."

What could I say? That I didn't like it. That I wanted her to quit even knowing she used the money to help her family. "Will you be short this month for your grandmother's housing payment since you didn't work last weekend?"

"No. The overtime from this week will more than compensate for it."

I suddenly had an idea. What if I could offer her more overtime work on the weekends? She could help me with my cases instead of bartending at the club. I certainly had enough to keep her busy. But now wasn't the time for the discussion as we'd just pulled up in front of the church.

My mother stood there as if she was waiting. I noticed the relief on her face. Almost as though she'd worried about whether or not I would show up. Today would be hard as they'd be talking about a man I never knew. A man my mother believed deserved the good things said about him. I would figure out a way to be okay with a new angle on an old history.

"You okay?" Kendall asked before we opened the doors. This time she focused on me fully with her body turned.

My hand took hers as if it was the most natural action in the world. "Ask me later. Come on. Let's unload the best food anyone in this town will have ever eaten."

Just smelling it made me hungry. But knowing how hard she'd worked on everything humbled me. It also made my chest tight; I was aware of how tired she must be now.

The next hour was a blur. Since there were plenty of church volunteers to help Kendall, I had no choice but to go with my family into the church. There sat the urn. At least I could be thankful there wasn't an open casket. Seeing him yesterday had been hard enough.

Sitting still during the service was near impossible. I sat next to my mother, swallowing down the bitter taste while I listened to the kind words the preacher had to say. It was all I could do to remain cordial while people expressed their condolences after the service.

Once we went into the reception hall, I grabbed a moment to myself, slipping out the back door to breathe in the frozen air. I had no coat, yet I didn't feel the cold. A voice brought me out of my internal thoughts.

"There you are, handsome."

I turned toward the door to see Tonya. We'd dated for all of two months in high school. Although she'd aged well and still had a rockin' body, my dick didn't even stir in her presence.

"Hello."

"You, uh, interested in finding a quiet corner? Warmer than having to escape outside."

I was, but not if it included her.

It was as if she read my mind. "Try downstairs where they

have the day care. They have restrooms down there if you need a minute."

"Thanks, Tonya."

"Anytime, sugar."

I took a breath when I heard the door shut again. Perhaps I would take a moment and go downstairs to collect my thoughts. I went back in and skirted around the back though I did catch a glimpse of Kendall. She looked lovely in a black wrap dress. Her hair was back in a low ponytail, and she was happily manning the food tables. I could already hear the murmurs of people's compliments about the catering.

It took me a minute to find the stairs down, but once I did, it was just as Tonya described. Quiet. I went into the men's room and splashed water on my face, afterward studying my reflection in the mirror. My eyes were drooping. My face pale. I was tired. And in dire need of a good, punishing work-out. The type to get my blood flowing and my mind back where it needed to be. Tomorrow couldn't come fast enough for my return to California.

Anger unexpectedly coursed through me. I cursed out loud, talking myself down from hitting a wall or a mirror. I wouldn't. No. I was in control. Only I could feel it slipping. Feel the careful façade I'd built over the years, the one exuding confidence and composure, start to crumble. My skin was tight. My breathing uneven. Maybe I was having a nervous breakdown. Or an anxiety attack of some sort. The sound of a soft knock took me off guard.

Chapter Twenty-Five

KENDALL

The food was a hit. Liam's mother came up to thank me profusely for such a lovely spread, making all of the stress and hard work worth it. Not even the snow had kept a crowd of sixty from coming out. I was happy to provide what little comfort I could to her and the family.

Allison walked up with her youngest daughter on her hip. "God, these meatballs are the best thing ever. Well, maybe not compared to the quiche or these little salmon things. You are in the wrong job, Kendall. You need to cater."

"Thank you. I'm just glad it worked out okay."

"I would guess it worked out better than the food from the place in Blacksburg." She scanned the people in the spacious room. "Have you seen my brother?"

"No. Not since after the service." I'd seen him walk out. He'd looked a bit lost. And I'd had to keep myself from going up to take his hand. But in light of what I may or may not have said early this morning, I kept my distance. My thoughts were hazy as to whether he'd carried me to my bed. And as to whether I'd told him it wasn't the way I'd imagined. Or maybe it had been part of my dream? I'd been so tired I'd been delirious.

One of the church ladies approached me with a smile. "Did you bring any coffee to serve with the desserts, my dear?"

"No. I didn't." My shoulders sagged as I realized I should've thought of it.

"No worries. We have some. It's downstairs in the storage room, though."

"I'll go get it if you give me directions."

I set off for the coffee with explicit directions: go down the steps and turn left past the restrooms until you hit the room at the end of the hallway.

As soon as I came up on the men's restroom, however, I heard a loud curse followed by some muttering. Huh. It sounded like Liam. I paused, about to move on when I heard it again. This time there was no mistaking his voice. I felt like I'd recognize it anywhere.

Not knowing what to expect, I knocked on the men's room door. When there was no answer, I let out a soft, "Hello."

Liam opened the door and, for a moment, looked completely out of sorts.

"You okay?"

"Fine. What are you doing down here?"

He didn't look fine. He looked as if he wanted to run far, far away.

"Oh, one of the ladies told me to get coffee from the storage room. I guess it's at the end of this hall. I heard you in here, but I didn't mean to intrude."

His face softened. "You didn't. Come on. I'll help you get the coffee."

We walked in silence to the end of the hall where we

found the gray door the church lady had described. Opening it revealed a small closet with shelves on one side containing staple items like coffee. On the other side were brooms and dustpans. I reached up to the tall shelf, but it was a good six inches too high. Thankfully, Liam reached over me for the assist, giving me one of his rare smiles.

We both froze at the woman's voice behind us. "There you are. Although I would've preferred the restroom, I can certainly take your mind off of things in the supply closet just as well, sugar."

I turned around, realizing Liam's body was blocking me from view. Tonya had thought it was only him in front of the closet.

His gaze met mine, a mixture of annoyance and humor in the depths of it. "You okay with another fake rescue?" he murmured, drawing my hungry gaze to his full lips.

"What did you have in mind?" My voice was breathless. My mind raced with the possibility of pretending to be his girlfriend again.

He turned to face his high school ex. "I'm down here with Kendall, but again, I appreciate you telling me where we could get some privacy."

I peeked around him to watch her face turn red, and I parroted his words. "Yes. Appreciate it."

But she didn't leave right away. Not until Liam faced me, placing his hands at my hips and leaning down as if he was about to kiss me, pausing at the last second.

I barely registered the sound of her walking away. Instead, my hands found their way around his neck, my body inching closer to his until we were touching. I should have pulled away now that she was gone. But I couldn't. Instead, we closed the gap, and suddenly his mouth was on mine.

His full lips soft to the touch, yet possessive in his exploration. Heat coursed immediately through my body with the contact.

A throaty moan was my response when he moved the kiss to my neck.

"We should stop," he whispered against my ear.

"Uh-huh. Or we could ensure she gets the message in case she comes back." It was an excuse. A flimsy excuse to keep kissing him.

He nibbled my bottom lip. As soon as his tongue entered my mouth again, I seized it, sucking on it lightly and causing him to growl. It was as if a switch had been flipped. No longer were we tentative and exploring. We were carnal.

His hands gripped my ass, and he lifted me up onto the shelf while he kicked the door closed.

The darkness was immediate, but I didn't care once he stepped in between my legs. Oh, God, I could feel him hard against me. I practically rolled my hips into his at the erotic contact. I needed him. It was clear by the way his hands were quickly moving my dress up that he needed me, too. We were both desperate for more. My hands fumbled with his belt while he made quick work out of yanking down my thong. Next he began searching for what I assumed was his wallet.

"Shit, no condom."

My hands halted, disappointment hitting me hard. "I'm not on the pill." Not that pregnancy was the only reason we shouldn't go bare.

He cursed, bending his head to my neck. The sensation of his heavy breath in my ear was giving me shivers. So was the fact that we were unbelievably close.

Suddenly he turned around. It sounded as though he was pulling up his trousers. I seemed to be on my own for getting down from the shelf. I clumsily did so, pulling up my thong and trying to straighten my dress.

I was at a loss for words, waiting for him to say something.

Finally, he opened the door, letting in the light.

While his back was still turned, I smoothed my hair down. I was sure my lips were swollen, making me appear like I'd been fucked senseless.

The thought we'd been doing this in the basement of the church holding his father's funeral instantly shamed me.

"Are you okay?" I asked tentatively.

He finally spun around and made eye contact. Barely. His expression had regret written all over it. Even his voice was small. "I need to get back upstairs."

Right. To return to his grieving family. This had been a bad idea all the way around. "Of course. You should go." I needed a moment to calm myself before I could be seen again.

He took a step, then turned back toward me, opening his mouth but evidently deciding against whatever he was going to say. Instead, he simply left without another word, leaving me there with tears in my eyes and shame heavy on my shoulders.

What the hell had I done?

Chapter Twenty-Six

LIAM

*E*scape could not come quickly enough. My heartbeat was pounding in my ears, and the only thing I could think of was how I'd almost fucked my assistant in the supply closet down in the basement of the church.

Self-loathing wasn't a strong enough word for what I was feeling. Simply put, I'd been ready to use her against a storage room shelf. If I'd had a condom, there was no doubt I'd still be balls deep inside of her. Had I even touched her to make sure she was ready? Nope. I'd been ready to rut against her like a selfish bastard.

I'd screwed up.

Royally.

I was in a daze as I climbed the stairs to the funeral reception. I had to get out of here.

"You okay?" my sister asked, coming up to me with her brows drawn together in concern.

"No. I need a drive. Can you drop Kendall off at the house?"

"Sure. But are you all right? You don't look so hot." If I

appeared one-tenth as bad as I was feeling, it was no wonder she was concerned.

"I will be. Just gotta leave."

"Okay. Call me later or at least text. Or if you want to come over—you can."

"I'll let you know."

I drove to a local place, three miles away, and took a seat at the old wooden bar. "Bourbon neat," I ordered. "Can you leave the bottle?"

The old barkeep looked like he could play Santa during December. "You got it," he said with a kind smile.

I tipped back my first swallow. God, it burned. No top shelf here.

What the hell was I going to do? Would we be able to work together again? Would she accept my apology? Was she already calling HR? It might be unfair for me to automatically jump to the conclusion she'd take it there, but then again, I wouldn't blame her. Especially after I'd simply left her following my manhandling. I was no better than her last boss.

Another swallow went down, burning less this time. My phone vibrated with my mother's number displayed. I silenced it and then threw back another shot. Numb. I wanted to be numb to the fact I was a horrible son, a terrible boss, and an even worse human being.

One of the older men two stools down tapped the bar top. "You Fred Davenport's son?"

My gaze focused on him, trying to place his weathered face, wire-rimmed glasses, and crooked smile. "Who's asking?"

"Name is Chuck. Chuck Lassiter. Used to work with him. You resemble your old man. I mean when he was younger. Was sorry to read his obituary in the paper."

That made one of us. "Thanks."

"Anyhow. Hope your mom is doing okay. She was always a nice lady."

Yes, she was. And if ever I believed in divine intervention, this was it. I wouldn't sit here and get drunk like my father would have. I'd man up and be there for my family. Face my screwup with Kendall. "My mom is all right. Thanks for asking." I threw a hundred down on the bar and motioned to the barkeep. "Next drink for Chuck is on me. Keep the rest. Thanks."

I WALKED into a darkened rental house, having come from my sister's place. I'd gone straight there from the bar, spending the rest of the afternoon with both my sister and my mom. It was important for me to be there for the both of them.

Ally had asked Kendall to come over, but she'd opted instead to be dropped off at the rental. I couldn't blame her. Not only had I made it awkward for her to be around my family, but I also doubted she wanted to see me.

It was after nine o'clock, and I wondered if she was already in bed. My question was answered when I walked down the hall and saw the light on under her bedroom door.

Part of me wanted to take the chickenshit route and just go upstairs, but there was too much at stake to avoid talking to her tonight. *Deep breaths. Don't apologize too quickly or come off as guilty. Feel her out and see where her head is first. If she hates me, then talk to her and try to fix this before it goes to HR.*

I held up my hand to knock when the door opened to reveal her in a messy bun and dressed in only her Ram's jersey—apparently fresh from the shower.

"Hi," she greeted tentatively.

I tried unsuccessfully not to breathe in her fresh scent. Nothing like a distraction when my entire career was held in the balance. *Named partners did not have flings with their assistants.* "Hi."

We both stood there, staring at one another. I was trying to work out what I would say when she beat me to it.

"I'm sorry about earlier. In the storage room. I didn't mean to take advantage. I wasn't thinking, and then I really wasn't thinking. And I apologize."

"What?" What in the hell was she saying? Why the hell was she apologizing?

"It was your father's funeral and you were feeling vulnerable and having a tough time. It was supposed to be a fake kiss, then it— Well, you were there to know the rest. I've beaten myself up over and over about the timing. I know you had serious regret on your face, and I caused you to leave which—"

She could not be serious. "Stop." I couldn't let her continue to feel one ounce of responsibility in this. So much for proceeding with caution. Her candor took me completely off guard. "This was not you. It's on me. I'm the one who screwed up. If you plan to go to HR about me, I wouldn't blame you, but I'd like for you to give me the courtesy of discussing it first."

She was shaking her head. "What are you talking about?"

The words were bitter on my tongue. "I crossed a line. A big one. It's inexcusable." She was twenty-four. I was her boss. I'd insisted she come here this week. I was in a position of power, and I'd abused it. I was unprepared for her temper.

"Is this because I reported my last boss? Am I now that girl? I know the damn difference between getting an unwanted grope of my ass at a Christmas party and taking part in a consensual kiss."

"No. Jesus. I didn't mean to imply you were. I have no clue where your head is regarding what happened." If she wanted to, she could threaten everything I'd ever worked for.

"You think I'm trying to use this to—what? Get you fired?"

My temple throbbed. "You very well could if you wanted to."

She studied me. "I'm trying to figure out if something happened to you to make you this cynical in general, or if this is personal toward me."

"It's not personal, Kendall; it's just—" I *was* cynical. I took a deep breath. "I need to know that come tomorrow morning we can be back to normal. Can we do that?" What I wanted to say was could I trust her? Or would this end up being the worst mistake of my life?

"We can be normal tomorrow. You have my word on it."

Here was hoping I could trust her.

Chapter Twenty-Seven

LIAM

*M*y alarm went off way too early. Not even the shower could make me feel human with the hangover I was sporting. After speaking with Kendall last night, I'd gone up to the office and polished off my bottle of bourbon. It hadn't been my wisest decision. Chalk it up to a day full of bad ones. Since I was normally cautious about how much I drank, I was a serious lightweight when it came to paying for any overindulgence. I slurped water from the tap, took some Advil, and dressed slowly. Then I had to pack.

By the time I went downstairs, I could tell Kendall had been busy. The trash had been taken out. All of the files were packed. Her suitcases were already placed by the front door. She was currently wiping down the counters and table.

"What can I do?" I asked, my voice sounding rough.

She barely made eye contact. "Nothing, except take a shower and pack. There's coffee in the pot if you want it. If not, then I'll throw it out."

She was almost cold. Efficient, but cold. She was acting as if it was before we'd sat in this living room over wine and spilled our guts.

"I'll drink the coffee. Is everything all right?" I decided to put a toe in the water to see if she was still upset with me over yesterday.

Her expression softened. "Yes. Fine."

"Anything else we need to do with the house?"

"Nope. You gave the wood to your mom, and the flights are on time."

When I went outside to load the truck, I expected Kendall would already be sitting inside it, but instead she was in the yard, attempting to make a snowman with the four inches we'd gotten. She wasn't having any luck getting it to form.

"Here, I'll show you." I made a ball and rolled it along by the illumination of the porch light.

She smiled and did the same. None of the balls we made were very big, but we soon had three of them on top of one another. She was beaming with pride, taking out her camera phone to snap a picture with the flash. "My first snowman."

"It's kind of sad," I remarked wishing we had a chance to do the whole carrot nose and face for it.

She held up a snowball, grinning at me. "Take it back."

I shook my head. "Nope. It's sad and without a face."

She let the ball fly. It did no damage since it basically fell apart.

Unable to resist, I reached down and formed a good one, pelting her on the chest of her coat with it.

She smiled, picking up more snow, pressing it into a ball, and chucking it at me. This one managed to hit me smack in the face.

"Oh, shit. I'm sorry. I wasn't aiming there." But she was in a fit of giggles.

I took her down to the soft snow, holding up a snowball above her face.

"You sure about that?"

She was grinning. "Yes. Please spare me."

"Mm. I don't think so." I only took a chunk off, but plunked it on her nose, causing her to squeal.

"Shh, too loud." It was early morning on a Friday, and there were plenty of neighbors.

One moment we were both breathing hard and laughing, the next, my lips were on hers. I hadn't meant it to happen, yet the kiss seemed like the most natural thing in the world.

Then her arms wound around my neck. Her tongue invaded my mouth, dueling with mine. Damn. This time we couldn't excuse our behavior on a fake girlfriend act or my vulnerability over my father's funeral. I could feel her shifting, almost as though she was trying to put her legs around me.

I wanted it, too. More than anything. But the puffy jacket was like a chastity coat, preventing either one of us from making a further mistake. Or making us miss our flight. I pulled away reluctantly, getting to my feet and helping her up beside me.

"We shouldn't have done that."

She nodded. "I know. I'm sorry."

Her apology once again took me off guard. She was so free with it.

Reaching out, I cupped her chin. "I'm sorry, too. I'll get the bags loaded if you want to start the truck."

She was probably freezing from having lain in the snow.

We drove in silence, only stopping for a coffee place when my stomach demanded I put some food in it. I settled for a latte and croissant while she passed.

Finally, unable to stand it anymore, I had to bring up the kiss. "Are you upset?"

She glanced over. "No, why would I be?"

"Because we crossed a line. Again."

"We already both admitted it was a mistake. I'm not telling anyone. But I'd rather not talk about it, either."

Okay. God, I wanted to believe her. I truly did. Deciding a change in subject was in order, I asked the question: "Did you upgrade your flights to first class?"

"No need. I'm good with coach."

"When we get there, we'll ask the agent."

"You don't have to."

"What if I need you to work and be in first class with me?"

She sighed. "Then, by all means, upgrade me."

THERE WERE NO UPGRADES AVAILABLE. Despite the fact I'd used work as an excuse to try to get her into first class, the truth was I didn't have anything for her to do during the flight.

As with our outgoing trip, we had a brief layover in Chicago, but we barely had time before boarding another plane. Once we landed in LAX, I waited for her to come down the sky ramp.

"Do you need a ride home?" Since we both lived in South Bay, I figured I could give her a lift.

Although she seemed surprised by my offer, she simply replied with, "No, thanks."

"I'm in Manhattan Beach, so Torrance isn't far from me."

"It's okay, but thanks. Have a good weekend, Mr. Davenport. I'll see you Monday in the office."

I was being dismissed. She sped up and went into the ladies' room. I briefly spotted her at baggage claim, but she didn't so much as glance my direction. Instead, she took her suitcases up the escalator to where she was probably catching an Uber home.

Stepping into my empty house after the forty-minute drive in traffic, I waited for the relief over being home to hit me. I'd bought this place as my first major purchase. Three point five million. A view of the beach from the top floor, three bedrooms, three baths. Ultra modern. Just like the Tesla I used to commute to the office every day. Yet neither the vehicle nor the house was giving me the pleasure they normally did upon returning home to them.

I took a hot shower, a short nap, and then ordered in takeout Chinese food while looking at the clock. It was eight in the evening. I imagined Kendall was getting ready for work about now. I should probably put in a couple billable hours to make up for losing so many yesterday, but I didn't. Instead, I sat there sipping water, trying to talk myself out of what I was about to do.

But considering I was already up and getting dressed, it was clear I wouldn't be talked out of this. I texted Chance Maxwell, an occasional client, to ask to be put on the list for tonight. Chance was the owner of the Cheetah Club and others like it. I was sure not all of them were above board, especially in the foreign locations, but I didn't ask, and he certainly didn't tell me.

His text back came almost immediately. *"Consider it done, my friend."*

Chapter Twenty-Eight

KENDALL

*A*fter I arrived home from the airport and took a much-needed nap, I felt like a brand-new person. I hadn't slept well last night, thinking way too much about Liam and our kiss. Then this morning's snow-time activity hadn't exactly inspired sleep on the plane, either. Instead, I'd been thinking about my newfound attraction to my boss. What was most disconcerting was the fact it was more than a physical thing. I was finding myself emotionally invested, too. So when he'd suggested I might go to HR to report him, I felt both a simmering anger and a healthy dose of hurt.

Then again, he was a man who seemed to have a single focus. To become a named partner. Any possible threat toward that aspiration would cause him to panic. This was exactly what he'd done. Ugh. I needed to stop obsessing and get my butt in the shower so I could get to work.

I only wished my roommate, Chloe, was around to go into the club tonight, too. Being without her made it lonely. But she deserved a weekend at home with her family. At least I'd be so busy tonight, it would go by quickly. It always did.

Dressing carefully, I chose my favorite pair of Daisy

Duke denim shorts, fishnet nylons and a crop top. Although I'd never wear these clothes out in my normal daily life, they definitely fit in with the club. I capped the look off with a smoky eye and red lip.

The club was already filling up when I took my place behind the bar. Jose, the other bartender, whistled. "Damn, girl, you're fire tonight."

I smiled. Jose might be gay, but I'd take any male attention I could get right now. My self-esteem evidently needed it. "Thanks, Jose. Are we fully stocked?"

"Yep. I don't think we're out of anything."

That was good news. There was nothing more frustrating than being down someone's favorite liquor. Since this was a busy club, top shelf went quickly. I couldn't see paying five hundred dollars for a bottle of Patron and some juices to go with it, but people did it every night using our bottle service.

An hour later I was into my rhythm. The club was set up with five bars. The one upstairs catered to the VIPs with the private rooms while the four down here were on all the corners of the large space. We were two bartenders to a bar, filling everything from the individual orders of people who came up to the bar to the group orders from waitresses serving the majority of patrons who didn't want to get up out of their seats.

As far as dance clubs went, this one was upscale. Not that I had a lot of knowledge of nightclubs, but the people I worked with definitely did, and everyone said this one was classy.

"Your girl not here tonight?" Jose asked over the loud music.

"Nope. Chloe is up in Canada visiting her family this weekend."

"She missed you last weekend. Hey, suit at the end of the bar is staring at you."

I turned only to have my breath catch.

Liam.

What the hell was he doing here? And why did he have to look so handsome in a white button-down shirt with a charcoal gray sport jacket? He was without a tie, his shirt unbuttoned enough to show the barest hint of skin at his neck.

"I, um, I got him."

I walked over to where Liam had positioned himself at the last stool. Unlike the other men waiting on drinks, who were staring up at the stages where beautiful women in very little clothing danced to the music, his gaze was completely transfixed on me.

"What are you doing here?" I had to shout over the loud music.

"I wanted to see what this place was about."

Oh. I scanned the place, trying to guess what he was thinking. Currently, it was nuts. And totally not his scene. At least I wouldn't think so. "Do you want something to drink?"

He hesitated. "Yeah. I'll do a beer."

"What kind?"

"Amber lager or something."

I poured our amber on draft and handed it to him. "It's ten dollars," I said, rattling off the price as I normally would.

He handed me a twenty. "Keep the change."

"Thanks." His intense eyes were still on mine, but I had a full bar of customers. I couldn't linger.

I worked the bar the next half an hour, but every time I glanced at the end of the bar, Liam was still there. Still watching me.

Noticing he was getting low on his beer, I used it as an excuse to go back down there. "You want another?"

"No. But when do you get a break?"

My heart beat harder. "Why?"

"Because I want to talk to you."

"I don't get breaks where I can talk to customers." I'd have to go to the private employee area, and there was no way I could take him back there. "I'm off at two thirty. We could talk then?"

He glanced at his watch, frowning and probably realizing that was four hours away.

"I've gotta get back. Sorry."

I stepped away to help two college guys ordering Flaming Doctor Peppers, and when I turned back, Liam was gone. I fought my disappointment. What did I expect? Him to sit there and watch me all night?

Jose sidled up next to me. "The suit is talking to the floor manager."

My gaze tracked to where my boss was, in fact, talking to my boss before heading upstairs to the VIP rooms.

"You two a thing?" Jose asked.

"Nope." The p popped on the response as if it would hurt less.

"Then, why do you look like someone kicked your puppy, beautiful?"

I didn't bother to try to mask my disappointment with a smile, knowing all too well some of the upstairs activities included strippers for paying guests. "Because I'm a stupid girl." I took a deep breath. "Who needs to get back to work."

I shook martinis, I poured whiskey, I fixed shots. I was trying to get back into my groove, so when the floor manager came behind the bar to tap me on the shoulder five minutes later, I startled.

"Sorry, didn't mean to scare you. I've got someone in

room four upstairs who wants ten minutes with you. He said his name is Liam."

I opened my mouth, but the floor manager interrupted.

"It's not to strip. He said he just wants to talk? The owner verified him."

I sucked in a breath, completely taken aback by the lengths he'd gone to. "But what about the bar?"

"I'll cover. If you don't feel comfortable, then you don't have to go—that's straight from the owner, Mr. Maxwell himself. Remember, there are cameras, and you only need to give the peace sign to signal someone to come in if you're in trouble."

Chloe had once told me the symbol was the universal distress sign to signal security about something getting out of hand. Not that I'd have to worry about that with Liam, but it was comforting to know the club had such precautions.

"Okay. I'll go." I was way too curious not to.

Jose was already giving me a wink. I weaved my way through the crowd and went up the stairs. The second floor consisted of private VIP booths which overlooked the dance club, but the third floor was closed off to club members unless you were on a separate list. Security was obvious, but when I approached the big man standing there, he simply unfastened the velvet rope without a word. Upon finding room number four down the funky hallway with rainbow lights, I turned the knob and opened the door.

I walked inside, eying the pole and small stage in the center of the room.

Liam had opted not to sit on one of the two leather couches, but was instead standing with his back to me, looking out the large picture window toward the club floor.

"Hi. You wanted to see me?"

He turned with the sound of my voice and walked closer

to me. "I hope this is all right. I wanted a quiet place where we could talk for a few moments."

With his gaze on me, I wrapped my arms around my exposed midriff. "What do you want to talk about?"

"I have an offer for you."

"What kind of offer?" Because I could think of plenty I'd like him to make me. Not one of them appropriate to our work relationship, but all of them getting my hopes up. Perhaps this connection I'd imagined wasn't one-sided.

"I'd like for you to work for me on the weekends to earn overtime instead of here at the club."

I could only stare at him, trying to figure out his motive. Was this an excuse to spend more time with me, or did he truly need someone on the weekends? I had no doubt he probably had the work, but why now? "Why?"

He shifted his feet. "Because you need the money for your grandmother's care, or for your clothes, or whatever, and I have plenty of work to do on the weekends."

My temper snapped. "For my clothes?"

He sighed. "It's not my business, but clearly you're funding your designer wardrobe in addition to supplementing your grandmother's care."

"You're right. It's not your business." Although I may have been tempted to accept his offer, he had to go and piss me off. But even without his insult, spending any more time with him was a bad idea all the way around. "I appreciate the offer, but no."

His confusion was obvious. "Why not?"

"Because I don't want to. I prefer to continue working here."

"You're angry."

"Yes. I am."

"Why?"

He truly seemed clueless. Time to enlighten him. "Because you're making assumptions. My designer clothes are used. My Tory Burch flats were forty dollars. Most of my outfits, under a hundred. It took me an entire year to get a wardrobe fit for the law firm by socking away a hundred dollars a month."

He winced. "I'm sorry. I shouldn't have commented, let alone judged."

Although his apology seemed to be sincere, it didn't matter. I couldn't work for him any more than I already was. "I need to get back downstairs." I turned until his next words stopped me.

"Is it because of our kiss?"

"You mean kisses, don't you? The ones you seem to think I'll report to someone?" I countered.

He ran a hand through his short hair. "I didn't mean to make more assumptions. I just have trust issues."

"Why?" I wondered if I was missing something before, but now I knew I was.

"I don't have time to get into it now."

I checked the clock on the wall. "I have nine more minutes."

He moved closer to me until he was a breath away. I wondered for a moment if he'd choose not to tell me. To my surprise, he did. "As I've gotten further into my career, I see it all around me. People losing respect, money, their jobs because of mistakes they make. Because of the wrong people they trusted."

"What happened between us was consensual. You can trust I won't ever tell anyone."

"It still shouldn't happen again."

At least he sounded conflicted but still obviously not wanting to take the leap. I fought my disappointment. "Less likely to happen if I don't work with you on the weekends, don't you think?"

He sighed. "I don't like you being here. Do you have any idea what happens on this floor?"

"I've heard rumors, but this is my first time up here."

He instantly looked relieved.

His expression made me ask my next question. "How do you know what happens up here?"

"The manager told me."

"Oh." Made sense. "Is the only reason you came here tonight because you wanted to offer me more work?"

"If I tell you no, would you think I was a stalker?"

I fought a grin. "No. Nor would I think it was stalking if you wanted to wait for me until I was done with my shift." There. I'd put it out there.

He sucked in a breath, his gaze burning into mine. "I don't know if it would be a good idea."

Hell, neither did I. But the connection was something I couldn't deny. But my pride wouldn't let me push it any further than he was willing to go. "Let me know if you figure it out. My time is up."

Chapter Twenty-Nine

LIAM

atching Kendall walk out of the room solidified one thing. I wanted her like I'd never wanted another woman. Although the hurdle about romance in the office might end up getting resolved in a few months with her leaving the firm, ultimately she was a relationship girl. She wanted a husband and children. She'd said as much to my sister. But I didn't see a family in my future. Not at all.

As I was exiting the room, contemplating whether to stay until Kendall was off, one of the large security men came up to me. "Mr. Liam Davenport?"

"Yes."

"Mr. Chance Maxwell asked me to escort you to his private suite once you were done."

I hadn't anticipated Chance being in town, let alone at this club tonight. He spent a lot of time traveling. "Of course," I replied and followed the man down the hall.

I'd expected to be escorted into a suite similar to the one I'd just left. With Chance on a couch, a woman on each side waiting to do his bidding, and a stripper pole being utilized in the center. At least that had been his scene four years ago when I'd last met him at one of his establishments.

But this time I was ushered into an office on the third floor. A huge, wall-sized window looked down into the club. He was seated behind his desk and rose with my entrance.

"Hello, Chance. It's been a while." I crossed over, meeting him halfway and taking his extended hand in a firm handshake.

"It has, my friend. Which is why upon hearing you were making a night of it at my club, I had to drop by." He hadn't changed a bit. Perfectly groomed, dressed in expensive clothing, and with an expression some might call aloof but which I knew was always calculating. He was definitely a shrewd businessman.

Although I was on friendly terms with Chance, I also knew I had to be careful not to share too much. The man was reputed to enjoy games. The last thing I wanted was to have Kendall become part of one.

"Yes, well. It's been a while since I've been out."

He laughed. "Cut the shit, Liam. You're not one for the nightclub scene, and my manager already told me you paid five hundred dollars tonight for ten minutes with one of my bartenders. I'm the one who cleared it, by the way, as that sort of thing goes against protocol." He walked over to the window, looking down to where I could see Kendall back working behind the bar.

"The pretty brunette, right?"

I didn't bother to lie. "Yes."

He turned to me, thoughtful. "Your girl?"

"I might be working on that part." Perhaps if I was frank about my interest, he'd ensure she had extra protection from the male customers.

He grinned. "Must be a change for you. You don't seem

like the type to have to work too hard for a woman's attention."

"She's different." In so many ways. And because we were being honest, I said my next words carefully. "Although I'm not happy about her spending her weekends moonlighting at a club, it did give me some reassurance to find out it was one of yours."

He regarded me for a moment before giving me a nod. "Appreciated. And I can assure you this club is above board. Regardless, I take the treatment of my staff very seriously."

My gaze didn't leave his. This was a man in power. But he wasn't the only one. It needed to be crystal clear I would accept nothing less than his word on her safety. "Happy to hear it."

"Since you're here, I do have some business to discuss with you if you have a couple minutes."

He indicated a chair next to the window. I was grateful for the view of Kendall while we were talking. "Of course. Always happy to discuss business with you."

"This is of a delicate nature." He grabbed a decanter of amber liquid. "Still a bourbon man?"

"Yes, I am. And of course, anything you say is in confidence."

He poured four fingers and handed me a glass before pouring his own.

Taking a sip, I realized it was Blanton's, my favorite.

I'd met Chance over ten years ago when I'd been an associate. I'd worked with him on his first business acquisitions—not the sort of thing I did very much anymore since I was now mainly focused on litigation. Even a decade ago, it had been clear he didn't trust many. And since it sometimes paid to have friends in high places, I didn't mind being trusted. He understood I had a limit: our conversations had to be on the right side of the law. He undoubtedly dabbled in some questionable activities, but thankfully he kept that part of his business for his personal attorney.

"I need a private investigator."

I quirked my brow. This was something he could probably get any number of ways.

As if he anticipated my question, he said, "It regards something of a personal nature, which is why I want to go outside of my inner circle. Has to do with my brother."

"Which one?" He was the oldest of four—or was it five? I couldn't keep track as there were some halves and steps in there. His father had been married a few times.

"My younger brother Reed. The one who's working for a security firm in Dubai. It's his fiancée I need investigated."

"Gold digger?"

He sighed. "Worse. Anyhow, if you have anyone who can be discreet, I'll pay expenses."

"I have a guy in LA. He's willing to travel." We'd used him on a number of cases. He was a top-notch security guy. Former Special Forces. He might be overkill for what Chance wanted, but I knew the nightclub owner would expect the best.

"If you could help me arrange it, I'd appreciate it. I'll send everything to your personal email?"

In other words, this was off the law firm books. "Yes. I'll set it up."

"Good. You want my manager to cover for your girl so you get some more time?"

It was tempting, although what else would I say? She'd left the ball in my court. "No. It would only piss her off. She takes her job seriously."

"I hear she's one of my most reliable. I assume you're waiting until she gets off?"

He was giving me the excuse I'd been searching for to stay until Kendall was off work. "Yes."

"Good. The staff cars are parked in a garage underground on the P3 level. I'll let Mikey, the bodyguard who escorts them out, know to clear you. Like I said, we take security very seriously."

Now all I had to wonder was what would happen when she saw me by her car.

Chapter Thirty

KENDALL

*I*t continued to be a busy night after I returned to the bar. The only difference from before my trip upstairs was that now I kept searching the room for Liam.

Damn. He'd made me miss him already. Which made no sense. Before last week, I'd have done just about anything to get him off my mind. How the hell had he gone from being the bane of my existence to meaning something to me—in merely a week?

I understood why he was hesitant to start something with someone he worked with. It made sense, considering the firm was his life and he took seriously both the position he held and the one to which he aspired. As for me, I truly did plan to quit the firm within the year. I might not know exactly what I wanted to do with my life, but I did know the firm wasn't my end game.

Thankfully, Jose didn't pry once I returned. Not that we had the time to chat. But even so, I was so confused about Liam's behavior in showing up here tonight—but then not wanting to pursue anything—that I wouldn't have wanted to talk about it.

Two thirty finally rolled around, allowing me to take the deep breath I took at the end of every shift. I was exhausted. We worked quickly to clean up the bar and ensure we could get out on time.

"You're done, my love. Go home." Jose had already turned over the registers and was writing down what we needed to restock for tomorrow.

"You sure? I can do some mixers."

"Nah. Plenty of time. Go. Get some sleep. See you tomorrow night."

"See you then."

Mikey met me at the elevator as he always did with the girls. Although the parking garage was secure, you could never be too careful. We waited on a couple others before he pressed the down button. Although I typically took the bus to the law firm during the week, I drove to the club on Fridays and Saturdays, so I wouldn't have to deal with public transportation at this hour.

Coming off the elevator, I walked toward my Honda Civic, only to stop dead in my tracks.

Liam was leaned against it.

Mikey was by my side. "Mr. Maxwell said he was cleared, but you say the word, and I can unclear him right now."

Mikey was a good few inches taller than my boss and could probably use me as a free weight. He was intimidating as shit, so I had no doubt he would do as he said. "No. No. He's good."

I walked up to Liam, watching him push off my car while distractedly staring over my shoulder, probably at the mountain of the man behind me.

"Your bodyguard doesn't look happy to see me here."

"He's not generally happy about much. I'm surprised you

stayed." I wasn't above wishing he'd ask me to come home with him, but what the hell had changed since we'd talked four hours ago?

"Do you, um, think we can talk some more?"

Considering how dead on my feet I was, talking might be the only thing I was capable of at the moment. "Here?"

"No. I could come to your place, or you to mine? Or we could find an all-night diner. Or hell, this can wait until tomorrow when you're not exhausted."

I knew for a fact if we waited until tomorrow, one or both of us would chicken out. But there was no way I'd have him over to my tiny studio apartment where my suitcase had exploded, strewing my clothes all about. And a diner wouldn't afford us privacy. "How about I go to your place?"

"Do you want to leave your car here and drive in mine?"

My heart kicked into overdrive. "How about I follow you? I'll need my car in the morning." I didn't want to have to come back to downtown LA to get my ride.

"Okay. I'm in the dark blue Tesla. I'll wait outside the garage for you."

I followed him down the 110 freeway south and onto the exit leading toward the beaches. I'd known he lived in Manhattan Beach, one of the wealthier neighborhoods, but nothing could've prepared me for his beautiful house. As I crossed this last personal line, reality started to set in.

He opened his garage, but I noticed he didn't pull in. He opened his driver's side door and got out to come around to my now open window. "Go ahead and park in the garage. I'll go in and meet you in there in a minute."

"Okay." I wasn't sure if he was hiding my car, or if he was simply being a gentleman with the offer to have it parked inside, but at this point, I wasn't sure I cared. I was beat.

Once I pulled into the garage, I got out of my car and shut

the door. I walked around toward the door, using my cell phone to light the way.

Before I reached it, he opened it from the inside. "Come on in."

Shit. He looked awkward as hell to have me here. And my butterflies were about to have a mutiny. Especially since the first thing I usually did after a shift was to shower. I was still all sweaty from working all night. Not exactly sexy.

"Do you want a tour?"

"Sure." Not only was I curious about his house, but I also hoped this would ease my sudden nerves. But it didn't. Because after touring the gorgeous home with gleaming hardwood floors, a modern kitchen, and three spacious bedrooms —one of which was obviously the master—I'd never been so wired. The house clearly showed how we came from two different worlds. I was way out of my league with a man of his wealth. It now made sense to me when he'd said he had a lot to lose by trusting the wrong person.

"What are you thinking?" he asked, as we ended up back in the kitchen. He poured a glass of water and handed it to me.

"You have a beautiful home. What did you do the whole time you waited? Did you stay upstairs?" Color me curious as to if he was partaking in the club activities offered.

"No. I did some work from the car."

My relief was immediate.

He fidgeted with straightening his dishcloths before turning toward me. "Sorry this is awkward."

It really was. "Are you having second thoughts?"

He expelled a breath. "Yes and no, but I promise it's nothing personal toward you. I want you here. I just—"

"—have a hard time trusting?" I finished for him.

"Yeah. How about we eat, then talk? I'm not much in the kitchen, but I can make some sandwiches."

I was starving. "Sounds good. Uh, is it too weird if I ask if I can use your shower? I sort of smell like booze and sweat."

His brow arched at my request, but he seemed to take it in stride. "Yeah, sure. You can use the shower in the master bathroom. There are clean towels hanging."

"Thank you."

I went up the stairs and quickly started the water in the largest shower I'd ever seen. Stone tiles made it elegant. As I stripped off my clothes, part of me fantasized about him joining me. That would be a hell of a way to start things.

I left my hair up so as not to get it wet and washed my body quickly with his mint body wash. I was thankful I'd shaved this morning, but once I was out of the shower, I realized I didn't want to go and put on my dirty clothes. Opting instead for a towel, I wondered what he would think about me coming downstairs in nothing but.

Talk about sending a message. But I definitely didn't have the nerve to pull that off. I'd been with exactly two boys. Emphasis on boys. Not a man. Most certainly not a man with as much experience as Liam probably had.

After my shower, which had been divine, I opened the bathroom door to see the object of my thoughts standing in his bedroom with a clean T-shirt and soft sweat shorts folded in his hands. His expression was priceless as he gazed down at me wearing nothing but the soft terry towel.

Chapter Thirty-One

LIAM

My eyes were glued to the beauty in front of me. "I thought you might want clean clothes." My voice was thick. My erection was going to be difficult to hide if I stayed in this room. "Why don't you get dressed? Then we'll eat and talk downstairs in the kitchen."

A few minutes later, she walked down my stairs in my white cotton T-shirt and way-too big-for-her athletic shorts. My eyes tracked her all the way. She must have been dead on her feet. Yet she was still here. "More water okay? Or I have wine."

She grinned. "I think wine would make me fall asleep. Another glass of water is good."

While I filled two glasses, she hopped up on the granite countertop, grabbing the sandwich and taking a bite. It was simple turkey and cheese, but she made a sigh as if it hit the spot.

My brow arched at her choice of seat. "I have a table and chairs."

"Do you now?" She took another bite, humor dancing in her eyes.

"I do. Or stools on the other side of the counter."

"Mm. But this was much more convenient."

My lips twitched at her sassiness until I realized this dynamic might bleed into the work place. "This is what can't happen on Monday morning."

She cocked her head to the side, trying to fight her grin. "You think I'll hop up on your desk at work. Maybe eat your sandwich?"

"Perhaps I just need some reassurance that you won't."

"I won't."

She made it sound so simple. Although there was no rule against sleeping with my assistant, it would be a shit show at work should the other partners find out. With a conservative board voting on it, this situation could ruin my chances for named partner.

"If you don't believe me, Liam, then I should go."

I swallowed hard, not wanting her to leave. Trying to figure out a way to voice my concerns, I said, "It's complicated, Kendall."

"Actually it's not. You think you're the only one with something to lose here, but you're not."

"What do you have to lose?" I instantly regretted my words when I saw the way her eyes narrowed.

"My heart, you stupid jerk." She attempted to hop down off the counter, but I was able to catch her, lifting her back up and caging her in for a moment. My arms were on either side of her thighs, her face inches from mine.

"Believe it or not, it's not only my career I'm trying to protect. I'm not a relationship sort of guy. I don't have room for one in my life. And I know offering you any less than that would be wrong. It wouldn't be what you want."

My gaze held hers.

"Can't we play it by ear instead of deciding this would be

a relationship? I'm not sure why you showed up at the club tonight. Or why you stayed until after closing. But I do know I was happy to see you."

I leaned closer, inhaling her scent.

She shivered at the contact.

"I showed up tonight because I already missed you. Does that even make sense?" I was completely baffled myself as to how matters had changed. I'd tried so hard to avoid having a personal connection with this woman, but now I couldn't go more than twelve hours without seeing her.

"It doesn't make sense. Yet I feel the same way."

As if she'd given me the green light I'd been craving, suddenly my lips were on hers. There was no going back after this moment. No more restraint. I was tired of fighting it. I needed her. My hands traveled down to her hips, pulling her center against mine. The way she whimpered told me she could feel the evidence of my desire. "Hook your legs around me."

She didn't hesitate. No puffy green coat to stop us this time. I handled her weight easily, walking her up to the master bedroom where I set her gently on her feet. Tucking her hair behind her ear, I whispered, "Are you sure you're okay with this?"

Her eyes were full of mischief, with a touch of vulnerability. "I'm sure."

My hands attacked her clothing. I couldn't get her shirt over her head fast enough. Once she stepped out of her shorts, though, fully naked, I took a step back, hardly able to catch my breath.

Jesus. I'd been with my share of women, but seeing the vision in front of me was a whole new experience. I regarded her from her perky breasts with rosy nipples to her trim waist and flared hips. I about swallowed my tongue once my gaze got to her pussy. Perfectly groomed with just a patch of hair. I could feel myself harden fully, thinking about all the ways I wanted to sink into her. Her legs were shapely and, as the rest of her, perfectly in proportion. But it was the glow of her skin that really got to me, making her appear as if she'd been kissed by the sun everywhere.

When my gaze finally lifted to her face again, I could see it. The self-doubt from my appraisal—as if I'd find her lacking. Then again, why wouldn't she be insecure given my past stinginess with compliments?

"You're absolutely stunning," I whispered, meaning it.

Her face lit up at my words. "And you're overdressed."

I was indeed, considering I was still in suit pants and a shirt.

She reached out, almost shyly, her hands shaking as she worked my belt buckle.

I took her fingers in mine, stilling her motion. "Are you nervous?"

"A little. It's been a while, and I've only been with two other guys."

Her admission floored me. It also fueled a possessiveness inside of me I didn't dare to examine.

I let her finish undoing my belt, then untucking my shirt before working open the buttons. The way she looked up at me with sweet mischief in her eyes, like she was opening a surprise present, created the most sensual moment I'd ever experienced.

Once my dress shirt was off, I fisted the back of my T-shirt, drew it off and let it also fall to the floor. Next, I stepped out of my trousers, leaving me in only my boxers and socks. Already missing her sweet kiss, I captured her face between my hands, concentrating on exploring her delectable mouth.

In the back of my mind, it occurred to me I should be setting ground rules. I needed to define the boundaries of this sexual relationship and how it would play out at the office. Given her lack of experience, I should ensure I didn't raise expectations that might end up hurting her. But there was no way I could stop to have the conversation. Not now. Not when this moment had been building for days, and I was on the verge of having her beneath me. Especially not when her skin was so incredibly soft.

My fingers trailed down her sides before sliding back up to cup her breasts. They were perfect. Bending my head, I took one of her nipples into my mouth, enjoying the way she shivered at the action. One of my hands then went lower, over her stomach, feathering, until finally I had to touch her where I most ached to do so.

As soon as my fingers went between the lips of her pussy, she moaned low and hard. Damn, she was wet while I was practically drilling a hole through my cotton boxers. And once she brought her hand down and circled my length, I knew I was on borrowed time.

I was too overstimulated to last long if she kept touching me. I pulled back, ready to shed the rest of my clothing. But I didn't want to rush this. I'd bungled things before by doing so in the basement of the church.

"Get on the bed. Up near the top so you can rest your head on a pillow. Then spread your legs for me. I need to taste your pussy."

She sucked in a breath, blinking hard. Shit. Were my words too blunt for her experience level?

"Sorry. Too much?"

She grinned while shaking her head. "No. I just—" She giggled, not finishing the thought but moving toward the bed.

"You just what?"

She hesitated, biting her lip while she got comfortable on the bed. Christ, she was sexy displayed against the backdrop of my blue comforter.

"Tell me," I said, grabbing her bare calf and kissing up to her knee.

"I just— Oh, God—" She lost her train of thought as I trailed my mouth up her inner thigh, spreading her legs wider to accommodate my shoulders.

Now it was my turn to grin. She was so damn responsive. Getting closer to my target, I inhaled her scent, getting drunk on the heady combination of my mint body soap and her unique sweet smell. Blowing a breath over her clit, I enjoyed the way a shiver snaked through her.

"You just what?"

My finger penetrated into her slick heat. She was perfectly tight and wet for me. But she was quickly losing herself in the moment when I wanted her to finish her thought. As I removed my finger, I chuckled at her mewl of protest.

"Tell me."

She took a deep breath. "I just didn't know you'd be so good at this part. I mean you freaked out when you saw my thongs in the suitcase. I thought you might be a bit more reserved in the bedroom."

Her assessment brought out a smile. It also made me want to tease her as I got my first taste, swiping my tongue along her seam.

Her hands reached out, clutching the bedspread as if trying to anchor herself.

The gesture only made me want to drive her completely mad with lust. She gasped when I curled my two fingers up, hitting her outer wall while I bent down to suck on her clit. Pumping my fingers harder, I glanced to see her writhing with pleasure. Then boom, she came spectacularly, tightening around my fingers like a vise grip while yelling something incoherent with a lot of Gods involved.

I withdrew my fingers, only because I wanted a better taste of her. I wanted to take my time to feast on her completely. After her second climax, I glanced up to see the surprise etched in her expression.

"I didn't know multiple orgasms were possible—Jesus."

I enjoyed being the very first man to make it possible for her.

Chapter Thirty-Two

KENDALL

*H*oly shit. Mr. Robot. Mr. Icy. Mr. I-had-like-fifty-ways-I'd-like-to-see-him-suffer only a week ago was a master at eating pussy. And he wasn't done with one orgasm. Jesus. I'd never been happier to see his overachievement in action.

The second climax ripped through me like I had a live wire attached to my body. My eyes rolled back, my hips arched up, and light exploded in my head. I'd never had an orgasm so intense. Vaguely aware that he was now crawling up my body, landing kisses against my skin on the way, I tried to catch my breath.

But he wasn't giving me much of an opportunity. He fixed his mouth around one nipple while toying with the other between his fingers. When he bit down softly, I had to suck in my breath. I wasn't normally a fan of my breasts getting the attention. Since they were on the smaller size, I'd assumed he'd skip over them. But nope, he teased the rosy buds until they were practically begging to move in with him permanently.

Whoa. Bad internal thought. I banished it almost immediately. I couldn't go there. Just because the guy knew how to give a girl an orgasm did not make this a relationship. This had the potential to become complicated enough without me making it more so.

"Hey, you okay?" he said, hovering over me, a worry crease in his brows.

My internal thoughts immediately got shuffled to the back of my brain. "I'm better than okay." I leaned up to kiss him, rolling my body and tangling up in him.

His body was incredible. Muscled, hot, and oh, so very hard for me. I moved to return the favor of putting him in my mouth when he stopped me.

"Some other time. Right now, I need to be inside of you."

Although I was disappointed not to have the opportunity to taste him, I wouldn't argue. I was anxious to have him inside of me, too.

He moved to the side of the bed and opened the nightstand drawer to take out a condom while I had to keep myself from wondering how many times he'd done this particular movement since he executed it so gracefully. Nope. Don't go there. It stood to reason he'd be much more experienced than I was.

Luckily, by the time he'd sheathed himself in the condom, I was reduced to only one thought. And it was carnal. My eyes swept down his muscled chest to his delicious abs before focusing on his long, thick cock. He was perfect. There really was no other word.

He lined himself up to my opening and pushed the head in. We both groaned in unison with the welcome intrusion.

"Fuck, you're tight."

Yes. I was. And he was stretching me with each inch he eased inside of me. My hands gripped his biceps while I wiggled to better accommodate him. I was incredibly full.

Finally he stopped, studying my face as if to ensure I was okay. The gesture was both sweet and unexpected. I leaned up, taking his lips to make sure he knew I was ready.

He pulled out slightly, before slamming back home. My hips arched to meet him. "God, you feel incredible," he whispered, encouraging me to run my hands down his back and pull him in deeper.

I loved the way it was his turn to gasp with my movement. Then he was kissing me, his tongue demanding and hot, and completely possessive. His hips moved, finding a rhythm which had me close.

As a girl who never orgasmed with straight sex, I moved my hand down to alleviate the building pressure. But he wasn't having it.

"Let me." He put his hand between our bodies, working my clit like he was a master at knowing how to touch me just right.

"Oh God, oh God," I shouted, feeling my orgasm wash over me.

He was quick to follow, growling out expletives as he ground out his climax on top of me.

We both lay there, his weight pressed into mine, and tried to steady our breathing for a few minutes. Then he moved, giving me a quick kiss before hopping out of the bed and going into the bathroom. I stayed where I was, my body feeling heavy with exhaustion. It was four thirty in the morning, no wonder.

"Time for sleep, unless you want more food? You didn't finish your sandwich."

"Mm?" Although I could probably eat, I wasn't sure I could move. My eyes opened to see him coming back to bed fully nude. "I'm not hungry. But I'm a big fan of this look on you."

He gave me a boyish grin, crawling into bed, and gathering me close. "I think I could get used to wearing it just for you."

MY EYES FLUTTERED open to an unfamiliar sight. Liam's bedroom in full daylight. Turning over, I could see his side of the bed was empty. But my purse was sitting on the nightstand. He must've brought it up from downstairs. Grabbing my phone, I gasped.

Crap, it was close to noon. Shit. I had to go. I had laundry to do, grocery shopping, and school stuff to get in order, all before I went to work tonight. Since Sunday was my family day, Saturday was the only time I had to get things organized for the work week.

I hurried into the bathroom, feeling nosey as I searched under his cabinet sink for an extra toothbrush. Luckily, he didn't disappoint and had a whole package of them. I made quick work out of brushing my teeth, pulling my hair up, and using the facilities. Deciding there was no other choice, I put on my jean shorts from last night, but I coupled them with Liam's T-shirt. I'd have to return it later. Lastly, I swiped on strawberry gloss before walking down the stairs.

My shoes were at the front door but no sign of Liam. Not in the kitchen. Not in the living room. Shit. What should I do? Just leave? Write a note? Search for him? Ugh. Non-relationships after sex with your boss were tough.

After slipping on my shoes, I fished out my keys and jumped at the sound of his voice.

"Where are you going?"

I turned to see him standing there. Oh, man, did he look hot in his jeans and black T-shirt with bare feet. His hair still looked damp from the shower. "I need to get home. I have a lot to get done today. I didn't mean to sleep for so long."

He seemed to consider my words for a moment before replying. "You want something to eat or drink before you go?"

"No. I'm good. I did find a toothbrush under your sink upstairs. Hope you don't mind."

"I don't mind." His intense stare gave nothing away.

Awkward. Only made weirder by the fact I really did need to go. "Um. Can you open the garage for me?"

My words put him into motion.

"So, I guess I'll see you on Monday," I said.

Did I kiss him goodbye? Did I give him a hug? Shake his hand? Hell if I knew how this was done.

"Yeah, Monday," he responded, holding the door open for me.

My reminder about the office made him do the little jaw thing he did when he was stressed or irritated.

Sensing this was about to dissolve into more awkwardness the longer I stood there, I gave him a *thanks for the sex* wave and went out the door to my car.

He stood by the entrance and hit the garage door opener button, still frowning.

He watched while my hands fumbled with my phone in the charger. It was almost dead. Next, I hit the GPS so I could find the fastest route from here to my apartment. Eighteen minutes. Not bad. I'd just put the car in reverse when the knock startled me. He was at my window.

I hit the button to open it, wondering if he was about to lecture me on his expectations regarding Monday's in-the-office behavior, but he shocked me by moving to take my lips. He absolutely possessed my mouth, flicking his tongue against mine. Then he suddenly pulled away. "Brakes, Kendall."

Huh? I was mildly disoriented when I realized the car was moving backwards. Oops. I put it back in park, giving him an embarrassed grin. "I didn't realize."

But he was back, kissing me. Jesus. I was about to unbuckle and skip all responsibilities for the day. My willpower was completely obliterated by this man. But he ended it before I could contemplate further poor choices.

"Strawberry lip gloss," he muttered, putting his forehead against mine.

"What?"

"Strawberry lip gloss is my kryptonite. Drive safe."

Chapter Thirty-Three

LIAM

Once Kendall backed out of my driveway, I pressed the button to close the garage door. The taste of strawberry gloss lingered on my lips.

Although I'd been tempted to wake her when I'd gotten up, I'd let her sleep, knowing she needed it. Then I'd gone downstairs to try figuring out how to talk to her this morning. She probably thought we'd spend the day together. How would I let her down easy? Despite the temptation to spend more time in bed with her, I had work to do. This was the reason I didn't want a relationship. Because of the demands on my time.

But never one to do what I expected, she was ready to leave when she came downstairs. I'd forgotten what a busy girl she was. She probably had a lot to do after having been gone last week. No doubt she'd be seeing her family tomorrow since she'd missed seeing them last weekend.

What a contrast to my weekend plans, which included work, work, and more work. Jesus, only fifteen minutes after she left, I was sitting here in my living room feeling—was it lonely?

When other women stayed the night, I was anxious for them to go the next morning, but when Kendall had been in a hurry to leave, I'd felt oddly disappointed. Then I'd kissed her because I couldn't help myself. It turns out strawberry lip gloss wasn't merely an incredible smell but actually tasted like strawberries. I was a goner. Especially if she wore it to the office.

The thought of Monday left me anxious. My leg tapped involuntarily just from my thinking about it. How would she act? What would the dynamic be between us? Could she sustain the professional line? But the bigger question was how would I react? I was already wishing she was back in my bed, under me.

By midnight, although I had more billable hours left in me, I was too distracted to log any more time. I found myself up until two thirty, when I texted her.

"Are you off?"

"Almost," came her reply.

"Call me on your way home?" I lay in my bed waiting for her reply, hoping she would. It had been tempting to go to the club. However, I considered one night there stalkerish enough.

Still, I hated the thought of her being out at this hour. I'd seen the way she'd dressed last night. Like pure sin. Although she had a bouncer accompany her in the parking lot at the club, there was no one at her apartment building to watch over her.

When my phone rang with her number, I picked up immediately. "Hi."

"Hi."

"How was work?"

"Busy. How was your day?"

I'd gone for a run. Worked on the deposition. Billed hours

on two other cases as well. My day had been boring. Uninspiring. Uneventful until the moment I heard her voice. "Better now."

"Me, too."

I wanted to ask her to come over. For a guy accustomed to his solitude, it was a strange sensation to want her here with me. "You still there?"

"Yeah. I looked for you tonight. Is that weird?"

"Not any weirder than me being tempted to show up again." It was on the tip of my tongue to ask her to drive here now, but the timing of her yawn reminded me she hadn't gotten much sleep last night. "You seeing your family this afternoon?"

"Yeah. I'll do dinner with them and head back up."

"What time do you think it'll be?" It was a vague way of asking if she might be open to coming over.

"Not sure."

Either she was too tired to realize what I was asking or it was her way of avoiding an actual answer. "You almost home?"

"Mm. Almost."

"Will you stay on the phone with me until you're inside your apartment?"

"Do you have ten minutes of conversation in you at this hour?"

"I'm a litigator; I always have something I can say." Of course that was in a court room, not with personal chitchat, but with her, I wanted to know more. "Tell me what you like to do for fun."

"Hang out with my family. Cook. Bake. Binge the Food Network shows."

She was definitely in the wrong field if her hobbies included her passions. "Sounds like you need to be a chef."

"Someday, maybe." My suggestion elicited a sigh. "How about you? What do you like to do for fun?"

"Work out." I'd thought it was a fair answer until she laughed.

"Working out is your idea of fun?"

I was a bit defensive with my reply. "It's necessary to stay in shape."

"And I did appreciate that fact earlier this morning."

She not only knew how to soothe an ego, but also how to make me blush. Now I was thinking about having her back in my bed.

"But what do you do to unwind? What were you doing this evening before you called?"

"Working." Then, because I could practically hear her eyes roll, I added, "It's not easy for me to relax."

"Why not?"

"I'm always thinking of what I need to do next." *I wasn't enough, therefore I constantly push myself to do more.*

"Mm. Perhaps we need another cooking lesson."

It had been surprisingly relaxing. "If I recall, I wasn't very good during the first round."

"I could entice you into another round by wearing nothing but an apron."

Damn. I was hard. "Sign me up."

Her laughter was contagious, making me once again wish she was on her way here. But I wouldn't ask. We chatted a few more minutes about what type of pasta we'd make next time until she said, "I just pulled into my parking lot."

"Talk to me while you go inside. Do you live in a safe neighborhood?" It bothered me to think of her alone at this time of the morning.

"It's not bad, although I must admit without my roommate here, I'm happy to be talking to you while walking up to my apartment."

So was I. Not that there was a lot I could do by sitting here in my bed. Instead, I waited for the sound of her locks.

"I'm inside. All locked up."

I let out the breath I'd been holding. Feeling protective over someone other than my family wasn't an emotion I'd been expecting. But here it was. "Good. Glad you're home."

Her yawn reminded me of how exhausted she must be from the trip, her job, and not sleeping much this morning. "I know you're tired, so I'll let you go. Have a good day with your family tomorrow."

"Thanks. Guess I'll see you Monday."

"Yeah. Monday. Bye."

On Sunday, I lasted until six o'clock before I had to reach out to her. I rationalized we needed to talk so we could be on the same page tomorrow when it came to our first day in the office, but the truth was there. I missed her.

Sending her a text was the safest bet in case she was in the middle of something.

"You still at dinner?"

"Yep. It's Christmas at Plum Creek. I really can't stand Nellie Oleson. She shouldn't have Bunny."

I had no clue what she was talking about. *"Have you been drinking?"*

"Not a drop. Watching Little House on the Prairie. Bunny is Laura Ingalls's horse. She sold her to the horrible Nellie Oleson to afford a stove for her mother for Christmas. Gets me every time."

I couldn't help grinning at the complete obscurity of her text message, and her thinking her explanation would make me understand better. But at least I remembered her mentioning her grandmother loved to watch this show.

"Does she get Bunny back?" It felt only right to ask, after all.

"It takes years and a bit of drama where Mrs. Oleson wants to put Bunny down because Nellie pretends to be paralyzed after she's thrown, but yes. Eventually it has a happy ending."

"Sounds serious."

"You have no idea."

I sent my next text before I could overthink it. *"Do you want to come over tonight?"*

Nothing came back. Shit. Was I pushing too hard too quick? Was she getting the wrong impression? I forced myself to take a deep breath. I was already far too anxious for my health.

"Sorry, was finishing up and saying goodbye. I have to take my nan back to the center, and then will be heading up. Is eight o'clock okay?"

"It's good." Maybe if I typed it, I would learn to be good by the time she got here.

SIX MINUTES PAST EIGHT O'CLOCK, Kendall dialed my number.

I picked up on the first ring. "Hello."

"Hi. I'm in your driveway. You want me to park in the garage?"

"Yeah. Hold on." I was up and outside, pressing the button. I felt a bit guilty in hiding her car, but I didn't want to take any chances with other attorneys I knew who lived in the neighborhood. It wasn't as if any of them were prone to snooping, but all I needed was for someone from the office to recognize her car.

She didn't seem to mind parking in the garage if her smile was any evidence.

"Hello," I greeted.

"Hi."

When she came up and stepped into my arms, it felt natural to have her there.

I hit the button to close the garage and kissed her. Strawberry lip gloss greeted me.

"You and this gloss," I said, taking her hand and leading her inside.

"Now that I'm aware you're a fan, how can I not wear it always?"

"Dangerous words." Which reminded me. We needed to talk. "I think it's a good segue into tomorrow and what to expect."

She quirked a brow. "Is this a conversation about rules and boundaries in the office? Because if so, I'm gonna need wine."

I probably would, too.

We went into the kitchen where I poured two glasses of red.

She immediately hopped up on the countertop where she'd been the other morning. Shit. I was already fighting an erection from simply recalling that moment.

Her amused expression let me know she was most likely thinking about the same thing.

"You're a big fan of my countertop?"

"It holds some special memories." With a wink, she sipped the wine I handed her.

It was time to remember she was all of twenty-four, and I'd poured the wine for a reason. Our talk. "Look, I don't want you getting attached. This isn't a relationship."

The way her eyes narrowed told me my words had come

out wrong. I tried to do damage control. "What I mean to say is we want different things long term."

"After sleeping together once, I wasn't aware we were talking long-term plans."

"We're not, but I wanted to make sure we're still on the same page."

"We are on the same page. If it changes, I promise to let you know. I would hope for the same in return."

"Good." This had been simpler than I'd thought. I set down my glass and stepped in between her legs, loving when she twined them around me, pulling me closer. "So I have a question."

She gasped when I trailed kisses behind her ear. "What's that?"

"Why on earth did they name the horse Bunny?"

Chapter Thirty-Four

KENDALL

I didn't leave Liam's house until five o'clock the next morning. Oh, yeah, there was nothing like leaving your boss's bed the morning before seeing him in the office a few hours later to establish truly professional boundaries.

After returning to my apartment, I showered, put on my favorite black skirt suit with a crisp white shirt and black-and-white pumps. I was ready to look the part at least. On the inside, however, I was a nervous mess. What would it be like to see him in the office today?

My arrival was on time at eight thirty despite the fact I'd had to drive in so I could lug the files back. They were in the trunk of my car, back in their boxes. I would need to get the cart later to bring them up to our office floor.

Figuring Liam was already in his office, as typical, I sat down at my desk and took a deep breath. Then I booted up my computer and logged in. I needed to think of this as a typical Monday, which meant not picturing him rolling me over in his bed last night and riding him. Not imagining the way he'd used his tongue after, leaving me completely spent.

Nope. No sex thoughts. Instead, I needed to get his breakfast as per usual. I got up, giving a brief rap on his door like I did every day, and opening it when he said to come in. "Good morning, Mr. Davenport."

Why was my heart threatening to pound of out my chest? My face heated as soon as his gaze hit mine.

"Good morning, Ms. Tate."

Jesus. When did that statement become so hot? "The usual for breakfast?"

"Yes. Please."

The please was a new word. I turned to go, unable to help my smile. I went downstairs to the cafeteria to get a veggie omelet, side of fruit, and a coffee with cream and sugar, putting it on to his account.

Balancing Liam's food, I knocked on his door again. When I entered, I noted he didn't hesitate to fix his baby blues on me. No more ignoring me by staring at his monitor. Instead, he was tracking me with his gaze like I was the prey and he was the predator. The thought made me both want to giggle and to hop on his desk like I swore I wouldn't do. Before I could go too far with my imagination, I set his tray with his coffee on his desk.

"Thank you," he murmured, causing me to smile again.

"You're welcome."

"Did you bring the files back in?"

"Yes. I'll need to get a cart to bring them up. I can do it now if you like."

"I can help you. I should've taken them with me so you didn't have to haul them in."

"It's not a problem. I can get one of the guys from facilities to help me."

He was about to respond, but we were interrupted with a knock.

It was the managing partner, Phillip Kinkaid, peeking his head in. "Hello, Liam."

My boss immediately stood up.

"Good morning, Mr. Kinkaid," I said, taking my leave.

The impeccably dressed and always polite older man gave me a warm smile. "Good morning, Kendall."

"I'll go get those files now, Mr. Davenport," I said, excusing myself.

By the end of the day, I had to say that staying completely professional hadn't been so difficult. Probably because I couldn't imagine being flirty or sexual in a place that sucked out all of the fun the minute you walked through the door. Aside from carting up the files and getting Liam lunch, I'd had no other interaction with him. That wasn't a surprise considering he was one week before the deposition. He was basically hunkered down, completely focused on the case.

By the time five thirty came around, I did as I normally did. Logged out and didn't bother to say good night. We hadn't bid each other goodbye before last week, so doing it now seemed like it would come off as awkward.

Tonight was my first class of the winter quarter. I tried, but wasn't very successful, in not getting bored with the topic of organizational leadership. This quarter also included a class on business-oriented computer applications. After these two mind-numbing classes, I only had two more left until I earned my degree. I couldn't wait to be done. Yes, balancing work and classes was exhausting, but frankly, the subject matter bored me to tears. Hopefully, the payoff would be worth it once I could put a bachelor's degree on my resumé.

Once I was done with class at nine, I checked my phone, but nothing from Liam. I hadn't expected him to text me, but I did find myself disappointed.

Non-relationships were turning out to be tough to navigate. It was proving difficult to avoid breaking the rules of something I didn't really know how to play. I was officially the uncoordinated girl in the back of the relationship step-aerobics class, hoping I didn't trip and fall on my face.

The bright spot was when I returned home to see Chloe was there. I'd missed her over the last week.

"Hi," she squealed bounding off of the couch to hug me.

I happily hugged her back. "Hi. Gosh, am I glad you're back."

"Me, too. Catch me up. What happened during a week with your hot dick boss?"

Oh, God, was her metaphor about to take on a new meaning. Only, wait. I couldn't talk about it. Right? I'd told him I wouldn't tell anyone. But then again, she was my best friend and roommate, not someone we worked with. I was torn and decided to change the subject for now.

"I'll tell you, but after you tell me about home."

Immediately, Chloe's smile disappeared. "Nothing much to tell. It was unfortunate family drama stuff."

"Your brother?" Her older sibling had become involved in drugs, leaving his mother with a mountain of debt while still caring for two younger children. The reason Chloe worked two jobs was in order to help them.

"Yeah. But I can't talk about it without getting angry. Tell me about your boss. Was it horrible? Awful? What? I've been dying to find out."

"I need wine for this." I figured I'd stick to the basics, starting with my ugly, puffy, olive green coat, him freaking out about the house, his father, and family.

We were down two glasses by the time I finished. "Wow, that's a lot."

Definitely an understatement. It made me anxious to keep silent about the physical part of our relationship or the way he'd come to the club this last weekend, but I fought the sensation.

Hell, now that it was going on ten o'clock and I hadn't heard from him, our non-relationship could be over, and I simply hadn't heard yet. Sure, I could initiate the text or call, but something told me if I reached out, I'd fail whatever the criteria was for casual.

213

Chapter Thirty-Five

LIAM

I operated on autopilot over the next four days, barely eating, sleeping, or socializing, while consumed with the deposition prep. Hell, if there hadn't been a dress code, I doubt I would've shaved or showered on a daily basis.

Of course, Kendall was there in the office, but we were back to our previous coolness. I made an effort to be more appreciative and say thank you and please, but otherwise you would never guess we'd spent last weekend naked in my bed.

Now, sitting at my desk on a Friday afternoon, I should feel relief that she hadn't gotten weird in the office. But instead, I was unsettled, not knowing where we stood. Shit. Maybe I should've sent her a text at some point this week. Especially since I was due to leave for Hong Kong on Saturday night and would be gone for five days.

I was exhausted from putting in so many hours, but I finally felt prepared for the deposition. I was always ready. Anything less was not acceptable.

My intercom buzzed with Kendall's voice. "Ms. Owings is here to see you."

I wasn't in the mood for Tabitha, but then again, I seldom was. I'd put her off the entire week telling her I could carve out fifteen minutes on Friday. Clearly, she hadn't forgotten.

"Thanks. Please send her in."

Tabitha came in like she normally did, with eyes only for me and a big smile. "You've been working hard."

"Yes. I've been wrapped up in this deposition prep."

"I noticed. I also heard about your father. I'm sorry," she said, taking a seat across from my desk.

Word traveled fast. Of course, I'd had to tell the managing partner why I was flying to Virginia and taking my assistant. "Thank you."

"Did you really take your secretary with you for the week?"

Leave it to Tabitha to want to start up some gossip. I decided to shut it down. "Yes, I did. This deposition is a vital element in an important case to the firm. I couldn't afford to get behind despite a death in my family."

"No, no. Of course. I mean some people may have thought it odd, but I suppose it makes sense." She almost sounded jealous.

"I don't care what people think." At least it was what most believed.

"Of course. I completely get it. When do you fly to Hong Kong?"

"Tomorrow night." I was not looking forward to the lengthy flight even if it was in the luxury of first class. Frankly, I'd rather be with Kendall in my bed.

Whoa. Where had that thought come from?

"Good. You have plans for tonight?"

Aside from waiting on my assistant to get off her moon-lighting job and come over to spend the morning in my bed, no. But I didn't come up with another story quickly enough.

"Before you say you're busy, let me tell you I have two tickets to the most coveted charity event in the city, the Feed the Homeless campaign. It sold out months ago because of all the celebrities attending. You know who else will be there?"

I knew immediately who she meant. "Stephen Walsh."

Her brilliant white teeth flashed. "In the flesh."

Stephen was the CEO of one of the biggest tech companies on the West Coast and our firm had been trying to land him as a client for years. With him now facing possible litigation from some investors, it was a prime time to get in front of him and try to sell the firm. This fundraiser would be a good opportunity to do just that.

"What's in it for you?" I hated to be blunt, but Tabitha didn't do anything without motivation.

She held up her hands as if in peace. "Look, I'm a tax attorney. But if you land his litigation business, perhaps it opens the door for us to take on his tax work in the future. Plus, it's a boon for the firm."

"And?" I knew her too well to think she didn't have an agenda.

"And I want a percentage of origination credit. I'm trying to make equity partner, so it would go a long way."

"Ten percent."

She smiled. "Twenty-five. After all, these tickets don't grow on trees."

"Fifteen."

"Twenty."

"Fifteen. Or I don't go. You may get me in the door, but I have to do the work to sell myself." Frankly, there were any number of people from whom I could wrangle a ticket with a simple phone call. If I hadn't been dealing with the funeral and this deposition, I probably would've already called in a favor to obtain a ticket.

She sighed. "Deal at fifteen percent. It's black tie, by the way."

At least it would give me something to do tonight instead of simply sitting at home and waiting until three o'clock in the morning when Kendall got off work. The thrill of hunting a new client always brought an adrenaline rush. And Stephen Walsh could mean millions, which would go a long way toward getting my name on the front door.

Tabitha stood up and moved to leave. "Pick me up at eight o'clock tonight. I'll text you my home address."

It would be easier to simply meet her there, but I didn't have the energy to argue. However, I was thankful she'd said the words behind the closed door, for I didn't want Kendall to overhear them and get the wrong impression about tonight being anything but business.

Chapter Thirty-Six

KENDALL

I pretended not to care when Tabitha went into Liam's office and closed the door. My eyes stayed glued to my computer even after she came out fifteen minutes later.

Ordinarily, she would simply ignore me; however, this time she stopped at my desk.

I glanced up, schooling my voice. "Can I help you with something?"

She was tapping on her phone. "Perhaps. If your boss asks you to book a car for our date tonight, can you ensure it's a limo? I'd like to have privacy."

"Certainly." The word was hard to choke out.

"Good." She didn't so much as glance up from her phone as she turned and walked away.

I told myself I didn't care. Liam was free to go out with who he wanted, when he wanted. It's not like we'd talked about exclusivity. Still, it hurt to think that just Monday morning I'd woken up in his bed. Now, in the same week, he had another date. With Cruella de Vil, of all people.

During the rest of the afternoon, he didn't mention it, and I didn't bring it up.

Later that night while I worked the bar, I pictured them together. All dressed up. Drinking champagne. Her hand on his leg during dinner. Him laughing about something sophisticated and smart that she'd said in a lawyerly way I'd never master.

"Whoa, whoa. What are you thinking about while you're mulling the mint?" Jose asked.

I was certainly putting a lot of aggression into making a mojito. "Sorry. Guess I have some contained rage."

"Anything to do with the suit from last week?"

I gave my coworker a smile. "Good guess." I'd even put a new entry in my secret document: I hoped he got food poisoning tonight and barfed all over Tabitha's dress. Petty, yes. But then again, the high road wasn't something I was capable of taking this evening.

At twelve thirty I stepped in back for my fifteen-minute bathroom break. I shouldn't have looked at my phone. But I couldn't help myself. No messages. What had I expected? Knowing I had to go back to the bar for another couple hours, I found myself typing a text to him.

"Are you home alone?"

The dots appeared instantly. *"No."*

My breath left me. Of course he wasn't alone. I immediately turned off my phone. I was officially a stupid girl. Wiping my stupid tears, I put my stupid phone back in my stupid pocket and left it there.

"YOU WANT to hit the diner for pancakes?" Chloe asked me on our way out to my car after our shifts.

We went out for breakfast from time to time, but right now, there was nothing more I wanted than to go home and to bed. "Nah. Not today if you don't mind."

"I don't mind. But are you okay?"

I gave her a small smile, not wanting to get into my stupidity over everything with Liam until tomorrow, when I could cry on her shoulder with a tub of ice cream within reach. "Yeah. Just tired. Sorry."

"Um, Kendall?"

"Yes?" I glanced up from the ground to her face.

"Is that your boss?"

My head swiveled in the direction of her stare. Sure enough, there was Liam leaning against his Tesla in our employee parking lot, looking incredible in a tux.

"Yeah. It's him."

"I feel like there was a lot from last week you didn't mention. What is he doing here?"

"I'm not sure." Why was he here after he'd said he wasn't home alone?

Chloe smiled. "Why don't you go talk to him? I can wait for your text letting me know if you're coming home with me or with him."

"'Kay." I was already closing the distance between us.

I cinched my long belted sweater over my waist, covering up my short black skirt and shiny, off-the-shoulder red top. Seeing him in his tux, I felt it was never more evident we lived in very different worlds. "What are you doing here?"

"You didn't answer my text messages."

"The one telling me you weren't home alone. Yeah, I wonder why."

His brows furrowed. "You didn't see my other messages?"

"There was no need. You had a date with Tabitha. Then you said you weren't home alone. I get it."

He pushed off his car and stepped toward me. "I had a business engagement with Tabitha. And I answered your question with no, because I wasn't home. Not because I was with her or anyone else. I then sent you a text asking if you wanted to come over. Then I asked if you wanted me to come to the club to meet you here. You didn't answer either."

Oh. "I shouldn't have asked the question to begin with."

His expression was serious. "Why did you?"

I sighed. "Because I'm a stupid girl."

He stepped closer, stroking my cheek. "No. You're not."

"Can I ask you something?"

"Sure, but can we do it from the car on the drive to my house?"

"Your answer has a lot to do with if I get into the car."

"Okay." He looked apprehensive. Probably because we both knew I was about to commit a non-relationship foul.

"Are we exclusive? Sexually?"

"If this is about Tabitha, nothing happened."

"That wasn't the question, counselor," I retorted.

His lips twitched as if he was fighting a smile at my response, then he let out a long breath. "I worry about what saying we're exclusive will mean to you."

"Again, not an answer to the actual question. And how about I'm the only one who worries about what something will mean to me. Let me put it this way: I'm an only child not used to sharing. And the idea of you sleeping with someone else while we're sleeping together doesn't sit well."

He grinned. "I don't like the idea of you sleeping with anyone else, either."

Okay, this was progress. "So, we are exclusive sexually?"

"If I say yes, will you get in the car?"

His flippant answer irritated me. "Not if you don't mean it."

His expression softened. "I mean it, Kendall. We're exclusive. Now, will you please get into the car?"

"I thought you'd never ask." I pulled out my phone to send a quick message to Chloe telling her I'd see her tomorrow.

Her response came quickly. "***Okay, but I want all the details then.**"*

"Please tell me your friend doesn't also work at the firm?" He glanced over while pulling out of the garage.

"No, but she's my roommate."

"Okay, but you didn't tell her I was your boss??"

"No, I didn't."

He exhaled a breath of relief, which I knew would be short lived.

"But you showing up tonight pulled the cat out of the bag."

"What do you mean?"

"Don't freak out. But she saw your picture when I started working for you. She knows you're my boss." And I wasn't about to apologize for it.

"I'm not freaking out. But I am curious. Why did you show her a picture back then?"

My face heated. "I, um, I mean she was curious about what my new boss looked like."

"Interesting. What did you say to make her curious?"

My lips twitched with a barely repressed smile. His ego was enjoying this far too much. "I may have mentioned you weren't entirely terrible to look at."

He chuckled. "I seem to remember you insisting I wasn't your type."

"I seem to remember you panicking that I was trying to woo you with my culinary skills."

I'd turned toward him and watched him drive. Damn, he was a treat to watch. Gorgeous in his tux, with his gaze concentrating on the road.

"One more bad assumption on my part," he said. "But now I want to know. What is your type? Since I was sooooo not your type."

I found it interesting he remembered exactly how I'd put it, drawing out the "so." Evidently, it had stuck with him. But there wasn't an easy way to say, *when you're a complete asshole, you're not my type.* "Let's just say I had an impression you might be too conservative and uptight for me."

He glanced over, mischief dancing in his eyes. "Sounds like you basically thought I was an asshole."

"In all fairness, I hardly knew you."

"Are you saying that now that you know me, you don't find me conservative and uptight?"

Dammit. Never get into this type of discussion with a lawyer. "You're definitely neither of those things in the bedroom. But I don't think spontaneity comes naturally to you."

He frowned. Crap. Maybe I would've been better off saying yes, I'd thought he was an asshole instead of calling him conservative and uptight. But it was true. I mean what guy sees a woman dressed in his T-shirt and shorts, fresh from the shower, sitting on his countertop and reminds her he has chairs? It wasn't natural. Which was adorable in its own way. But I didn't think he'd appreciate me saying that, either.

"Give me an example."

Hilarious. His wanting an example was, in fact, an example of how he was conservative and cautious. To give him an illustration, I decided to take matters into my hands, literally. Reaching over, I ran my hand down his thigh, moving it toward his groin.

His voice sputtered. "What the hell are you doing?"

"Giving you an example."

He sucked in a breath when my hand skimmed over his cock. I could feel it growing with my touch.

"I don't think this is the time. We'll be at the house in ten more minutes."

"Hm. Maybe I can't wait that long. Maybe I need my mouth on you now." I'd never given road head, but hell, there was a first time for everything.

He frantically glanced my way. "I don't want you taking off your seatbelt while we're on the freeway."

Safety first probably was a good idea. "Then, I'll just have to wait until we're in your garage to put my mouth on you, but I can still do *this*."

I unfastened the leather belt at his waist, before unzipping his trousers. Glancing up, I could see the way he was gripping the steering wheel. My hand then circled around his growing length, pumping up and down. I enjoyed the sound of garbled words hissing out between his teeth. There was nothing I wanted more in this moment than to take away his control. To make him lose his mind. "I can't wait to taste you. To have you grab my hair and thrust inside of my mouth."

He closed his eyes for a brief second. "Christ. This is crazy."

"Probably." But I was empowered by the fact I was taking him out of his comfort zone. That I could bring him this level of pleasure despite my lack of experience.

I played with him for the eight minutes it took until he pulled into his driveway. I'm guessing he must've sped the entire way home. He was leaking pre-cum and gritting his teeth by the time we pulled into his garage. The door wasn't even down before I'd unfastened my seatbelt and pounced on him. I licked his crown like a lollypop, curious about the taste of him. It was a combination of salty and sweet. Wanting more, I opened my throat and took him all the way to the back of it. After a few minutes of bobbing up and down on his cock, alternating deep throating with shallow, I noticed his legs start to tremble.

"I can't last much longer."

I swirled my tongue up and down his shaft, sucking up and down on his length. Good, I didn't want him to last. I wanted him to explode. I could feel his hand tangled in my hair, but still, he was hesitant to apply pressure. I needed more.

"Lift your hips," I murmured, needing his trousers to come down so I had more room to move. The moment I circled my lips around him, he was cursing, groaning, and writhing in pleasure under my touch. I fisted him again, taking him deeper and rubbing his balls with my other hand.

"I'm coming. Oh—"

Hot streams hit my tongue and went down my throat. I swallowed once, then twice, and wow, a third time. His breathing was still labored while I licked him clean.

Chapter Thirty-Seven

LIAM

$\mathcal{M}$y world had just been officially rocked. I couldn't recollect half the drive home. Instead, I'd been in such a lust-induced state of mind, my body had operated on autopilot. After Kendall sat up, I realized we were sitting in the complete dark in my garage.

"You okay?" she asked, sounding a bit unsure of herself.

"Yeah. Remind me not to question how I'm conservative ever again."

She chuckled. "Shall we go inside?"

"Yes." I was slowly regaining my wits. At least there was light when she opened her passenger door, so I could see what I was doing while I redid my trousers.

We didn't speak until we were inside. I still hadn't recovered when she said, "I'm heading up to take a shower if it's okay?"

"Yeah. Sure."

She gave me a small smile before climbing the steps.

It occurred to me she was right. I wasn't spontaneous. Hell, I wouldn't even say I was adventurous. I liked control and the feeling it gave me. However, I'd enjoyed surrendering it completely, too. To be taken off guard and completely overcome with passion had been wonderful. The sensation was foreign, yet I suddenly craved it again.

I was up the steps two at a time, stripping off my clothes once I hit my bedroom. The sound of the shower came from my bathroom. I was hard again, thinking about her in there, wanting her with a carnal attraction I wasn't sure was completely sane. I didn't care. I needed her. I wouldn't let the thought freak me out.

At the sound of the glass shower door opening, she turned, her eyes wide. I enjoyed the way her hungry gaze raked over my body and how free she was to express it. I didn't hesitate, just framed her face and kissed her hard, not caring if I tasted myself still on her lips. I backed her into the corner, feeling the hot water on my back and needing to possess her.

"Are you clean?" I asked lifting her up against the stone shelf.

"Yes. But remember, I'm not on birth control."

Shit. That should've been something we discussed.

"I'm sorry," she whispered, looking as if she'd done something wrong.

"Nothing to apologize for. Hold tight." I walked out to the bedroom and grabbed a condom from the nightstand, trying not to freak out. See, this was why I couldn't lose my mind. Because the consequences could be disastrous. She could very easily not have reminded me, and then we'd be dealing with my worst nightmare of an unplanned pregnancy.

Kendall's eyes met mine hesitantly when I walked back into the shower. Although I had a condom on now and could've picked up where we'd left off, I didn't. Instead, I cupped her face and kissed her softly. "I'm sorry for not remembering."

"I could probably go on the pill."

"I don't want you to do anything you're not ready to do." I meant it. Plus, condoms were safer and wouldn't send the wrong message.

"My appointment is next month. I'll talk to my doctor about it."

"Okay." This was dangerous territory. Relationship territory. I think my dick realized it too because it was starting to soften.

Apparently noticing the problem, she took me in her hand. "I think we should stop talking and start making out again."

I grinned. "I'm on board with that plan."

WE SLEPT for a few hours before I woke her up with my tongue. Now who was unspontaneous?

After two orgasms, she was all smiles, stretching in the bed. "Someone is out to prove me wrong, isn't he?"

I crawled up her body with kisses, loving the way her body quivered against my lips. I was quickly becoming addicted to her taste. "Prove that I'm not boring? Maybe."

She giggled, sucking in her breath when I fastened to one of her nipples. "I never said you were boring. Oh God—"

My fingers were back inside of her. "You were saying?"

"I was saying how you always are so unpredictable. So adventurous."

I nuzzled her neck, flipping her on her side. "Mm-hmm. And how adventurous would you like to be?" I swiped her wetness back to a place I'd never been but had always fantasized about.

She only gasped when I breached her slowly.

"I've never done that."

"Mm. Me neither. I think we could get adventurous." The thought fueled my anticipation.

She shifted, squirming with the new sensation of me working her both places. I knew her body; she was getting close. She exploded, screaming my name and arching her body up with a loud moan.

I wasted no time putting the condom on and entering her from behind. It was the first time I'd had her this way. I was deep in her pussy, so I went slow.

"Harder," she rasped. "Faster and harder."

Jesus. This girl was about to be the death of me. The slapping sound filled the room, as did both of our growls when we both hit our climaxes at the same time. I'd made sure of that with my fingers on her clit. Afterward, we lay there in the bed, her naked body curled up to mine until I had to get up to take care of the condom.

Once I was back in the bed, I blurted out what was on my mind. "I have to fly out for Hong Kong tonight."

She laughed. "I'm acquainted with the girl who does your schedule, so I'm well aware."

I grinned, kissing her neck. Of course she knew. Why I'd thought she'd somehow be affected by the fact I was leaving for the next week, I didn't know. This was just amazing sex. This wasn't a relationship. Maybe if I repeated it fifty times, I'd learn to believe it.

Chapter Thirty-Eight

LIAM

$\mathcal{M}$y arrival in Hong Kong was Monday morning local time. I went straight to the hotel from the airport to shower and change into a fresh suit. Luckily, I'd slept some on the plane because it definitely hadn't happened Friday night. Not with Kendall in my bed. I kept waiting for it to be awkward, but thus far we hadn't hit a saturation point. She made it easy to be around her.

Normally, with any new sexual experience, I'd find my interest waning after a few times together. But with her, if anything, I only found the attraction growing. Her teasing, sexy, and sometimes downright sassy attitude turned me on like nothing else. It made me miss her already if I was being truthful with myself.

All the more reason to use this week apart to gain some perspective.

What I needed was to focus back on the job. This case was everything. My adrenaline was pumping as it often did when it came to a deposition or trial. It was moments like these when I could say I truly did love the law.

It would be a long five days. I was in business mode, or as

my fellow partners liked to call it, "the zone," which meant I had to dismiss all other thoughts. Especially those about Kendall. We kept our emails back and forth professional. No phone calls. No text messages. Nothing personal. By the end of the week, I was ready to get back on the plane and be home.

Arriving in at seven o'clock on a Saturday night, I drove directly home. Glancing at the time, I saw it was now after eight. Kendall would be at work in the club. I'd missed her.

I felt some regret that I'd made it all business between us this last week, but I'd needed to test myself and prove I was still capable of doing so by putting up barriers. She'd put in a lot of hours. Even after her classes, she'd logged in to help me. I recognized part of my success with this deposition was due to her diligence.

I spent the next few hours prepping for Stephen Walsh, who'd agreed to come in and interview me and the firm this week. It had been worth enduring Tabitha's company at the charity function to get this shot at his business.

At one o'clock in the morning, I got in my car and drove north toward the club. I didn't bother to go inside but waited for Kendall out in the parking lot. The big dude escorting some of the ladies out recognized me.

"Your girl isn't here tonight," he said in his gruff tone.

"What do you mean?" Why wouldn't she be here?

A blonde I recognized as her roommate came up. "You're Liam, aren't you?"

"Yes, I am."

"I'm Chloe."

"Nice to meet you. Where's Kendall?"

"She's at home. Sick in bed."

"What? Since when?" We'd just emailed one another

yesterday about my flight confirmation. Had she been sick all week long?

"She's been barely sleeping all week, between both jobs and school."

Although Chloe wasn't laying the blame at my feet, I was busy doing it for her. All the guilt. All the blame for having Kendall work so many hours. "Can I follow you to your place to check on her?"

She assessed me for a moment before agreeing. "Yeah. I'm driving in her Civic."

I followed Chloe down the freeway to Torrance, where we pulled into the parking lot of a garden-style apartment building. It wasn't fancy, but it looked safe with its well-lit parking lot, and cameras mounted on the entryways.

She led me up the stairs to the third floor. As soon as I stepped into the small studio apartment, I spotted Kendall's petite figure huddled up on a twin bed in the corner of the room. I didn't hesitate in kneeling down by her side and stroking her hair.

"It's me. How are you feeling?"

I put the back of my hand to her forehead, immediately feeling the heat.

She stirred under my touch. "Not good. When Almanzo got a fever, they put him in a tub of ice, but I don't think I want to do that."

I glanced up at Chloe who came from the bathroom with a wet washcloth in her hand. She shrugged at Kendall's incoherent rambling. "She was binge watching *Little House on the Prairie* on her laptop all day."

"Do you have a thermometer? We should take her temperature."

Chloe put the cool washcloth on Kendall's head. "We don't, unfortunately."

"Have you been throwing up?" I asked Kendall.

"No. I'm stuffy. Achy. Cold."

"We should get you to the doctor to see if you have the flu." But it was after three o'clock in the morning. That would mean the ER. At this time of night, it was a crapshoot as to how quickly she'd be seen. Suddenly, I was struck with an idea.

"My neighbor is a doctor. I'll take her to my house, and he can come over."

Chloe pursed her lips in thought. "He'll come over at this hour?"

"Lucas is a friend." Not to mention, he owed me a favor. I wasn't above cashing it in if it was for Kendall's well-being.

Hoping to put her at ease, I took out my phone. "If you give me your number, I'll send you a text message to let you know what he says."

"You promise you'll take care of her? No work?"

What kind of monster did she think I was? The thought of the answer made me sick to my stomach. "I promise."

LUCAS OWED me for help with his messy divorce, which was why he was willing to come by at three thirty in the morning. The man was accustomed to making house calls at all hours, so he came in looking crisp and professional in a button-down shirt, slacks, and with his bag full of items.

I led him up to the master bedroom where I'd tucked Kendall into my bed.

Her eyes fluttered open to his soft, soothing voice saying her name. I watched her take in his movie-star good looks, bouncing her gaze from me back to him. "You're definitely not Doc Baker."

He chuckled. "Afraid not. But thankfully, we have better medicine these days than they did in Walnut Grove."

She gave him a smile. "Probably for the best as I'm fresh out of chickens to give you for your services."

He looked at me with a grin. "She's adorable."

Yes, she was. And first thing tomorrow I was binging on *Little House on the Prairie* simply because it bothered me to learn Lucas knew the reference and I didn't.

He took her temperature, which read one hundred two degrees, before doing a throat swab.

He came back a short time later with the results. "Good news is she's negative for the flu. But she has a virus of some type giving her the fever. Make sure she stays hydrated. She can also take Tylenol and a cold decongestant. I'll write down the one I recommend, so you can get it from a drugstore. If she develops a cough or a severe headache or any signs of an earache, call me."

"Thanks, man. I owe you."

He shook his head. "No. I owed you. I'll come by later today to check on her again."

Once we were left alone, I sent Chloe a text message letting her know Kendall didn't have the flu but did have a virus of some sort. I couldn't blame her for worrying or for being pissed at me for exhausting Kendall to the point she'd been susceptible to such a illness.

I stroked her hair. "Hey, beautiful, I'm running to the store. I'll be back in a few minutes." I needed to get her medicine and some things she'd be able to drink and eat.

She merely mumbled something like "okay" before rolling over and going back to sleep.

After driving to a twenty-four-hour pharmacy and buying the items Lucas had suggested, in addition to chicken soup, Gatorade, and Kleenex, I arrived back home an hour later.

I went straight up to my bedroom to see an empty bed. Panic hit me. Then I heard the water. Was it the shower? I opened the bathroom door a crack and sighed in relief to see her in the glass enclosure. However, upon further inspection, I could see she was bracing herself against the wall.

I wasted no time stripping out of my clothes and joining her. "You okay?"

She turned, putting her head on my chest. My arms went around her. "No. I was sweating through the sheets and wanted to get clean. Then I got in here, and I'm so weak with the hot water."

"I've got you. Come on. Let me wash you real quick, then get you warm and into a clean bed so you can take some medicine."

"'Kay."

I made quick work out of washing her, including her hair. I tried to be gentle, and provide comfort instead of focusing on my erection. Evidently, he wasn't getting the message that she was sicker than a dog.

After getting her dried off, I helped her dress in shorts and a T-shirt her roommate had packed for her. Then I went about stripping and re-making the bed. Finally, once she was in it, I had her sit up to drink some Gatorade and take some Tylenol.

"I'm sorry you're stuck taking care of me," she said.

I took the hair brush out of her bag and came back to the bed with it. "I'm not stuck with anything. I'm happy to take care of you especially since I'm responsible for you getting sick."

She scooted up, letting me sit in back of her to get a better angle on brushing out her hair. Who would've guessed brushing hair would be this intimate?

"How are you possibly responsible for me getting sick?"

"Because of all the hours I had you work. You got run-down."

"I'm sure it has more to do with me taking public transportation on a daily basis. It's cold and flu season, and I obviously came into contact with someone who had something."

"Still, I feel terrible." I brushed the knots out of her long hair as gently as I could.

"So guilt is what made you bring me here?"

"No. I came to the club to pick you up from after work and was surprised to see you weren't there."

"Bet this wasn't the way you thought we'd be spending the morning."

I grinned. No. It hadn't been. Yet, there was something immensely satisfying in being able to take care of her this way. I found myself taking on the role without any qualms. "I'm sure it's not the way you'd have preferred to spend it, either."

After her hair was brushed, I got up to get her a dry towel to get some of the moisture out. I wished I'd thought to pick up a blow dryer while I'd been at the pharmacy. "You okay with staying here a couple of days until you feel better?"

Her eyes widened. "Are you?"

"I'd prefer you did. You can rest here, and Lucas will be by later to check on you. Your roommate can come over tomorrow if you'd like her to."

"Really?"

"Yeah. She's worried. Unless you're still planning to go see your family today?"

"No. I wouldn't want to pass it on especially not to my nan. Better I quarantine myself."

"Did you work the bar Friday night?"

"No. I got there and Jose took one look at me and sent me

home. As much as I was disappointed, I'm glad I didn't spread it around."

"Me, too. I'll pay you for wages you lost over the two nights."

"You'll do no such thing."

"Yes. I will." I was adamant she not come up short this month for her grandmother's care.

There was temper in her eyes. "No, you won't. You're the one who said nothing should change just because we're sleeping together. I have a bad cold. I missed work. It is what it is. You didn't cause this. And I'll have enough overtime from last week to cover anyhow."

Most people had no trouble asking for money or even taking advantage. The fact that Kendall wouldn't take my offer said a lot about her character. It also made me regret ever questioning her integrity. "Anyone ever tell you how stubborn you are?"

She gave me a tired smile. "It's a bit of the kettle calling the pot black, don't you think?"

"True. You should get some rest. You won't be able to go in Monday. And I'll work from home."

She snuggled down into my bed. The one I enjoyed seeing her in. "You don't have to work from home for me."

"I know, but I want to." More than I cared to admit.

Chapter Thirty-Nine

KENDALL

I woke to the smell of coffee and my stomach growling. Sitting up in Liam's bed, I rubbed my eyes. My muscles ached, and so did my head. I hadn't eaten yesterday, so having my appetite back was a good sign I might be on the mend.

"Hey. How are you feeling?" Liam's voice came from the doorway. He crossed over to take a seat beside me on the bed and put the back of his hand to my forehead. He was dressed casually in jeans and a T-shirt, making me smile. He looked awfully handsome in his suits, but this was a side of him I knew most didn't get to see.

"I'm feeling better."

He dropped his hand into mine. "You don't feel hot any longer, which is a good sign. You hungry?"

"Definitely. What time is it?"

"A few minutes after nine. Your roommate texted this morning. I assured her you were sleeping and feeling better, but she'd probably like to hear it from you. You're welcome to have her over, too."

"But you have work—"

He was already shaking his head. "I had Sunday brunch delivered and rented *Little House on the Prairie*. Thought we could binge watch on the couch downstairs if you don't mind me being on my laptop. Or if there's something else you'd rather do, we can."

His thoughtfulness was overwhelming. "I think what you have planned sounds perfect. I'll text Chloe."

After Liam spent the morning taking great care of me, he took off for the gym.

An hour later, my roommate arrived. I could tell the moment Chloe stepped through his front door she had a million questions. Thankfully, she didn't start in right away. "You look better. How are you feeling?"

She took a seat on the couch next to me, surveying the place, her eyes wide. I didn't blame her. The house had the same effect on me the first time I'd seen it.

"I feel much better. Thanks for helping Liam get me here."

"I know you said things were casual, but it sure didn't seem that way when he came over."

I sighed. "I'm sure that had to do with guilt. He thinks he overworked me into getting sick."

Her pretty face turned pink. "My little comment about hoping he didn't put you to work if he brought you back here probably didn't help. But I have to say, guilt usually means he'd buy you flowers or check in to see how you're doing. Guilt isn't calling a doctor friend to come over in the middle of the night or inviting you to recover at his place. I think it's more."

Maybe, but I wouldn't allow myself to go there. My emotions were already unbalanced. This morning, he'd sat on the couch with me to start the first season of *Little House* after ensuring I took my medicine. Suddenly, this didn't feel like casual sex. It felt like something deeper. If I was being honest, it was starting to become something I could easily get used to. "If I go thinking this is anything but what we agreed on, I'm liable to get hurt."

She frowned. "I don't know much about relationships, but I have to believe it's natural to develop deeper feelings as things evolve."

Sure. But what if they only evolved on my side? Before I had a chance to think it through, the front door opened and in walked Liam in his workout attire, giving me a smile. "Hi."

Chloe turned to whisper only for my ears. "Jesus, the way he looks at you makes me blush."

I grinned, feeling my own face heat. "Hi. Um, you remember Chloe."

He came into the living room and took a seat on the ottoman. "Yes. I certainly do. Nice to see you under better circumstances. You two want lunch? I'll order, then take a quick shower, and be down to join you."

Sounded too good to pass up.

By Tuesday morning, I was feeling much better. After Liam left for the office, I decided to return to my apartment and my own space. Get back into my routine. Not because I didn't enjoy staying at Liam's house, but rather because I enjoyed it too much. Hell, he'd even given me a key this morning in case I needed to come and go.

It was too easy to see him as the doting boyfriend instead of what he actually was. Frankly, I wasn't sure exactly how to define what he was to me. All I knew was it would be easy to let myself fall for him. Hell, who was I kidding? It was already too late. He'd been so sweet, doting, and attentive the last couple of days—even choosing to work from home on Monday, which before now, he'd never done. My feelings were growing deeper. But I had no clue if he shared them.

Once home, I showered and dressed for the office before setting out for the bus. I couldn't afford to get further behind in my classes and didn't want to use any more sick time. I knew Liam would prefer me to spend another day resting, but my fever was gone, and I was getting restless. My boss would just have to get over it.

Once I arrived at the office, I knocked on his door. I peeked my head in when he said to come in. "Good morning, Mr. Davenport. Did you want the usual for breakfast?"

His response was terse. "No. Come in, Ms. Tate. Shut the door."

I did as he requested, feeling butterflies in my stomach. His charcoal suit with the light blue shirt did funny things to me. We hadn't been sexual in over a week due to the Hong Kong trip and then my sickness, which meant my libido was taking notice. Holy inappropriateness. Didn't it know these were business hours?

As soon as the door closed, he stood up. "What are you doing here?"

"My fever is gone. My cold is manageable, and I can't miss school again tonight. It was time for me to get back."

His jaw clenched. "You should take another day."

"You should get over the fact I'm not going to." As much as I appreciated him taking care of me, I was in fact a grown-up who could make her own decisions on when to return to work.

We were in a standoff. The kind that made me want to sit up on his desk and show him just how much better I was feeling.

"All right. I'll get over it. I already grabbed something for breakfast."

I smiled. "Thank you. What else can I do?"

"The deposition is in a good place. But I have Stephen Walsh coming in later this morning."

"He's the tech guy from last week's charity?" He'd explained the so-called "date" he'd had with Tabitha had actually been a new business opportunity.

"That's him."

"Do you need a conference room? Refreshments?"

"I have one on the eighth floor reserved. I believe there are drinks being delivered."

"I'll confirm." Our facilities team was great about catering, but this was a big meeting.

"Thank you." He stood up, moving one more step in front of me to lift his hand to my face. "You sure you're okay?"

I leaned into his touch, appreciating it more than he could know. "Yes. I'm much better thanks to you. You took really good care of me."

"I was happy to do it." His hand dropped as if he'd just remembered we were standing in the middle of his office.

Guess I needed to remember that, too. Back to purely professional.

Later in the morning, I informed Liam that Stephen Walsh had arrived in reception. Typically, I went to get most of our guests, but considering Stephen was a big deal, my boss went downstairs to greet him personally. I hoped the meeting would be a good one.

I was sitting at my desk when the conference room line rang through. Immediately, I worried something was wrong, but I'd checked earlier, and things seemed to be in order.

"Hello, this is Kendall," I answered.

Liam's voice was on the other end. "Yes, Ms. Tate. Can you please see about getting kombucha sent up to the room?"

"Kombucha?" I repeated the unfamiliar word, trying to place where I'd heard it.

"Yes. It's fermented tea."

"Certainly." I hung up and called the cafeteria. I was happy when someone answered. But no kombucha.

Next recourse was going downstairs and three blocks over to the Whole Foods. The receptionist assured me they'd definitely have it. I forced myself to walk as fast as I could in my gray skirt suit, ignoring the pang in my side from the post-sickness rushing around.

I'd been gone more than ten minutes by the time I took the elevator up with two bottles of kombucha. I wasn't sure which kind I should have gotten. Steadying my breath, I went through the glass conference room door, hoping to get in, drop off the drinks, and get out again unnoticed.

But it wasn't to be. All three men focused on me. Liam frowning. Phil, the managing partner, appearing relieved to see I'd brought the bottles of kombucha, and the guest of honor looking at me with a big grin on his face.

It turned out Stephen Walsh was a good-looking man. In his forties, perhaps, he had short-cropped black hair, deep hazel eyes, and a megawatt smile.

"I apologize for the delay with the kombucha," I said.

Stephen stood up. "None necessary, considering you're the one delivering it. Miss—?"

My boss was on his feet now, too. Phil stood as well. Liam did the introduction. "This is my assistant, Ms. Kendall Tate."

"Lovely to meet you. I'm Stephen Walsh."

I put the bottles down on the table so I could take his extended hand. Here was hoping I didn't get our potential top client sick by spreading any germs. "Pleasure to meet you. I, um, I brought two kinds of kombucha."

He didn't spare a glance for the kombucha. "I'm sure they're both great. Tell me, Ms. Tate, what are you passionate about?"

My gaze flicked to Liam's face, which showed surprise at the question but provided no help. "Pardon?"

"What are you passionate about? I assure you, there's no wrong answer. Sorry, it's a bit personal putting you on the spot in front of your boss and his boss, but you see, I always like to know who I'm working with. Not just the lead attorney, but also who else works at the firm."

Oh, boy. It was clear by the intense way he was staring at me, I could only go with the truth. "I'm passionate about food. Cooking, baking, learning new recipes from different cultures."

His eyes lit up like a beaver in a forest full of trees. "Excellent. Food is a passion of mine, too. Now then, if you had unlimited funds, what would you do with that passion?"

I glanced over toward Phil, who was giving Liam a nervous look. Crap. I didn't want to ruin this opportunity to get Stephen Walsh as a client for them by saying the wrong thing. "I'd probably open up a catering business."

"Ah. And would you do big, fancy parties?"

"No. I'd prefer more intimate affairs in someone's home or maybe cooking prepared meals that could be dropped off for a family hoping to eat healthy during the week."

He smiled. "And tell me, what would you do with all of the leftover food?"

My mind recalled the event Liam and Tabitha had attended had involved a charity for the homeless. The right answer was to feed the homeless. But if I said that, it would appear rehearsed.

As if he was leading me to water, Phil piped in. "Would you donate the food?"

Stephen gave him a sigh of disappointment as if the older man was ruining his game.

I finally answered. "Maybe, but I'm not a huge believer in simply feeding the homeless."

Now Stephen's attention was back on me. "Then, what would you suggest?"

I licked my lips, nervous regarding what I was about to say. "I read this article a few weeks ago about a community setup in Texas. They built these tiny houses, taught the homeless how to grow their own fruits and vegetables, and set up a community. They taught people job skills. They were subsidized in the beginning, but before long, the once homeless were self-sustaining, selling goods to pay for the ones they needed to buy. The project was deemed a short-term success."

Stephen's gaze didn't leave mine, but he leaned forward. "Why do you think that worked?"

"Because they developed a sense of community and pride. I'm not opposed to feeding the homeless, Mr. Walsh, but that's only one meal at one time, and only a few hours later, they will be hungry again. If I had unlimited funds, I'd find ways of teaching the population to self-sustain. Or put dollars into programs to help get people off the streets. Of course, it's easier said than done with mental illness prominent in the population, but I also believe there's hope based on the results of that experiment."

There was a silent pause. One that Phil obviously felt the need to fill. "I think we can all agree it's a nice dream."

In other words, he thought I was a silly girl. I didn't bother to meet Liam's eyes, afraid I'd find disappointment reflected in them.

Stephen interrupted. "John Klein ran that experiment.

He's a former engineer and very passionate about finding ways to help the homeless. I have nothing but respect for him."

Either Stephen knowing about the man and experiment worked in my favor, or he was about to tell me how he didn't believe in it. My breath held as I waited for his response. Then he smiled.

"You are a delight, Kendall, if I may call you by your first name. And your vision is one I think we could all use more of in this world. Good things can happen when someone believes they can."

"Thank you." What else could I say?

He turned toward Phil. "Without dreams, we'd never change things for a better future. Now that would be a real shame."

Huh. His words had the managing partner turning red.

Stephen wasn't done. "Gentlemen, I'll be signing with your firm today. Thanks again for the kombucha, Kendall." He picked one up and put it in his bag. "Take the other one. It'll change your life." He handed it to me with a wink before walking out with Phil scrambling after him to escort him out.

I simply plopped down in the conference room chair, giving Liam a dazed look. "What just happened?"

He grinned. "I believe that was a test. One you just kicked ass at passing."

Chapter Forty

LIAM

here had been something incredible about watching Kendall handle her own with Stephen Walsh. Then she'd taken it a step further by owning him with her sincere answer to his question. She'd been amazing, and it had been immensely satisfying to watch, not to mention a huge turn-on.

As soon as she popped her head in to inquire about lunch, I could feel my pulse race. Feel the magnetic pull toward her. I was aching to touch her.

"Hi. Salad or sandwich today?"

"Salad is fine. Thank you."

As soon as she left, I breathed easy, then thought about jerking off. It would be a first to do so in my office. But considering she'd be back soon, it would have to wait.

Once she returned with the food, I found myself standing up and helping her take the tray to put it on my desk for the excuse to touch her hand.

She glanced up at the same time I caught a whiff of strawberry lip gloss.

"How are you feeling?" I asked in an intimate, husky tone

that was very different from how we normally spoke to one another in the office.

"Good, actually. I think I'm ninety percent."

As if she'd given me the green light I'd needed, I crashed my lips to hers. Crossing one of the unbreakable lines I'd promised I never would by touching her in the office. But unfortunately, once I had a taste, there was no way I couldn't have more.

I pulled away, moving to flip the lock on my door. "Is anyone expecting you during this hour?"

"No, but I may still be contagious."

"I don't care." And I didn't. I pulled her back into my arms and met her lips again before trailing my kisses down to her neck and behind her ear. "I promised this would never happen here in the office. That we wouldn't do this here."

She kissed me back, igniting my need to have her. My hand dove under her skirt, swiping her thong to the side, fingers searching for her pussy. Jesus. She was wet. Clearly as turned on as I was with this impromptu make-out session.

"I need you," I muttered, unable to stop this madness.

She was working my belt buckle. "I need you, too. It was too long of a week to go without touching you like this."

Yes, it was. "I need a condom."

"Do you have one in your wallet?"

"No. Shit. Wait. I think I have one in my desk."

My answer earned me a raised brow, making me amend that remark. "It was for a campaign for safe sex for a client we were representing. They gave them out. I stuck mine in a drawer." God, I hoped I still had it from months ago. Otherwise, this wasn't happening.

After rifling through my bottom drawers like a madman, I pulled it out like a prize. "Aha."

She giggled, coming around to move my keyboard and sit

up on my desk in front of my chair. All laughing stopped once we reached for one another again. We were frantic. Me with sliding off her panties. Her with undoing my trousers and taking out my cock.

"This will be quick, but I promise to make it up to you this weekend."

"I'm holding you to your promise. Now, how do you want me?"

"On your feet, bent over the desk with your ass in the air." It was like a fantasy to watch her assume the position.

My hands massaged her globes, wishing I had more time to play. "We have to be quiet. Can you do it?"

"Uh-huh. Just fuck me, Liam."

Jesus. She had no idea what her words did to me. I quickly sheathed myself in the condom, wincing when I realized it was a bit snug, but it didn't matter as I had the perfect woman over my desk. I wasn't about to waste this opportunity after having thought about her all week.

When I pushed inside her, we both groaned, though trying to keep the volume down. She was both snug and wet. Perfect. I pulled out slightly before pushing home again. I'd give anything to pound into her harder and faster, but I knew it would be too noisy. Too risky to make loud sounds. I relied on measured thrusts, reaching around to play with her clit. She went off in record time, turning her mouth into her arm to keep from crying out. I followed quickly, grinding out my orgasm deep inside of her.

We were both still panting when I pulled out slowly. I was already wishing I had more time, so I could spread her out on my couch and pleasure her with my tongue.

She stood up and watched me tie off the condom, careful to wrap it in tissues so no one would see it in my trash. While I zipped up, she found her panties and straightened her skirt.

"Well, that was unexpected," she said, grinning.

I couldn't return the grin. Instead, reality started to sink in. I was now reeling from the fact I'd crossed a line. A big one. If the wrong person had come looking for me, it could've cost me everything. "This was a mistake."

Her face fell. "Why do I feel like I'm the one getting the lecture here when it was you who initiated it?"

"I'm not lecturing. I'm simply stating a fact." Shit. I was being an asshole and couldn't seem to stop the runaway train. I was freaking out at the line we'd crossed. "We can't do this again here."

"Don't worry. At this point, you could've left out the last word." She then turned and walked out.

———

SELF-REFLECTION RAN deep later that night as I nursed a bourbon in my living room, replaying the afternoon in my head. I was a dick. Kendall deserved an apology. I'd taken out my frustration with myself for crossing a line I never thought I would directly on her and it hadn't been fair. Did I mention I was an asshole?

I texted her with, *"I'm sorry."*

Nothing came back, but she was in class, so I waited. By the time nine o'clock rolled around, and she still hadn't replied, I dialed her number.

"Hello," she answered, sounding out of breath.

"Hi. Did I catch you at a bad time?"

"I'm at the grocery store. I didn't get a chance to shop yet this week."

"I wasn't sure if you were ignoring my text or just still out."

"A bit of the first and all of the second."

I smiled at her sassy response. "I took out my anger at myself for crossing a line on you. For that, I'm sorry."

Her sigh was the only sound on the other end.

"Are you still there?"

"Yes. I am. And we can agree to no more office sex, but just don't talk down to me ever again."

I swallowed hard at the reminder of what a prick I'd been. "I won't. Are we okay?"

"I think so. I mean boundaries are tough considering we work together. Do you still want me to come over after work on Friday?"

Relief finally made the tightness in my chest ease. "Yes. Definitely."

"All right. Have a good night, Liam."

"You, too." I hung up, wondering not for the first time if I could treat her the way she deserved.

Chapter Forty-One

KENDALL

$\mathcal{I}$'d never been the type to hold a grudge. That's why accepting Liam's apology two days ago had been easy. But it didn't mean, as I sat at my desk on a Thursday afternoon, I didn't second-guess if in the long term, this relationship, or lack thereof, was a good idea. Case in point, Valentine's Day.

It was the Hallmark holiday today, and I kept telling myself it didn't matter, yet I kept wondering if he'd do something. Send secret flowers. Send a text asking me to come over for dinner tonight after class. Get me a box of chocolates. Something. But so far, it was after lunch and nothing. Because nothing was what a non-boyfriend did. Right?

I found myself disappointed. Then again, we'd see each other tomorrow night. Maybe he'd have something romantic planned then? I glanced up mid-thought to see Phillip, the managing partner, walking up to my desk.

"Good afternoon, Mr. Kinkaid. Mr. Davenport is finishing up a conference call." My phone set's panel showed Liam's light was still on, but I knew he only had a few minutes left.

"Thanks. I'll talk to him after he's done, but first I wanted to speak with you."

"With me?" My voice went up an octave while my mind instantly went back to Tuesday when Liam had me bent over his desk at lunchtime. Had someone heard us? Was something reported?

Phillip gave me a kind smile. "Yes. It seems Stephen Walsh was quite taken with your fresh perspective on the homeless which, as you're aware, is a passion of his. Anyhow, he gave us an invitation for two people to attend a black-tie dinner tomorrow night at his home in Beverly Hills. He asked for you to be one of those people."

Phillip was studying me as if I'd know why a client would do such a thing. "I, um, that's a surprise." Shit. I could feel my face turning red.

Then the door to my boss's office opened. Liam did a quick glance between us, a frown marring his otherwise perfect face.

"What's going on?" he asked a bit too forcefully with a hint of accusation. Or maybe it was my imagination.

Phillip was the one to speak because, frankly, I didn't know what to say.

"I was telling Kendall about Stephen Walsh's request to have her attend the dinner tomorrow night."

Narrowed eyes, throbbing temple. Stiff posture. It was as if we were back to the beginning, before we were sleeping together, where I was just Ms. Tate, and he was still the dick I wrote secret entries about in the document I'd deleted last week. Perhaps it had been premature to do so.

"I see," Liam finally said.

Phillip smiled. "Don't worry. I'm sure she'll make a much better date than I would. Can you make it tomorrow night, Kendall? I realize it's last minute. The event starts at seven o'clock. As I said, it's black tie, and the firm will pay for a car to pick you up."

The timing couldn't be worse. I had to work at the bar. I didn't have a thing to wear. And I didn't owe the firm this inconvenience in my life. On the other hand, it was flattering to have made an impression on a client. One who'd requested me. One who didn't seem to care I was only a secretary. Unlike Liam, who appeared absolutely annoyed with the idea.

Perhaps he thought he should be taking someone like Tabitha instead of a girl who was still finishing her degree. Too bad. "I'd be honored to go."

Phil appeared pleased with my answer. That made one of them. Although Liam had his icy poker face in place, I could definitely say he wasn't pleased.

"Excellent." Phil then turned toward my boss. "If you have a few minutes, Liam, I have a number of things to discuss with you."

"Certainly." He didn't give me another glance as they went into his office.

Liam said nothing to me for the rest of the day. The only thing I knew was the party started at seven tomorrow night.

After class, I went home and tried to enlist the help of Chloe with the one problem I could manage. A dress. Unfortunately, she wasn't my size even if she'd had something formal to wear to a black-tie event.

"Can you hit the thrift shop tomorrow?"

"I'll be cutting it close, but I can go during lunch." The secondhand store I frequented was in Hollywood, and I could take the subway there, but I'd still have to find something my size. Here was hoping the dress gods were with me tomorrow.

"Your hot boss picking you up for the date?" Chloe asked.

"A driver is picking me up from the office. As much as I

hate the idea of getting ready for a fancy event at work, I won't have time to come all the way home, then try to drive in rush hour traffic to the party in Hollywood. I believe Liam is leaving from the office, too, although he hasn't confirmed. In any case, it's not a date." I tried not to let that bother me. But I was quickly finding out it was starting to. Maybe because he seemed weird about it. As if I had somehow gotten myself invited on purpose. As if he was uncomfortable with me being a part of his world. Hadn't he told me I'd rocked Stephen Walsh's test? So then, why was he being a jerk about it now?

"I'll tell everyone at the club that you're almost better, but won't be in tomorrow. I think they appreciate you not wanting to infect anyone," Chloe offered.

"Thank you." At least I had a plausible reason for missing work. Still, I felt bad they'd be short-staffed. I'd missed more days in the last month than I had in the whole two years I'd worked there. A small part of me was tempted to back out of the party. Maybe this was more trouble than it was worth. Yet I found myself curious as to why Stephen Walsh had asked for me specifically.

"How can you say it's not a date?"

"I mean it's a work function. And we're not telling people we're together. Not that we *are* together. We're just— I don't know."

"Did he do anything for Valentine's Day for you?"

I stared down at my hands before looking up at her again. "He's not my boyfriend, so I didn't expect anything."

She offered me a sad smile. "Does it mean you'll be okay with him not doing anything for your birthday next month, too?"

To be fair, I doubted he knew my birthday was in March. "Probably not."

She reached over and squeezed my hand. "I'm sorry. I don't want to see you get hurt. He does seem to genuinely feel something for you. You could see it by the way he took care of you when you were sick. I guess the question is if it's enough for you?"

It was the question indeed.

ON FRIDAY, during my lunch hour, I took the subway to my destination, praying I'd find a dress at a reasonable price for tonight's swanky dinner. I'd brought in my black and my nude pumps, and also some silver sandals, hoping whatever I picked out would match. At least Chloe had helped me figure out what I'd be doing with my hair. The benefit of having long hair was it went up without a lot of fuss.

I was grateful there were no other customers at the secondhand shop when I walked in. "Hi," I said to the older woman at the front desk.

"Hello, dear, how can I help you?"

"I'm hoping you might have a dress in my size. One for a black-tie event tonight."

"We have lots of beautiful gowns. The upside of being in Hollywood. What size are you?"

"I'm a four, but I'm short and have a generous bottom half, which means sometimes I have trouble finding things that fit properly."

"Ah. I think I may have the thing if you're okay with showing a bit of skin."

I wasn't sure having my lack of cleavage on display would be a good idea, but as soon as she walked over and pulled a silver dress off the rack, I knew it was the one. It was pure Hollywood glamour with thousands of crystals strewn into the bodice. It was beautiful, but once she turned it around and I saw the back, I knew I had to have it. Holy shit. The back took this dress to another level. It was scooped out to show, as she'd said, a lot of skin, but it was the draping back jewels which really set it off. It was both sexy and sophisticated. The question was would it fit?

Five minutes later in the dressing room, I discovered it fit like a glove. And it was the perfect length, so I wouldn't have to hem it up like I had to do with most dresses given my short height.

"It was made for you, honey. You certainly don't need much in the way of jewelry. Maybe some small hoops, but no necklace. The dress takes center stage for sure."

It certainly did. "How much is it?" I didn't want to get my hopes set on it only to have it out of reach.

"It's three hundred. But it's been here a long time waiting for a home. How about I give it to you for half off?"

It was still out of my budget, but I couldn't not have this dress. I mean what else would I do? Once again, I was tempted to back out. But the thought of Liam seeing me in this dress— Well, I couldn't resist. "I appreciate it. I'll take it."

After forking over the money, I was back on the subway and back to the office with the dress in a garment bag.

Cinderella had her dress. Now I just wondered if my Prince Charming would be a dick at the ball.

AT SIX O'CLOCK, I dressed in the handicapped stall in the women's bathroom at the office. Was I glamorous or what? It was too bad this party couldn't have been on a Saturday where I could've taken more time at home to get ready. But at least I was getting a ride.

Luckily, there weren't a lot of people still there at the office at this time. After dressing, I touched up my makeup, and put my hair up with a number of pins.

My red lipstick finished the look and then, because I couldn't resist, I added a coat of strawberry lip gloss. Other than confirming the time for the car to pick us up, Liam had said little all day. I wasn't sure where his thoughts were. But I was determined to find out tonight. I assumed I'd go back to his place? Or at this point, maybe not.

After I walked back to my desk, I logged out of my computer, locked my laptop in the drawer, and turned to see Tabitha coming down the hall toward me. Her steps were hurried, her voice shrill when she asked, "Why are you all dressed up?"

"I was invited to Stephen Walsh's party tonight."

Her eyes raked over my dress, then flicking toward Liam who was coming out of his office in his tux.

"So, your secretary is your plus-one now?" The way she said the word secretary let it be known how she felt about someone with my title going to a party she didn't deem me worthy of attending.

I braced myself for Liam's response. But he surprised me. "She is the very reason I'm invited tonight. The reason Stephen Walsh is probably signing with our firm. He invited her directly."

I hadn't expected him to stick up for me.

Tabitha only sneered. "Yeah, I bet he did."

Liam bounced his gaze between me and his colleague. "A moment please, Tabitha." He ushered her into his office but stopped in the doorway, turning toward me. "I'll meet you downstairs in the car, Ms. Tate."

Chapter Forty-Two

LIAM

*A*s soon as my office door was closed, Tabitha started with her tirade. "What the hell, Liam? A secretary is attending Stephen Walsh's party? Seriously?"

"Seriously. And like I said, if it wasn't for her impressing him on Tuesday, I doubt very much anyone would be going."

"What did she do, promise him sexual favors?"

My temper hit a boiling point. "Enough," I said in a low tone, serving notice that I wasn't about to hear another disparaging word. "You need to stow your jealousy and figure out a way to deal with it. Not one more word to Kendall or to anyone about this."

"It's Kendall now, huh?"

For an attractive woman, pettiness made her uglier than ever. I'd had quite enough of her snotty attitude. "Yes. It's her first name. Just like you call Helen, your assistant, by her first name. You're still getting your fifteen percent origination, as discussed."

Her expression remained hard. "Fine. But I still don't like it. We have a pecking order here at the firm for a reason."

I didn't want to hear about her outdated views of how

things should be at a law firm. This wasn't a caste system. It was an organization, all the people of which needed to work well together in all aspects. "I don't give a fuck if you like it or not."

Her face went red before morphing into something else entirely as she adjusted my bow tie. "You're right, of course. I was out of line. Call me after. Tell me how it goes?"

I had to physically keep myself from recoiling, but it would do no good to upset her further. "I'll let you know in the office on Monday, Tabitha. Have a good night."

I let out a sigh of relief as I watched her walk out.

By the time I got downstairs and to the car, I had a raging headache. I was aware none of this was Kendall's doing, but her accompanying me to this event posed a number of challenges. Tabitha was only one of them. This was where the line between professional and personal threatened to get obliterated completely especially since I was sure Kendall saw tonight as a date. But it couldn't be.

"Hi," she greeted when I got into the back of the black Lincoln town car with her.

"Hi."

"Everything okay?"

I gave her a small smile. "Yes. It's fine." I was about to tell her how damn beautiful she looked, but I couldn't. The driver was a regular for a number of partners in the firm. "Were you able to deal with the club tonight without any issues?"

"Yes. They think I'm still recovering."

"How are you feeling?" This was at least a safe topic.

"Back to normal, thankfully. Lucas called yesterday to check on me—"

I shook my head, a finger to my lips, and watched her

shut down her thought. I didn't want her to mention her doctor was my neighbor or friend.

"Oh. Right."

I immediately winced when I saw her retreat. It reminded me of our ride from the airport to the Airbnb the first day we'd flown to Virginia. She gazed out the window, and we both were silent.

We arrived at Stephen's house forty-five minutes later. He had a large mansion in the Hollywood Hills with an amazing view. I got out of the car first, taking her hand to help her out, regretting when I had to let go.

As soon as she stepped in front of me, I sucked in my breath. Jesus, her dress was backless. Given the way it fit her ass, I felt like making her wear my tux jacket to cover up.

It was going to be a long night.

After we walked in through the front door, she took a glass of champagne that had been offered on a tray. She seemed starstruck as she looked around at the opulence of the house and all of the beautiful people walking around, some of them famous.

She turned to me. "Should I stay with you, or—"

"I think it's appropriate. But no touching or personal talk. We never know who might be watching or overhear us."

She stiffened. "I understand."

"Also go easy on the champagne." She'd just downed half of it in one swallow.

Her glare prefaced her words. "Good thing I have you here to tell me how to act at a fancy party. Or maybe I should be grateful you're talking to me at all considering you've barely had two words for me since I was invited."

Shit. Of course she was right. But not for the reason I was sure she imagined. "I didn't mean—" I was cut off from an explanation when none other than Stephen Walsh came up to us.

"Ah, Kendall, you look ravishing. Doesn't she, Liam?"

I wasn't sure what his game was. All I knew was he was one eccentric dude, and he seemed to have taken a liking to my assistant. "Yes, Ms. Tate looks lovely," was the best I could come up with.

He laughed, turning to Kendall. "Please don't tell me he's this formal all of the time."

She drained the rest of her glass. "Mr. Davenport is very professional."

I'd intended to set some boundaries tonight and had completely overshot. It occurred to me that we could've had a complete conversation about my expectations for the evening yesterday or even today if I hadn't been so intent on avoiding it. I hadn't brought it up because I'd been so uncomfortable with the blurring of personal and professional lines. So I'd simply pretended the whole problem didn't exist. Which obviously hadn't been the right choice.

Stephen shrugged. "I suppose it's a good thing Liam is professional. But you know, all work and no play is just no fun."

I managed a tight smile. "I'll be sure to remember that."

He chuckled. "Yes, well, I suppose fun shouldn't be what I rely on to get me through the next few months of litigation. Tell me, Kendall, is your boss as good as they say he is?"

She gave him a smile not reflected in her eyes. "You're in good hands, Mr. Walsh. There's nothing more important to him than his job or his clients."

A month ago, I would've taken her words for a compliment. But now I knew better. It was a bitter pill to swallow knowing she was right. I certainly hadn't prioritized her feelings but had instead treated her as if her invitation to this event had upset me.

"You must call me Stephen. Now then, let's get you a fresh glass of champagne. And go have you meet John Klein, the creator of the study you'd read about."

His hand was on her bare back, and he was leading her through the crowd before I could say another word. The jealousy hit me hard and unexpectedly. I had to tamp down on the urge to pull her back to me. To do what? Insist she stay with me? Make sure Stephen knew she was off-limits? What the hell was happening to me?

Unfortunately, all I could do over the next hour was watch for any signal she was uncomfortable and try not to appear like I was stalking her.

Chapter Forty-Three

KENDALL

Stephen was charming and nothing but a gentleman. A strange guy with a number of quirks, but in all, he seemed harmless as I learned more about him over the next hour. Considering he was giving me more attention and compliments than my date—who wasn't actually my date but my lover, oh, and also my boss—I was hard pressed to leave his company for Liam's.

"Tell me, how do you like working for the law firm?" he asked while handing me a fresh glass of champagne.

"I enjoy it."

He chuckled. "I don't entirely believe you. But the moment you want to search for other employment, I'd have a place for you."

My spidey sense told me this could get awkward. "Doing what, exactly?"

He smiled. "I don't know you, Kendall, but something tells me you wouldn't leave for another assistant job. As you said in that conference room, your passion is food. And I own a number of restaurants around the city. So you tell me."

"I'm not sure." My indecisive answer was like a broken

record. One even I'd tired of. I knew what I wanted, but it seemed I was afraid to announce it to the world. Plus this man was a client. Surely, I couldn't confess that I'd quit in a heart-beat if I could do what I loved and still make enough money to help support my nan.

"Relax, my dear. I can assure you this is a legitimate offer. You're a stunning girl but not my type."

He motioned over my shoulder toward my boss, who wasn't doing a very good job of looking as though he wasn't watching us. "Liam is much more my type, to be honest. Although I doubt he'd appreciate knowing it. Anyhow, I'm serious about the job offer. Keep it in mind." He pulled a card out of his pocket and handed it over discreetly. "This has my cell phone on it as well as my personal email address. I like to hire people who are passionate and aren't defined by their title or content to be treated as less than others because of it. Hell, if I had been content with settling, I never would've gone from working as a janitor while taking college courses to where I am today. Some may think I'm strange, but I have an innate ability to read people. You, my dear, deserve good things. You deserve to follow your dreams. Don't ever settle for less."

I had to keep myself from tearing up. His words resonated so very much. It was as if he could see I wasn't following my true desires. That I was settling. Not only with my job, but also with my non-boyfriend. I tucked his card into my clutch so very impressed with how he'd gone from being a janitor to achieving his dreams. "Thank you. I'll keep your words in mind."

Liam came up fifteen minutes later, glancing between the two of us with a strained smile. "You ready to take our seats for dinner?"

"Yes."

"What did you talk to Stephen about?" he asked once we'd put some distance between us and our new client.

"He introduced me to John Klein. We had a great conversation about the study he'd done." And we had. Stephen had treated me as if it was normal to introduce me to any of the famous people attending. He hadn't acted like I was nothing more than an assistant or a secret lover, not worthy of meeting anyone.

Shit. I was being unfair. I found myself having to tamp down on my kernel of resentment. This wasn't the place. And I'd signed up for exactly the way Liam was treating me. I'd known it going in, but the question now, of course, was if it was enough for me.

Shortly after dinner, Liam asked if I was ready to leave. Considering it was after ten, and I'd had enough of socializing, I was happy to depart. We said our goodbyes and stepped out into the chilly evening.

I pulled out my phone with the intent of calling our driver, but Liam surprised me. "I sent the driver home. I figured we could take an Uber instead." He took out his phone. "The car should be here in two minutes."

"Really? Why?"

"Because I want to take you back to my place without one of the regular firm drivers knowing where we're going."

That stung. "I thought the driver was taking us back to the office. Isn't your car there?"

He was studying my face. "No. I took a taxi in today. I thought we'd leave from here to my place. Unless you'd rather not come over?"

"No. I want to." As I admitted to him, and also to myself, that I wanted him despite my warring emotions, I realized I had to let the rest go. He'd been very clear about what it was he wanted, which didn't include a relationship. Either I was on board or I wasn't.

Judging by my choice to go over to his place, I'd made up my mind.

The moment we arrived at his house, and he ushered me in, he was on me. "You in this dress drove me crazy all night."

He'd certainly hidden it well. "It did?"

"Yes. You look stunning. Obviously, Stephen thought so, too, since he monopolized you for most of the night."

He was kissing down my neck now while my hands helped him shed his jacket. "Mm, Stephen doesn't swing my way."

He pulled back, his brow arched. "Huh. Really?"

"Yeah. He sort of offered me a job, and I must've looked like it creeped me out because then he confided I wasn't his type. That you, in fact, were more his type."

Liam chuckled. "Thank God."

Not the words I'd expected him to say. "You're happy you're Stephen's type?"

"No. I'm happy *you* are not."

He carefully unzipped my dress and let it pool to the floor. I could feel myself aching for his touch, expecting him to hurry it along. But he didn't. Instead he peppered kisses from behind me on my shoulders, trailing his tongue up along the base of my neck. Oh, Jesus. This slow, sweet seduction was doing things to my emotions. It would be easier to keep thinking of this as a non-relationship if he bent me over his desk instead of making love with so much intimacy.

Turning around, I met his lips in a scorching kiss, hoping to speed things along, but he wasn't having it.

"I don't think so. I plan on savoring you."

An hour later, I was completely sedated from his love-making, having lost count of the number of orgasms he'd given me. His hand trailed down my back while I lay curled up in his embrace.

"Did Stephen really offer you a job?"

"He did."

"He needs an assistant?"

My body instantly tensed. "Actually, he knows I wouldn't leave for another assistant job."

"Then, what would he offer?"

I sat up, looking down at him in the moonlight. "Are you implying I wouldn't be considered for anything other than a secretarial position?"

"No, of course not. I'm sorry. I didn't intend to make it sound that way."

His apology rang true, but it also triggered what was bothering me the most. Unable to help myself, I pushed, despite knowing that doing so would have consequences. "What do you think about us going out for breakfast tomorrow since we'll be up at a decent time?"

Now it was his turn to tense. "It's not a good idea. A lot of attorneys from the office live down here in South Bay."

My emotions were starting to get the better of me. "So what? It's not like there's a rule against us dating in the office."

"No, but I can't have people in the office finding out about our arrangement."

Arrangement. Why did that word seem so dirty? So clinical. "Right. Then, I should probably go home now." I climbed out of bed, trying not to tie his words to my self-worth. I'd never been ashamed of being an assistant, buying my clothes secondhand, or having to work hard for a living. I wasn't about to feel diminished now. It was clear this non-relationship was no longer working for me.

"What are you talking about? Stay until tomorrow. I can order breakfast in. Anything you want."

I found my panties first and then my dress in a pool at the bottom of the bed. Luckily, my phone was in my clutch, fully charged. "No, thanks. I need to go." Before I started crying.

I hated to head home at this hour, but flight was the only way I could think of dealing with this situation. After pulling on my dress, I typed in my Uber app, wishing instead of UberX, there was UberShame. It would be a car with tinted windows, extra panties, vodka to dull the pain, chocolate, and some tissues. Oh, along with a very sweet and understanding driver who would listen to my troubles and mutter words like, "he's a bastard," the entire ride home.

"What is happening with you? What am I missing?" Liam was out of the bed, pulling on his boxers and running a hand over his face.

"I don't know. I just need to get home." Because the tears had already started.

"Wait. What is this about?" He'd closed the gap between us and put his fingers under my chin. Urging me to look at him.

"I can't do this." It came out as a whisper.

"Can't do what?"

My Uber driver was ten minutes out. I turned, walking down the stairs in search of my shoes. I only stopped at the large entry mirror where I tried to do something with my hair that didn't scream I'd been fucked senseless.

He followed me down. "Kendall, talk to me. Please."

He deserved an explanation, even if it wasn't fully baked. "I want more."

"More what?"

"Thursday was Valentine's Day."

Both his brows went sky high. "You're upset tonight because I didn't do anything for you on Valentine's Day?"

"Yes. No. I mean it's more than that. It's the fact you don't want to get breakfast, dinner, or walk on the beach together."

If I was truly being honest, my strained emotions involved more than my settling for a non-relationship with him. It was about me settling, period. I had dreams, but I wasn't close to pursuing them. Instead, I'd been content to simply go along with life instead of getting what I wanted out of it. Our non-relationship was an example of a bigger problem.

He raked a hand through his short hair. "This isn't a relationship. We agreed on it."

His tone implied I was the one changing the rules. He wasn't wrong. "I know we did. But I also said I'd tell you if it became too much."

"It's too much because I missed a Hallmark holiday?"

Leave it to him to miss the point. Then again, I hadn't given him a lot to go on. "It's my birthday next month. It's my nan's birthday in April, and we're throwing her a party. I knew what this was, but I realize it's not enough for me any longer."

"You want a boyfriend?" He said the B-word like it was dirty.

"Yes. And I can tell by your tone that's not what you want."

"We work together."

Of course, he would be most worried about how this would affect him at work. If I'd ever doubted his priorities, this slammed it home. "I know. And don't worry. It'll remain professional." I reached up to kiss his cheek. "Goodbye, Liam."

Chapter Forty-Four

LIAM

y feet were rooted to the spot. I was completely at a loss how Kendall and I had gone from entangled in my bed to me watching her bolt out my door. My heart was in my throat, my adrenaline pumping, my mind racing. The thought of her leaving brought on unexpected panic. I couldn't take it.

Finally, my feet caught up with my brain, propelling me into motion. I wasn't sure what the hell I would give her long term, but in this moment, all I knew for certain was I couldn't let her leave. Couldn't let her walk out of my life.

I quickly pulled up my slacks, not bothering with a shirt, and sprinted down my stairs and outside to my driveway. I was in time to see her opening the back door of a black Toyota Prius, which I assumed was her Uber.

"Wait, Kendall. Please don't go."

She hesitated, glancing toward the driver, then back to me, allowing me to close the gap. "Liam, I—"

"Stay so we can talk. If you don't like what I have to say, then I'll drive you home myself." I had no idea what words I'd use, but the thought of her getting in the Uber and driving away from me evoked such a pang of loss I had to think of something.

"Please." I threw in the last word on a whisper, desperate in a way I'd never experienced. I needed her to come back inside. To not leave me.

"Okay, um—" She looked toward the driver.

Thankfully, my trousers still had my wallet in them. I grabbed it, pulling out some cash, not bothering to count it. "Sorry for your trouble."

The older gentleman shrugged. "Not a problem. You two have a good night."

We both stood there, gazes locked, while he drove off. "Let's go back inside," I finally managed.

Taking her hand, I led her into my house and straight into the kitchen. I needed a moment to try to sort out my thoughts. Time to figure out what I would say. "Are you hungry?" She'd only picked at her food at the dinner earlier.

She nodded. "I could eat, but I should probably change out of my dress first."

"You can change into one of my T-shirts and boxers. And leave some things over here going forward if you'd like."

Her eyes widened at the significance of my words. I found no regret in saying them.

"Okay. I'll be back down in a minute."

As soon as she was out of sight, I expelled a long breath and braced myself against the counter, closing my eyes. I needed to figure out what I wanted to say. Obviously, I wasn't a wing-it kind of guy given the way I prepared meticulously for a trial or deposition. I left no stone unturned and went over every detail. Everything was prepared, every word I said, every action I took—I even went so far as to school my facial expressions. Yet, this— this was different. It was personal. It was emotional. And I was completely without a script or the confidence I could win it.

She came back down the stairs in nothing but my T-shirt and boxers, making my heart race. Lord, she was beautiful.

"I have a frozen pizza. Or I can order something."

"Pizza is good."

It would be for her. Because she wouldn't care that I was offering her a mere four-dollar box pizza. She didn't put on airs or expect gourmet simply because I had money. Instead, she was simply appreciative. I could learn something from her attitude.

I busied myself with putting the pizza in the oven, then turned to see her sitting on the counter.

As if she couldn't stand avoiding the subject any longer, she waded in. "I know you said you don't have time for a relationship."

"Honestly, I've never taken the time to have one. As you said tonight at the party, my work is my priority." I was terrified of the type of demands a girlfriend would put on me. I had no idea what I'd have to give up in order to make someone else happy.

"I don't want to feel like you're embarrassed to be with me."

Shock jolted through me. Then it sank in. It was my words and the way I was hiding our relationship that had made her feel that way. Taking her hands, I kissed the inside of each of her palms, then her lips.

"I could never feel embarrassed by you. I was proud to be there with you tonight. I admire what you said to Stephen in the conference room and the way you can be so at ease, whether we're at a fancy dinner or simply bowling with my family. You think I give a fuck about your title? I don't. You're the hardest working, most genuine, incredible person

I've ever known. Hell, if anything, you're the one getting the short end of the stick with me."

I hesitated before going into the next part.

She beat me to it. "But…"

My sigh filled the air. "But until you are no longer my assistant, can we keep this thing from the people at the firm? Would you be okay with me being your boyfriend here but no more than your boss in the office?" There was no good way of explaining all of the whys without her taking it personally. In my mind, I wanted both my named partnership and the girl. Was it too much to ask?

She pulled me into her embrace with her legs, put her arms around me, and rubbed my back. "I had no idea you felt that way about me." Then she pulled back. "And obviously, I'm not in a hurry to tell everyone at work. Maybe I'm being oversensitive to things tonight."

"Why do you say that?" Perhaps if I could get to the bottom of what had triggered her feelings tonight, I could work to resolve it.

"Stephen hit a nerve. He talked to me about following my passions. I'm not."

It didn't surprise me she would come to this realization because anyone who knew her understood her calling was food and cooking. But what did bother me was that she'd talked to Stephen about it instead of me. Then again, it wasn't as though I'd afforded her the opportunity. That, however, was about to change. "You want to be a chef?"

"More than anything. But the responsible thing is to finish my degree."

"You're close. How many classes remaining?"

"Two more classes next quarter."

"A chef with a business degree isn't a bad thing. Especially if you ever want to open your own catering business.

So you'll finish school by summer. Then what?" Although I had some ideas, I wanted her to trust I would listen and not try to influence her decisions.

"Maybe I could go work at a restaurant part-time. Take culinary courses."

"But still working at the club on the weekends?" I hated to see her unable to trade in her late nights.

"You know I don't have a choice with working there."

Right. Because of her grandmother's care. It was tempting to repeat my offer to have her work extra hours for me, but I knew it would only insult her. She had to figure out what she wanted on her own.

However, I did decide to show her my commitment to being a part of her future by asking, "The grandmother I get to meet one of these Sundays for a family dinner?"

Her smile was immediate. "Do you mean it?"

"I do. But in all fairness, that means you're stuck hanging out at Disneyland with my sister and her family when they come to visit in May."

Her smile only got bigger.

There, had it been so hard for me to make future plans? No. The pain in my chest started to ease with the thought I'd still be with her in the months to come. However, there was a warning voice in my head telling me I was only prolonging the inevitable. Delaying the arrival of a known fact. And once we did break up, we'd be even further involved. Yet when faced with the choice between letting her go now or jumping into the deep end, I was jumping. The only question was whether I'd hurt her with the fall.

Chapter Forty-Five

KENDALL

Although my birthday wasn't until tomorrow, I was celebrating it with my family during our regular Sunday dinner.

And this time Liam was with me.

It had been a month since we'd redefined our arrangement as a relationship. Things had been great between us over the last few weeks, and we'd grown closer. I'd taken Liam's words at face value. He'd been reluctant to have a relationship because he'd never balanced one with his job. And so far, we'd managed nicely by keeping to seeing each other mostly on the weekends.

It made sense for us to keep it quiet at the office. While staying at the firm wasn't my long-term goal, it was definitely his. By landing the Stephen Walsh case, he was closer than ever to achieving his goal of becoming a named partner.

However, today would be the true test of how he felt about being my boyfriend. That's why nerves attacked me the moment we pulled up into the driveway of my parents' home. It seemed I wasn't alone in my anxiety if his pale expression said anything. "You having second thoughts?" I asked.

He shook his head. "No. I want to meet your family. But I'll be honest and tell you it's been a long time since I've met anyone's parents."

I squeezed his hand. "It'll be great." At least here was hoping. My nan would be a delight with some slightly crazy tendencies and repetitive stories. My mother would fuss about feeding him enough and would have nothing but smiles that I'd brought someone home. As for my father— Hopefully he'd be able to accept the fact Liam was a few years older than I was.

At least I'd talked Liam out of wearing a formal suit. Instead, he was in jeans and a sweater, same as me.

We each got out of his Range Rover and stood in the driveway.

"You told them we work together?"

We'd already covered this, but given our nerves, it was probably best to go over it again. "Yes. I told them you're an attorney, and we met at work. But they don't know you're my boss. And of course they don't know I work at the club to supplement my grandmother's care." I paused, wrinkling up my nose. "Geez, I sound like a liar."

Liam smiled, pulling me close in a side hug. "At least you're a cute liar. Don't worry, I'll keep your secrets." He blew out a breath. "Okay. Let's do this."

I was the one who was suddenly hit with second thoughts. It wasn't that I didn't want him to meet my family, but I worried I might be pushing him into something for which he wasn't ready. Maybe I was freaking him out. Making him reconsider a relationship.

BUT AN HOUR LATER, at the family dinner table, my worries were proving unfounded.

"I can see where Kendall gets her talent for cooking, Mrs. Tate. Dinner was delicious."

My mom smiled. "Thank you. It's our pleasure to have you here."

Liam might not have felt completely comfortable at the table, but he'd definitely won over my grandmother and mother with his manners and compliments.

My father was harder to please. However, the two of them had bonded over their love of the LA Rams. I found it fascinating to listen to Liam talk football as I hadn't realized he was into sports. Then again, I shouldn't have been surprised. He had to win clients and win over juries. Dealing with my family was probably a piece of cake.

I was calling this evening another win until my nan asked, "Do you know Kendall's boss at the firm?"

Liam stiffened but gave her a kind smile. "I do."

"He as big of a prick as her roommate says he is?"

I sucked in a breath. "Nan."

But she merely chuckled. Why did her memory have to be crystal clear just now? I could only imagine what Chloe must have told her when she'd visited while I'd been in Virginia.

Liam handled it with a smile that didn't reach his eyes. "He can be, certainly."

Oh, no. "He's not that bad. It's always an adjustment when you work for someone new. Now that I've gotten to know him better, we get along."

"Does that mean you got rid of the list you kept of ways for him to suffer?"

Damn. Grandma went there. My gaze strayed warily to Liam's face, but he was schooling his expression, casually taking a sip of wine.

"What types of things?" he asked as if he was amused by the idea instead of the one the list was about.

"It was harmless stuff," I quickly explained. "And only at the beginning. I deleted it over a month ago. It was immature and—" I realized I was sounding way too defensive when my mother's brow lifted.

Liam smiled tightly.

"Chloe only told me about a couple things. Funny stuff," Nan said on a sigh. "She said he's hot, too. Have to say it must be quite the law firm if all the lawyers are hot. They have a 'bring your grandmother to work day'?"

I'd failed to warn Liam that my nan could be a bit pervy. I blamed all of the romance novels she read with her friends at the facility.

"I think that's enough, Mother," my mom said, giving us an apologetic smile. "Sorry."

He waved her off. "No, no. It's quite all right."

But a half hour later when we got into his Range Rover, he was uncharacteristically quiet.

"Everything okay?" I asked.

He glanced over with a smile and took my hand across the console. "Yes. Sorry. Just lost in thought. Your family was amazing. I can see why you love spending time with your nan. She's a kick."

"She is indeed. She was very lucid tonight."

"She especially loved giving you the knitted throw for your birthday."

I was hit with a wave of affection for her. "She did. I cherish everything she's ever made me."

He squeezed my hand. "Thank you for introducing me to them."

Deciding now was my opportunity to bring up what had been said, I went for it. "I want to apologize for what my grandmother heard about you as my boss. And about the list.

Like I said, I already erased it. And I only vented to Chloe in the beginning about—"

"There's no apology necessary. I understand."

"I no longer feel the same, of course."

His smile was strained. "It wasn't as though I didn't deserve what was said, Kendall."

True. He'd been an asshole, but now that I understood him better, I realized his behavior had been a sort of armor to keep people from getting close to him. Now I wondered if hearing about the list was affecting him more than he was letting on.

He brought my hand up to his lips, kissing the knuckles. "Don't give it another thought. On to better subjects, are you ready for your birthday surprise?"

I was relieved he seemed to be taking it in stride. "I'm always ready for a birthday surprise. Especially if some of it includes you naked."

He chuckled, the tension leaving his face. "I think sex is a given, regardless of your birthday. And considering you're a big fan of picking places other than the bed, I'll make it ladies' choice."

Damn. The way his voice went low and sexy made my stomach flutter with anticipation. Our sex life definitely hadn't diminished in any way. If anything, the more we got to know one another, the more I eagerly anticipated his touch. "I'm looking forward to the options."

Once we walked into the house and made our way to the kitchen, I faltered in my step. On the counter were several wrapped gifts with big bows. I turned toward Liam. "How? When?"

We'd left together for Orange County from his place. How had he managed this setup?

"When I said I forgot my wallet, I went back inside and

took this all out of the hall closet. I know your birthday isn't until tomorrow, but I figured between work and school, you might want to open gifts tonight."

I put my arms around him, hugging him close. He'd not only listened to me last month when I'd told him I wanted more, but he was also putting in a continued effort to give me more. "Thank you."

He leaned back to cup my face. "You haven't opened the gifts yet."

"Doesn't matter. I just appreciate you coming with me for dinner and for thinking of me."

"There aren't a lot of times I'm not thinking of you."

Chapter Forty-Six

LIAM

here was something both touching and sexy as hell about Kendall cooking in my kitchen on a Wednesday night when I arrived home from work. I'd given her a key since she had no class tonight. She'd come over because we wouldn't have a chance to spend next weekend together since I'd be out of town. I found myself silently watching her go through the motions, not wanting her to know I was here yet.

It reminded me of the first time I'd observed her in the rental house in Virginia. You could see how much she loved to cook in every graceful movement she made. I especially loved how she was using the new pots and pans I'd given her last weekend for her birthday.

I'd enjoyed meeting her family on Sunday. However, I hadn't expected to hear that she'd kept a list about me and the ways, as her boss, I should suffer. Then again, I don't know why I was surprised. I'd been a prick. This wasn't news. But it was a reminder how far we'd come from the days we'd avoided one another in the office.

Now, with only a few months left of classes, I knew how anxious Kendall was to start on her next plan. I had been successful thus far in not meddling but rather allowing her to figure it out on her own. Honestly, as much as I'd miss her every day in the office, I'd also love to see her pursuing her dreams.

"I'm a big fan of finding you in my T-shirt upon coming home, but I thought we had a deal about you wearing nothing but an apron."

She turned, smiling at me. Damn. I'd never get tired of the way she lit up when she saw me. Like I was the best part of her day. God knew she was always the best part of mine. I'd find myself literally counting the minutes until she'd come into my office each morning to say good morning. And on Friday nights, I'd count the hours until she got off work and drove down to my place.

"Mm, but I don't have an apron."

I didn't hesitate to go over and put my arms around her from the back, loving the feel and smell of her. "I'm buying you one the next chance I get."

I nuzzled her neck, delighting in the fact we had all night together. As much as I'd worried about balancing a relationship with my work, it turned out I didn't get as much time with her as I wanted. Between our busy schedules and my travel, it only left me wanting more.

"I'll miss you this weekend," she said.

It was as if she'd read my mind. "I'll miss you, too. I wish I could've talked my mom into doing the reading of my father's will via video call instead of in person." I absolutely dreaded having to go home for it, but I wouldn't say no to my mother.

Kendall turned in my arms, laying a hand on the side of

my face. "I could maybe take a couple days off and go with you if you'd like."

Her offer meant more to me than I'd ever admit. However, I knew she couldn't afford to miss another weekend of work at the club. "It's a quick trip, but I appreciate you offering."

I noticed her ingredients on the counter. "Did you go shopping?"

"I did. I wanted to make lasagna."

She turned back around to start layering her pan with sauce and noodles. I wasn't sure where she got her energy, between working two jobs and going to school. Yet here she was, wanting to cook a gourmet meal. I tried not to groan when I saw there were two pans. I'd gladly hit the gym harder, so I could enjoy her amazing cooking, but I could only eat so much pasta. I also didn't want to hurt her feelings. "You're making a lot, huh?"

"Don't worry. The second one is for your neighbor, Lucas, for taking the time to come over and check on me last month when I was sick. I promised him I'd make him something, but he's been out of town the last few weeks. So I thought I'd drop it off tonight."

It was sweet. It also made me insanely jealous.

She arched a brow. "You're okay with that, right?"

"Yeah. It's a thoughtful gesture."

"Then, why the strange expression on your face?"

"Because I've seen women throw themselves at Lucas. Guess I was having a moment."

My admission earned me an arched brow. "A moment of jealousy?"

"Something like that. Sorry." I moved toward the sink to get myself a glass of water.

She laughed. "I kind of like seeing you a bit jealous.

Makes me feel better about getting annoyed when Tabitha looks at you like you're an item on the McDonald's dollar menu, and she's got a hundred-dollar bill to spend."

I nearly choked on the water I'd just sipped. "That's, uh, quite vivid," I chuckled.

She shrugged. "It's true."

"Now who's jealous? I hope you realize there's never been a moment I've ever considered dating Tabitha."

Her brow quirked. "Really? But you both have a lot in common."

"We're both lawyers. But that's about the extent of what we have in common." Being ambitious was probably something else we had in common, but it bothered me to think we were similar.

"I guess I thought you enjoyed talking to her given the frequency with which she comes around to your office."

"We always talk about business. And it's a chore." Glancing over to her laptop on the counter, I frowned at the webpage I saw up on her computer screen. "What are you searching Craigslist for?"

She sighed. "New roommate. Chloe accepted a job in Dubai for the next year. She leaves next week."

This was news. And not the good kind. I didn't like the idea of Kendall out on the internet searching for a roommate. Especially since it was a studio apartment, and they'd have to share such a small space. Before I could filter my comment, it was out. "Do you think it's a good idea to search for a stranger on Craigslist?"

"It's not ideal, but I asked around the club and the firm—no one is in the market for a roommate. And I need someone to split the rent."

"I don't like it."

She rolled her eyes. "You don't have to like it. It is what it is."

I realized I didn't get a lot of say over this. *Unless I wanted to offer her to move in with me.* The thought hit me without warning, and my pulse skyrocketed. People who moved in together were in a serious commitment. They were looking toward the future. Marriage. Kids.

Not for the first time, I recognized we were on a short track here without a lot more room to go if we wanted different things in the long term. So far, this relationship hadn't taken me away from work, but any further commitment had the potential to undermine all I'd built. I suddenly remembered her appointment tomorrow.

"You see your GYN tomorrow?"

"I do. I plan to talk to her about going on the pill."

I liked the idea of her going on the pill; it was more effective than using condoms. However, using both would give us even better protection. The worst possible scenario would be for her to get pregnant. "I was thinking we could continue to use condoms even with the pill. Would be good to have double the protection."

She paused. "Okay. I guess it's better to be safe."

Yes, it was.

THE NEXT MORNING, Kendall popped her head in my office. "Mr. Kinkaid's assistant called and asked me to schedule you for ten thirty. I put it on your calendar."

Although it wasn't uncommon for the managing partner to schedule meetings with me, Phil was typically less formal, picking up the phone or simply dropping by. It made me wonder what might be happening. "Yes. It's fine. Thank you."

She gave me a small smile. The intimate kind we only shared when we were alone. The type that hit me square in the chest in a way that both satisfied and terrified me.

"You're welcome. I'm off to my ten o'clock appointment and should be back in an hour or so."

That's right. Her GYN appointment. "Okay. See you then."

At promptly ten thirty, I went up two floors to the managing partner's office. Much to my surprise, Mr. Gerald Anderson of Lowry and Anderson was there with Phil. The older man had been retired from law for at least a decade, but he was known to drop in on his namesake from time to time. I'd only met him once before.

"Ah, Liam Davenport, how nice to see you again."

"It's nice to see you again, too, sir." My gaze traveled to Phil, and he looked pleased, which made me anxious. Thankfully, my years of being a litigator enabled me to keep a poker face

"Phil and I were discussing how much money you've brought in for the firm the last few years. And with the Stephen Walsh case, you're due to top our expectations this year. Well done."

"Thank you. Much appreciated." I accepted the compliments instead of deflecting them as I usually did. I'd worked my ass off for years, and I needed to feel as if I'd earned the respect given to me. But old habits were hard to break.

We took seats in Phil's sitting area, with Gerald and Phil on either side of the couch and me in the ornate wingback chair.

"You know what I admire most about your career, Liam?" Gerald asked.

"No, sir, what is that?"

"You haven't let anything get in the way. You're not out chasing skirts, you're not home changing diapers, you even managed to work through your bereavement leave. All that demonstrates you are purely focused on the prize."

"And what's the prize?" Did I dare ask? Did I dare get my hopes up to think my biggest dream was about to come true?

"Your name on the doors of this firm, of course. You want it, don't you?"

I didn't bother to be coy. "More than anything."

"Good. That's what I wanted to hear. It comes with sacrifice, of course. If you think you don't have a personal life now, well, hold on for the ride. You definitely won't have one if you become a named partner. In addition to the trial work you'd continue to do, you'd also need to represent the firm. As you may have heard, Alan Lowry isn't in the best health lately. And I'm getting up there, too. We want young blood to invigorate the brand. And I think Lowry, Anderson, and Davenport has an excellent ring to it."

It certainly did. This was why I hadn't cut back my hours when I'd made equity partner. This was why I'd sacrificed sleep and a personal life.

Shit. I briefly thought of Kendall, but pushed her from my mind. This moment wasn't about her. It wasn't about our relationship. And it certainly wasn't about choosing. There was no choice. I wanted to see my name on the door every day when I walked in. That's what I'd always wanted. "I would be honored."

"We have a board to convince. But with me being the head of it, and Phil agreeing with my mindset, I think we'll have a majority vote next month. I'd like you to meet with the head of the executive committee tomorrow in Chicago. Leonard Smith. Can you be there?"

I'd have to rearrange the flight I'd intended to take home to Virginia tomorrow. But I'd do it. "Of course. I'll fly out tonight if possible."

"Good. See, you're already in the mindset of named partner. The firm always comes first."

Chapter Forty-Seven

KENDALL

*A*fter walking the three blocks to my gynecologist's office, I signed in and took a seat. I tried not to let what Liam had said yesterday affect me—about not wanting to give up using condoms. It made sense; the double birth control would be better protection. However, my motivation to avoid getting pregnant was because I was waiting for the right time. His motivation centered around never. The whole thing was a reminder he hadn't changed his mind about having a family.

The thought was disheartening since I was already in love with him. But the thought of breaking up with him and not having him in my life was even more depressing. Still—did I want to stay in a relationship hoping he'd change? It wasn't fair to expect it. But while my head could be logical, my heart was busy trying to convince myself it was possible he'd change his mind. Hadn't he done so already about not wanting a relationship? It was enough to cause a headache for sure.

Once my name was called, I stood up and followed the nurse to the back into the exam room.

"We'll do your annual exam, but do you have any concerns?" the doctor asked when she came in. She was someone I'd found through a recommendation when I'd first started working downtown.

"No concerns, but I'd like to go on some sort of birth control."

She gave me a warm smile. "Certainly. Were you thinking about the pill or the shot?"

"Probably the pill if it means I don't have to come in as often."

"I have one I'd recommend which is a low dose of hormone." She went on to explain some of the benefits and possible side effects, also warning about the loss of effectiveness if I was on antibiotics. "Any questions?"

"No, it all sounds good."

"Excellent. We'll test the urine for pregnancy, then I'll do your exam and write your prescription."

Sounded fine to me. Only when she came back ten minutes later, she wasn't smiling. She wore a concerned-mother face.

"Your test came back positive."

I couldn't for the life of me comprehend what she was saying. "Positive for what?"

"The pregnancy test. You're pregnant, Kendall. We'll have to do some blood tests to figure out how far along you are."

I couldn't speak. I simply stared at her like she must be mistaken. Finally, words formed on my lips. "But we used condoms. Always."

She gave me a soft smile. "Not one hundred percent effective, unfortunately. Do you have anyone you'd like to call?"

Definitely not Liam. Oh, God. He would flip out. He'd

regret ever entering into this relationship with me. Tears leaked out of my eyes from merely picturing his reaction. "No."

"Tell you what—I realize this is coming as a shock to you. How about we take some blood and get some more information for you? Okay?"

I nodded, only half listening at this point.

Forty minutes later, I was back at my desk, staring unseeingly at my computer screen. Liam was clearly still in his meeting as he wasn't in his office.

Based on my hormone levels, the blood test had put me at approximately six weeks. Dr. Ling had given me a list of books, vitamins, and resources to call if I had questions. Unfortunately, she wasn't an obstetrician which meant I'd need to find one. She hadn't judged, hadn't asked hard questions about my relationship status, but had given me her on-call number in case I had follow-up questions.

"Ms. Tate." Liam's voice startled me.

I hadn't heard him approach. He was with Phillip Kinkaid. How in the world was I supposed to tell him this? And when? I had class tonight. Maybe after. Shit. Could I manage to hold it together if he asked what was wrong? "Yes, Mr. Davenport."

"Everything okay?" he whispered once Phil had preceded him into his office.

"Yes. Fine. Can I help with anything?" I didn't want to give anything away. This would be the absolute worst place to tell him the news.

"I need you to reschedule my entire afternoon. I have to run home after my meeting with Phil, then fly to Chicago tonight. And rearrange my flight for Virginia so that it leaves from Chicago tomorrow afternoon. Sorry for the last-minute changes."

If he was flying to Chicago, that meant I wouldn't get a chance to see him tonight. It meant he'd be gone for the weekend. My heart sank. Right now I needed someone to tell me it would be okay. Then again, would Liam be that person? Doubtful.

"Sure. I understand. I'll take care of it."

Chapter Forty-Eight

LIAM

*O*nce I was behind a closed door in my office, Phil went on and on about the privilege of being considered for a named partner.

Meanwhile my mind wandered to Kendall. What would happen if the board knew I was seeing her? I didn't have to guess. I'd lose my shot at becoming named partner quicker than I could blink. Given how unbelievably conservative the group was, they'd never understand a partner dating his secretary. They'd consider it drama the firm didn't need.

Then there was the part about Gerald saying my life would only get busier. I'd be traveling the country. Attending events and representing the firm. No time for a relationship. No time for a personal life. No time for Kendall.

I swallowed hard, focusing on Phil's next words.

"I don't have to tell you this is confidential until it's voted on and made official."

"No, you don't. I won't tell anyone."

"Not even Tabitha?"

My eyes narrowed at his question. "Especially not her. Why did you ask me that question?"

He shrugged. "She's implied more than once you two may have something going on."

"Believe me when I say there has never been something now, nor would there ever be. Named partners don't earn the title by sleeping with their coworkers."

I was a hypocrite. An absolute fraud to have uttered those words. Doing so made me question if I deserved the title of named partner.

I DIDN'T SEE Kendall before I had to leave for my flight. It was for the best as I had dread eating at my stomach. Even if she quit the firm in a few months, and we were free to date without any judgment, it was clear a personal life wasn't compatible with my new role at the firm. Bottom line was she deserved more than I would be able to give her.

Then, why was I hesitating? I had everything I'd ever worked for in one hand. I should have been elated. I should have wanted to celebrate. I shouldn't have been second-guessing whether it would be worth the sacrifice of love—of all things. Jesus, was it love I was feeling for Kendall? Why did this have to be so complicated?

It was near ten o'clock when I checked in to my Chicago hotel. First thing in the morning I'd go into the office to meet with Leonard Smith, the head of the executive committee for the firm. After the meeting, I'd be off to Virginia for the reading of my father's will. It was enough to have me downing two mini bottles of bourbon, trying to get a handle on my emotions. I was finishing off the second when my cell phone rang.

It was Kendall. Which was strange as she should still be in class.

"Hello," I answered.

"Hi. How was your flight?"

Her voice seemed off. "It was okay. Shouldn't you be in class?"

"I didn't feel like staying the whole time. Um, do you mind if I come over Sunday when you return? I really need to talk to you."

Something was definitely off if she'd left class early. "Sure. Or you can tell me now." Perhaps she sensed me already pulling away. Maybe she'd heard about Gerald coming into the office and realized the stakes had been raised, putting our relationship in jeopardy.

"I can't. It would be better face to face."

Again, her tone was strange. "Something's wrong. Is it your roommate search? Your nan?"

"No. It's not either."

"Just tell me now." I'd never been a patient guy, and this was making me anxious—perhaps she was ready to break up with me. Hell, I could've been more social with her family. Maybe she was tired of hiding things. Perhaps she'd come to the conclusion that she was better off without me before I had to say it myself.

"I can't tell you over the phone."

"Yes, you can." Then I remembered how she'd appeared off shortly after she'd returned from the doctor. "Was something wrong at your appointment today?"

Silence with what sounded like sniffling.

Fuck. Fuck. Fuck. Acid crawled up my throat as my mind raced toward a worst-case scenario. "Tell me, Kendall."

"I'm pregnant."

Whoosh. Blood rushed to my ears while my brain seemed to shut down completely. There only the sound of her breathing over the line. My voice, once found, was uncharacteristically high. "How?"

"I asked the doctor the same question. She said condoms aren't foolproof. I was thinking back to the time in your office with the condom you found in your desk. The timing is about right as they're putting me at six weeks."

"I knew I should've had a vasectomy." I'd put it off, but it would've been the smart thing to do. I hadn't realized I'd said the words out loud until she sucked in a harsh breath.

"And I knew I shouldn't have told you this over the phone."

I was pacing the hotel room. "I'm sorry. But I told you I don't want kids. I don't want a family. I don't want any of it. Jesus, the timing couldn't be worse. I found out I have a shot at named partner today. That's what the meeting was about with Phil. Gerald Anderson was there. I'm meeting the head of the executive committee tomorrow to gain his recommendation. They made it clear this isn't a position for a man with any personal ties."

I would blame the shock and alcohol later for my lack of filter. I was unprepared for her anger.

"Do you think I planned this? Being pregnant, now of all times, wasn't part of my plan, either. Just because I don't have named partner on the line doesn't mean this doesn't affect me, too. But don't worry. No need to wait until you have the title to break up with me. You can have your wish early."

I raked a hand over my face, cursing myself, about to respond with an apology, but the phone was cut off. Shit. If there was an idiot's guide about what not to say, I could have written it.

TEXT MESSAGES and phone calls to Kendall went unanswered. Finally, I gave up and employed a new strategy the next morning. I waited until she was in the office and called my line from the Chicago office, so she wouldn't recognize the number and ignore me.

"Mr. Davenport's office, how may I help you?" her voice answered. Amazing how much I'd missed it.

"It's me. Don't hang up."

"Unless this is work related, please don't call me."

"I need five minutes. Can you transfer this to my office and take it there for privacy? Please?"

I waited the ten beats until she finally said, "Fine. Five minutes."

Although I was a master at preparing what needed to be said, I was ill prepared right now.

Finally there was a click and then the sound of her voice. "All right. I'm here."

"First off, I want to apologize for last night. I could make a lot of excuses, but the bottom line is it was inexcusable."

Silence.

"What are you thinking, Kendall?" How was she feeling? Scared? Lonely? Disappointed in me? Probably all of the above.

"I don't know. I'm still processing things."

"About if you're planning to keep this baby?"

"Yes. Or from what I'm reading, the miscarriage rate is high, so maybe you'll get lucky."

Her shot hit below the belt, but I didn't blame her. Never in a million years would I wish for her to lose the baby. Nor did I want her to consider abortion. "I didn't mean it that way. I'm thousands of miles away trying to figure out what to say here, and clearly botching it all."

"I should've never told you over the phone. It was a

mistake. I knew you wouldn't be happy, but I wanted someone to talk to because it had come as such as shock."

Not for the first time, I realized how very selfish I'd been to only think of myself. "Kendall—"

"I'm not done. I need you to leave me alone for the weekend. Don't call. Don't text. Leave me to figure some things out. Rest assured, I'm not going to HR, nor do I plan on telling anyone in the office. Hell, I'm still on the fence about whether to tell my roommate. I've always known what your priorities are, and I don't expect you to change them for me or for this circumstance. Matter of fact, I don't expect anything from you."

I hated the way she said circumstance. It was cold. Clinical. I knew in my heart, I'd pushed her to this. She was in self-preservation mode because I had been such a prick. I also loathed the way she assumed I'd think she'd go to HR. I was beyond my trust issues with her, but hearing she didn't believe it was another blow.

"Can we talk once I return?" I was grasping at straws here, desperate to try to do damage control.

"Text me once you're home, and I'll let you know when I'm ready to see you. Also, one more thing."

"What is it?"

"I put in this morning for a transfer to the Century City office. They have an open secretarial position. No matter what happens, it would be best for me to make this move. I'm sure the coordinator will be reaching out to you. I'm hopeful you will be supportive of the move."

"If it's what you want." I'd lost her. She couldn't wait to get away from me. She had probably started another list of all the reasons why.

"It is. Again, I'm sorry I put this on you over the phone

on your way to Virginia. I hope everything goes okay with your family."

Leave it to her to apologize when she didn't need to. "It's me who should do all the apologizing. I'll text you Sunday."

"Okay. Goodbye."

Chapter Forty-Nine

LIAM

"**Y**ou look like shit."

Leave it to my sister to be blunt when she got out of her car to give me a hug. We were curbside at the Roanoke airport on Friday night.

Although I could've rented a car, Allison had insisted on picking me up. I was relieved to get the time alone with her. Because I needed someone to talk to.

"I look like shit probably because I feel like shit."

"What's going on, Liam?" she asked when we got settled in her minivan.

I sighed deeply. "The executive committee is taking a vote next month about making me a named partner for the firm."

"Congrats. But why so miserable? I thought it's what you wanted."

"I can't have a relationship with Kendall and at the same time be a named partner."

She was silent for a full minute. "I thought things were great between you two, last we talked."

"They were, but it's complicated."

She was shaking her head. "Then, uncomplicate it, Liam. It's what you do for a living. Break it down and solve the problem."

"She's pregnant. She found out yesterday."

At least this time she muttered a *holy shit* in response. I then proceeded to dump the rest on her, including my own less-than-stellar reaction to the news. I had to hand it to my sister; she simply listened until I was out of words.

"Do you think she did it on purpose?"

"No. Not at all." I raised my voice, glaring at her. I'd thought she liked Kendall.

"I'm not asking because I think that for a second, but I'm trying to ensure you're not idiot enough to believe it."

"If anything, it's my fault for using an old condom I found in my desk." Probably TMI, but Allison didn't flinch.

"Do you love her?"

I didn't hesitate. "Yes, but given the way I've already fucked things up, I'm a terrible boyfriend. I'll make an even worse husband and father. She deserves better."

"I call bullshit, little brother. You don't deserve her because you're making damn sure you don't. You're thinking if you can't be perfect and say all the right things, then you won't be worthy. But relationships don't work that way. You don't get a plaque for the wall or a title by your name for being successful at it. But I'd argue that what you do get is much, much more valuable."

"She hates me. And I don't blame her. For all I know, she may not even keep the baby."

Allison let out a long sigh. "She doesn't hate you. She's hurt. Although it's absolutely her right to do what she needs to do regarding the pregnancy, it's your right to tell her how you feel about the options. Do you want her to get an abortion?"

"Hell no." There wasn't a doubt in my mind.

"Then, unequivocally tell her that. Because I can bet she's feeling like a burden. She may feel if she were to terminate the pregnancy or have a miscarriage you'd be relieved."

"It's not how I feel. I need to call her."

She was shaking her head. "No more conversations via phone. I would think you'd already have learned that lesson the hard way. You need to do this face to face. And only after you figure out what you intend to do."

"I know what I need to do," I said with a sigh.

Allison heaved a big sigh. "Can I ask you something?"

"Anything."

"What happens after you get your name on the door? What's next?"

"What do you mean? It's a big accomplishment to become a named partner."

"It is. But will you see it that way? Or will you instead try to figure out what else you need to do in order to prove yourself? Will you try to increase the size of the firm? Double the revenue? Put the firm on the map in some other way?"

I always did more because I was never enough.

I didn't realize I'd murmured the words aloud until she pulled the car over into a parking lot, turning to me with tears in her eyes. "You were always enough, Liam. So was I. So was Mom. You deserve to be loved. Just as you deserve to sit back and celebrate your accomplishments instead of searching for the next thing that will—what? Somehow prove you're enough? Will your name on the building finally accomplish that goal?"

I shook my head, knowing deep down that it wouldn't. Everything I'd worked for, all the accolades, all the plaques, all the money, all the possessions—none of it was filling the void I'd tried tirelessly to fill over the years. I was broken. Irrevocably unrepairable.

"Don't. Don't you dare start thinking something is wrong with you."

"How did you know?" Fuck, my voice was gruff with emotion.

"Because I recognize that look. And if there is something wrong with you, then there's something wrong with me, too."

I took her hand, hating the tears that were tracking down her face. "There isn't a thing wrong with you. Except, perhaps, your bowling game needs work and sometimes you're hella nosey, but other than that, you're perfect."

She laughed, as I'd expected. "And there isn't a thing wrong with you, little brother. Except maybe when you're a dick to the people you love instead of being honest with them about your demons."

I blew out a long breath. "Damn. Tough love."

She squeezed my hand. "The toughest because of how much I do love you. Sugarcoating things doesn't do you any favors. And you weren't the only one who didn't feel enough growing up. I was also a little broken going into a relationship."

"How did you do it? With Warren?"

"Went to counseling. Talked about a lot of shit. The resentment. The feeling that if I'd been a better kid, perhaps Dad wouldn't have left. The feelings of missing him, yet wishing he'd never come back, then the guilt over being grateful he hadn't. The fear of allowing someone in and letting myself be loved. The bigger fear that I'd be like Dad when it came to parenting the girls."

"You're nothing like him."

She shrugged. "Not all fear is rational. But you're right. I'm nothing like him. It helps to have an understanding husband who knows my insecurities. But the first step in working on the problem is to be open about it."

I couldn't imagine telling Kendall the depth of my demons. But my sister had a point. I'd avoided relationships my entire life because they were never something I could trust I'd be good at. In avoiding love, I'd avoided leaving myself vulnerable; I'd avoided getting revealed as lacking in someone else's eyes. Instead, I'd chosen things I could control, things I could feel safe in doing. Money, possessions, titles. They were all empty goals, yet they were safe at the same time.

"Liam, the bottom line is I deserve to be loved. And so do you. Dad didn't leave because we weren't good enough kids. It wasn't because Mom wasn't a good enough wife. It was because of his alcoholism."

"What if Kendall deserves more?"

My sister didn't mince words. "If you won't be the man who gives her more, then you're right. She does deserve better. But if you're letting her go because you're scared, then you'll regret it."

She was right. I already did.

───────

MY SISTER'S words stayed with me the next morning when I met her and my mother at the attorney's office in Blacksburg. I had no idea why my father had a will, nor did I know what to expect, but it never occurred to me they'd play a video. I was so surprised I could only sit rooted to the spot, even when my sister grasped my hand.

It was him. The first time I'd seen him alive since I'd been a boy. Wearing a long-sleeved shirt and tie, he was seated in a chair in what appeared to be a small conference room in this building. He was fidgeting. "Is this thing on?" he asked the camera.

My mother started weeping at the sound of his voice.

I held my breath, muscles tensed.

Then he started talking.

"Um, I'm recording this in the event something happens to me. I haven't taken the best care of myself over the years, so the way that I see it, it's a miracle I've lasted this long. Anyhow, my lawyer advised I could just write out this will, but in case I don't have the balls—I mean courage, sorry—to face you all again, I wanted for you to at least see my face one last time and know I mean what I have to say with all my heart. First, I'm sorry. Sorry I let the bottle get the best of me. I was weak and driven by the next drop instead of focused on what mattered most. My family. I told myself if I can get one year sober, I'll come home. I'm twenty days away." He took a deep breath, rubbing his hands on his thighs. "Damn if I don't have regrets. I'd run out of video if I listed them all. But believe there wasn't a day I didn't think of the three of you. Not a day I didn't love you. Not a day I didn't wish I could've been the husband, and father you deserved."

He faltered for a moment, taking a breath.

My mother and sister were doing the same.

I was simply numb.

"I don't have much to leave you. But every penny I'd like to see go to my grandchildren. Not sure I'll get a chance to meet them, but since I screwed up with this generation, maybe the next one will remember me as more than a drunk and an abuser. At least it's my hope. It's what keeps me moving forward each day to add another sober one to the count. I love you all. I'm sure it's not obvious by my actions, but know I never stopped. I only hope I'll get a second chance to show you that. To begin to make up for all the bad times. All right. That's it. Hopefully, it'll be years before you have to see this."

It was the end of the video. I simply sat there, my arms around my mother and sister, with my emotions raw and reeling. It had been easier to put the man out of my mind permanently as a drunk abuser with no chance at redemption. Now, seeing him with clear eyes, hopefulness in his voice and regret in his words, I was faced with the very real possibility I'd screwed up by not accepting his calls.

After a short meeting with the attorney, I drove to the cemetery. I hadn't planned on coming here, yet here I stood in the cold. Walking over to the grave, a few down from where my grandparents were buried, I stopped at the headstone for my father.

It turned out my dad had a hundred-thousand-dollar life insurance policy he'd taken out many years ago. We'd all agreed it would go toward Allison's kids' college fund. Someday they would be able to say their grandpa had helped them with school. That he'd been a good man in the end. I thought it was the fresh start he'd hoped for.

Looking up at the clear, dark sky, I was forced to face a couple hard truths about my childhood. Although I was glad my father hadn't come back while we'd been growing up, I had never appreciated that had been a conscious choice on his part, that he'd decided not to return until he could get sober. And secondly, holding on to hate and resentment was helping no one, least of all me.

So I said the words out loud from my heart. "Thank you for leaving. You staying away was the best thing you could've done for us kids and for her. I'm glad in the end you changed. That you got sober." I could finally start to believe it was the disease that had made him abandon us and not anything we'd done wrong as kids. I could believe my future wasn't tied to a painful past.

"I'm sorry I never took the time to give you a second chance. But know you made Mom happy in the end. And I forgive you."

I swallowed hard and walked away with a sense of peace I hadn't felt in years.

Now I was anxious to get back to California. The problem was how to approach Kendall. Truth be told, my sister had been right. I'd never entertained the idea of a relationship or family because I'd been petrified I couldn't be enough for them. Instead, I'd focused on a career trajectory, something I could control and to which I would never feel vulnerable. A named partnership might have been something I'd worked for my entire life, but I realized the prize would be empty if I sacrificed Kendall and the baby for it.

Now I just had to plan how to win her back.

Chapter Fifty

KENDALL

rying to get ready for my Friday night at the club proved to be impossible since I kept crying my makeup off. I still kicked myself for telling Liam I was pregnant over the phone. It had been stupid. And now I was paying the price for it by playing his words over and over in my head. I'd always known his career was his priority, so then, why was I feeling so hurt to have that confirmed?

Simple. Because I was a stupid girl who might have thought for a moment he reciprocated my feelings.

Since his call at the office, he'd given me the space I'd asked for by not calling or texting again. I wasn't sure if I was more relieved or disappointed. Be careful what you ask for I guess.

Taking a deep breath, I tried to keep myself from sobbing again. I'd told him I wasn't sure what I'd do about the baby, but in truth, there was no doubt. I was absolutely keeping it.

A knock on the bathroom door had me taking in a shaky breath.

"Hey, Kendall. You okay?" Chloe asked.

I came out the door and just hugged her. She didn't disappoint, simply letting me cry it out without a word. Finally, when there was nothing left, she led me to the couch.

"Can you talk about it?"

"Yeah. I think so." After dumping everything on her over the next ten minutes, I waited for her response.

"That's a lot. What will you do?"

"Keeping it." I wanted to get that out of the way first of all. "Second, I'm transferring to another position in Century City. It would be nice to quit altogether, but I need medical insurance. And I wouldn't get maternity leave if I went and started a new job." It was tempting to quit school and work evenings at the club, but I couldn't. I only had another four months until I got my degree. I was too close. But I had to transfer away from Liam as soon as possible.

I'd also made another decision. I'd sent an email to Stephen Walsh asking about a job opportunity. I wasn't sure he'd hire a pregnant woman, or if there may be something for after I had the baby, but I hoped fate had put him in my life for a reason.

"Will you talk to Liam on Sunday night?"

"Probably. It's better than first seeing him Monday in the office and it being horrible. I'm hoping I can get transferred out of there in the next week."

"What will you say to him?"

"I'll tell him I don't need help. I'll raise this baby on my own. And he can go on to be named partner without ever seeing either of us again." I was determined to avoid a relationship where neither of us would be wanted.

"He still needs to help you financially."

He'd be on the hook for child support, but I wasn't in the right frame of mind to think about it yet. "Pride tells me I don't want it. Practicality tells me I'll probably need it."

"What about telling your family?"

They'd be disappointed. And I'd have to come clean about supplementing my grandmother's care. I wouldn't be able to work behind the bar once I was showing, but perhaps the club could find me a different position which would still allow me to earn extra cash to keep her where she was. "I will tell them eventually. Maybe after the first trimester."

"This is horrible timing with me taking this job and moving to Dubai on Sunday. I wish I was staying."

It wasn't as though her brother had left her much of a choice. She was hoping that working overseas would get her family out of the debt he'd put them in. "I know you do. But we each have to do what's best for us. We'll keep in touch. And I'll be okay."

At least I hoped so.

I went through Friday night mostly numb, wondering what it would be like to see Liam come Sunday night. I'd felt strong on the phone when I couldn't see his face. In person would be different.

I'd thought I'd been doing a good job of faking my way through things, but by Saturday, Jose took me off guard by taking me to a private room before our shift began. "What's going on, sweetheart? I'm worried about you. Especially with your girl leaving tomorrow. You okay?"

I shook my head before embarrassingly bursting into tears and told him everything.

At least Jose had been a nice shoulder to cry on. He'd even offered to talk to the manager about other possible positions I could do within the club. As much as I hoped Stephen Walsh might come through with something, he'd yet to reply to my email. Perhaps I could be a hostess or do the books on the side on the weekends.

Finally, after a long shift and then going to a diner for a goodbye breakfast for Chloe, I arrived home, more tired than usual. I'd read online that exhaustion could be expected, especially in the first trimester. Unfortunately, I could hardly chug a Red Bull to get my energy back up.

After showering, I plugged in my phone and was shocked to see a text message from Liam. Was he already home? I didn't think so. He wasn't due to fly back until this afternoon. But the text had come in over an hour ago while I'd been finishing up at the diner.

"Are you home from work?"

I was tempted to answer but instead simply went to bed. I couldn't do this. Couldn't deal with him yet. I just wasn't in the right head space at the moment.

By the time I woke up four hours later, I had missed two calls from him, but he'd left no voicemail.

Weird. However, I had no time to think about him because I had to take my best friend to the airport. There were a lot of tears as Chloe and I said goodbye, and we promised to FaceTime. Once home, I simply fell into bed again, intent on shutting out the world temporarily and pretending that everything was fine.

The sound of pounding woke me up. Rolling from the bed, I checked the time. Four o'clock in the afternoon. Was it Liam? I went to check the peephole and sighed. Guess it was time to get this over with.

The need to be with Kendall was so overwhelming I couldn't wait until Sunday to fly home. Instead, I headed out Saturday afternoon, and drove straight from the airport to the club with the hope of driving her home tonight. That was, if she'd let me. If she'd consider giving me a second chance.

The moment I spotted her working behind the bar, I felt the tension start to ease. She looked so unbelievably beautiful it made me physically ache to be a hundred feet from her. To know I'd hurt her. Not for the first time, I wondered how she was feeling. Did she have morning sickness? Was she scared? Did she plan on keeping the baby? The last thought alone knocked the breath from me. What if she thought I didn't want it and made a decision based on her false perception? Now more than ever, I needed to talk to her.

I could only hope if I bared everything, she'd take me back. The thought was terrifying. But nothing compared to spending my life without the woman I loved. And fuck, did I love her. The depths of that love— Well, without abusing the word, terrified me, too.

"Mr. Davenport." A suit with an earpiece came up to me.

"Yes."

"Chance Maxwell is upstairs. He's asking for a word."

As much as I wasn't in the mood to talk with Chance, doing so would eat up the time until Kendall was off her shift, and I could meet her in the parking lot. I was ushered into the same office as before, only this time Chance had already poured the bourbon.

"You look like shit, my friend, if you don't mind me saying so."

I could imagine I did, considering I hadn't slept or shaved in days. "I'm getting that a lot lately."

"Word is you and your girl broke up."

I eyed the man, trying to figure out his agenda. He wasn't soft-hearted, he wasn't one to gossip, nor did I believe he gave a shit about my relationship. "It's temporary."

"We may not be friends, Liam, but I respect you, and I like you, which is about as close to friendship as I get these days. And that's why I'll say I'm happy to hear it."

"Thanks."

He assessed me for a moment before pouring, adding two shots of Patron to our tumblers already on the table.

I waved him off when he pushed one in front of me. "I'm good."

"You'll need this for what I'm about to tell you." He paused, before blurting out, "She's pregnant."

"I know." Funny how calm I was in saying it. Yet he'd just reminded me how badly I'd botched things. I threw back the shot after all.

He threw back his own. "Guess it keeps me from having to break the news, then. You okay with it?"

No. Not at all. And yet knowing she was carrying my

child brought out a fierce protective side. "Getting there. How did you come by the information?"

"She talked to my lead bartender about other positions that might be available at the club after she starts showing."

I was already shaking my head. "She can't work at the club period. I don't care what job you think to give her."

He shrugged, sipping his bourbon. "I may be an asshole, but even I'm not so bad as to turn away a pregnant woman from work if she wants it. You sure it's yours?"

The murderous glare I gave him had him throwing his hands up in surrender. "You and I live in different worlds, my friend, but I'm glad you don't have any doubts."

"I fucked up, but I plan on fixing it."

"If a smooth talker like you can't fix it, I don't suppose there's hope for the rest of our species. Hell, if anything, having a baby sort of implies you're in it with her, no matter what. Guess it's a good thing you'd want to be together."

"What if I'm a shitty father?" I hadn't realized I'd verbalized the comment out loud until Chance's brow lifted.

Much to my surprise, he answered. "Shitty fathers don't worry about being shitty fathers, you feel me?"

His words were simple and succinct. Also true if I thought about it. "I feel you. In any case, I appreciate you wanting to tell me."

"Glad I wasn't the first. By the way, her roommate's last night is tonight. After work they're having a going-away breakfast at a local diner. You may want to wait until after to talk to your girl."

Once again, I appreciated the information. But it wasn't lost on me that Chance knew more about Kendall's plans than I did. But hopefully, that was about to change.

It was in my best interest to go home and shower, shave, and better prepare myself for talking to Kendall. I found myself practicing what I'd say. Having my counterarguments ready. It was the only way I could quell my anxiety, preparing as if this was the trial of my life. How long would breakfast take? Would she be home by now? An unanswered text message and two calls later, I finally realized I should be using the time to my advantage.

I had a plan; now I hoped it would actually work.

By late afternoon, I had everything in place and decided to drive to her apartment. I was relieved to see her car in the lot. I was also nervous. Jesus, was I nervous.

After knocking on her apartment door, I waited with bated breath for her to answer. As soon as she did, opening the door to reveal herself in shorts and a tank top, her hair piled high in a messy bun, every prepared thought went out of my mind.

"Hi," I greeted, drinking her in.

Her eyes were sleepy, her voice rough. "Hello."

"Do you think we could talk in private? Maybe go back to my place?" It's where I had something set up I couldn't wait to show her.

"I already took Chloe to the airport. You can come in here."

She moved aside, letting me into her studio apartment. It occurred to me my first plan, to get her back to my place, had already failed. Now that I was in her apartment, I was even more at a loss regarding how to proceed. At least she started the conversation.

"How was the trip home?" She took a seat at the small table for two.

"I, um, it was difficult." I took the other chair. "My father had a video will. We all watched it."

Her face softened with sympathy. "That must've been tough."

Leave it to her to think about me even now. "It was. But it was also closure."

"I'm glad. Um, not to be rude, but what are you doing here? I thought you'd text me once you returned, and we'd agree when and where to meet up."

I swallowed hard. This was where I put it all on the line and lay myself bare. "I took an early flight. Came to see you at the bar last night. I thought about staying but found out you had plans with Chloe. Also, I didn't think you'd be too happy to see me."

"I probably wouldn't have."

Despite all my practiced words, all my ways of trying to win her back, the only thing I could say was, "I've always tried to accomplish more because I never felt like I was enough."

Her eyes went wide with my admission. Then, because she knew me, she whispered, "Your father?"

I nodded. "My sister asked me a question. What's after named partner?"

Kendall scrunched up her nose. "What do you mean what's after? Isn't named partner your all-time goal?"

"That's the thing I'm coming to realize. It would be, until I attain it, still don't deem it enough, and go for the next goal. It's been that way my entire life. Undergrad. Law school. Partner. Always trying, with the next level and the next accomplishment or purchase, to prove it's enough. To prove I'm enough. It never is. It never will be if I stay on the road I've been on."

"If?"

I nodded. "I'm still working on that part. Probably need to see a therapist or something to help me through it. But hopefully, admitting I have a problem is the first step. I've always been terrified of failing, but I controlled that fear by putting everything into whatever I did. The law came naturally to me. It was comfortable. Relationships never were, and I was never good at them. I told you I avoided relationships because I didn't have the time. Didn't want to threaten my career by gleaning any of my precious work hours. Hell, it's what I told myself, too, but the truth is I'm terrified. Terrified of letting anyone in. Of failing to be enough for them."

"You were always enough for me, Liam. You weren't perfect, but nobody is."

Hadn't my sister said the same thing? "I've never felt worthy."

*M*y heart broke over his words. It blew my mind to discover someone like Liam could have such deep insecurity. Looking back now, with the advantage of hindsight, I suppose there were clues, yet I'd never picked up on them. He'd always seemed so confident about everything. And I'd believed he simply didn't want a relationship getting in the way of his career goals.

"You've always been worthy, Liam."

He stood up, walked over and took my hand, pulling me out of my chair and in close to him. Jesus, I'd missed him. Missed the feel of being in his arms.

"I'm working on that part. I promise. I've let go of my hate for my father. I'll have to live with the regret I didn't give him the chance he'd wanted, but at least I understand better why he left. Why he stayed away. Why my mother chose to forgive him. In the video, he was coming up on his one-year mark of staying sober. He explained he'd decided he had to be one year sober before he'd come home."

Liam took a deep breath. I couldn't imagine what it would feel like to see a father you hadn't seen in over twenty years, or how he'd look different through the eyes of an adult. I was happy he'd found closure. Happy he was working on things, but selfishly, I wasn't sure where that left us.

"Those words I said to you on the phone were all wrong. I made it all about what I thought I was losing instead of what I was gaining. I don't expect you to forgive me right away, but I want a second chance."

His hand splayed gently on my belly. "I want this baby. I want you. I prepared this great argument with all of the reasons we should be together, but it sort of went out of my head the minute I saw you. Because all I could think about was how I could breathe easy again. How I need you in my life. How I'm willing to do whatever it takes. I love you."

He wanted me. He wanted this baby. But I wouldn't be the reason he lost his dream. "I love you, too. But I don't want you to give up on becoming named partner. I don't want to take a chance you might end up resenting me or the baby."

"I'm not giving up. But I also refuse to accept I can't have one without the other. So if when I tell them I'm not willing to completely sacrifice my personal life, they don't want me, then it's their loss. Because my new goal, the one I absolutely won't compromise on, is to be a better man, so I can be a better partner to you and a good father to this baby. Please tell me you want to keep him or her."

Tears tracked down my face. He was already thinking of this baby as a boy or a girl instead of an it. "I'm keeping him or her."

He crushed me to him, exhaling a shuddered breath. Then, easing up, he pulled back so he could smooth the hair off my face. "Are you going to your parents' house today?"

"No. I begged off, telling them I had an exam to study for."

"You haven't told them yet?"

"No. To be honest, I'm not sure how my dad will react."

"I'd like to be there with you. We should tell them together."

"I'm not sure how it'll go." I could imagine they'd both be disappointed, to say the least. Would that freak Liam out?

"All that much more reason for me to be there. They may be surprised, but they need to know we're together, and we're committed to raising this baby. We could get engaged before we go."

I was already shaking my head. "I don't want the reason we get engaged or married to be because of this pregnancy. We can be committed parents without trying to plan a shotgun wedding beforehand. I was thinking I'd tell them after the first trimester."

He rubbed his hands down my back. "We can tell them whenever you're ready."

"I'm hoping to ask them next weekend if they're okay with me moving home. My transfer to the Century City office will be complete in two weeks. I already found a bus that makes the commute from my parents' house."

His lips went flat, but despite us working things out, there was no way I could continue to work for him in LA.

"The partner you'll be working for is a great guy. He's in environmental law, which shouldn't be as high stress as my practice. And he's near retirement. Are you hungry? You want to get some lunch and go back to my place? I have a surprise there for you."

I was relieved he wouldn't fight me on my transfer. "I'd love to."

After grabbing lunch at my favorite soup place, we pulled into his driveway, entering his garage as the overhead door opened. Here I'd thought I might never be back here.

"Come on. I have something to show you."

He led me by the hand into the house and then up the stairs. But instead of taking me to the master bedroom, he took me to the guest bedroom. I was confused until he opened the door and revealed a nursery. Or at least the start of one.

"It's not nearly finished, but I figured you want to pick a color of paint and any other decorations you'd want. Or if you don't like this furniture, we can return it. I was limited in my choices when I went out this morning since I wanted it the same day. We still need to get a hutch or dresser and a changing table, but it's a start."

He was rambling while I focused on the gorgeous mahogany crib and plush rocking chair with a fuzzy stuffed bunny on it. I couldn't speak.

"I wasn't sure if you wanted to find out the sex of the baby. Or if you don't like this room, there's the other one down the hall, but I figured you'd want one closest to the master bedroom. Or if you don't want to live here, we can find a different place."

I finally let his words sink in. "You want me to move in with you?"

He flashed a rueful smile. "I probably should've started with that question. I want you to move in with me, Kendall. Share all your nights and weekends with me. I know you aren't ready for a proposal, and the last thing I want to do is rush this, but it feels right to have you live here. For us to get ready for this baby together."

"I haven't had my first checkup. I'm not out of the first trimester. There's a chance of miscarriage."

His expression was etched in worry. "Then, we'd have to cross that bridge. But make no mistake, even if there was a miscarriage, this bedroom is destined to be a nursery, whether it's eight months from now or later down the road when we try again."

I was in shock.

"I want it all. You, me. A family." He took my hands, locking his gaze on mine with an intensity I'd never seen from him. "This pregnancy wasn't something either of us planned. But I've come to realize sometimes the best things to ever happen are those you don't plan. Like falling in love with you."

Tears started streaming down my face. "I love you, too, Liam."

His arms went around me, hugging me close. "This may not come out right, but I really want you to quit your job at the club. I worried before, but now it would be unbearable to think about you working late in a crowded bar while pregnant."

It wasn't my first choice, either, but I had bills to pay.

He beat me to the punch. "I know you need the money for your grandmother's care, but I want you to let me pay for it. And before you argue, let me tell you something. Aside from my mother and sister, my grandparents were the most important part of my life growing up. They aren't still with me, but if they were, I'd do this for them. Let me do it for your nan. Let me do this for us."

I wiped my tears, both relieved and guilty that he'd offer this. "You realize you're impossible to argue with, don't you? But we can compromise because with the money I'll be saving on rent, I'd still be able to pay a good portion of her care."

He opened his mouth as if he was about to argue with me but then grinned. "Deal."

"And I've been doing a lot of thinking. After we have the baby, I'm quitting the firm. I reached out to Stephen Walsh, and if he gets back to me, I'd really like to work in one of his restaurants."

He surprised me. "I think that's a great idea."

"You do?"

"You deserve to do something you enjoy. What better example for our son or daughter than for their mother to follow her dreams?"

My arms went around him. For the first time, I felt the positives outweigh any lingering doubts. Whatever was in store, we would figure our future out together.

Chapter Fifty-Three

LIAM

*A*fter moving Kendall's things into my place, we settled into our new living arrangement. Although I missed seeing her in the office each day, I was happier to have her to come home to. With each moment we spent together, I felt more and more complete. I savored hearing she loved me. Holding on to her every night. Knowing she was giving us a chance.

Being a part of her first appointment where we got to see our baby on the ultrasound screen filled my heart. Although I might still have some insecurities about my ability to be everything she and this baby deserved, at least I could acknowledge I was a work in progress.

But there was one thing I couldn't stop thinking about. One thing I wanted more than anything. So on a Saturday morning, I put my plan into motion while she slept in. As soon as I heard her in the bathroom, running the tap, I took a deep breath, ready to go. Game time.

"Morning," I said, walking in to watch her finish brushing her teeth.

She gave me a toothy grin. "Morning."

"I have a surprise for you in your side of the closet."

"Do you now?"

I nuzzled her neck and splayed my hand against her tiny baby bump, wanting nothing more than to get her back in my bed. But I kept my mind on my goal. "Go in and check it out."

She kissed me lightly before giving me a sleepy smile. "I'm intrigued."

I grinned when I heard her laughter. Following her into the walk-in closet, I took in the scene of her eying her green, ugly, puffy jacket hanging with her sparkly lavender boots lined up on the shoe rack below. She may have relegated those items to a storage box, but I'd made sure to give them proper placement in our closet.

Her brows went high. "I knew you had a thing for this coat and boots."

"From the moment I saw you swallowed up in that ugly coat in the Walmart parking lot, trying to get up into the truck, I was gone for you."

She quirked a brow. "You hid it rather well."

"Fought it, more like. Check inside the pocket. I think there's something in it."

She scrunched up her brow in confusion before wiggling her hand inside the outer pocket. She sucked in a deep breath when her fingers found what I'd hidden inside. After pulling out the platinum-set diamond ring, she looked toward me and pressed her hand against her chest.

"I know you said you want to wait until after the baby, and if it's truly what you want, we can. But I know what I want. And it's you, Kendall. I love you. And I want to share my whole life with you. If you want to quit the firm tomorrow and start your culinary classes or begin working at Walsh's restaurant, I'm supportive." I'd already told Phil

Kinkaid about my relationship with Kendall. He'd been shocked. But I was done hiding it. And if living with Kendall meant I wouldn't get the named partnership, then so be it. For once I wasn't the one hoping to feel good enough. I was flipping the tables, recognizing I didn't want my name on a firm that didn't value family.

"I wouldn't have insurance if I quit my job. Or maternity leave."

"You would have my insurance if you marry me."

"You want me to marry you for your health insurance?"

"I want you to marry me so we can fly both our families to Hawaii next month, and they can watch me stand in front of the very best thing that's ever happened to me and pledge my eternal love. I want to marry you because I dream of spending our weekends binge watching *Little House on the Prairie* with your nan—with the exception of that blind school fire episode which made *Game of Thrones* look tame —and learning how to make pasta, or maybe just eating it because, I'll admit, it's much sexier watching you do it than helping you. I want to have dinner with your family every Sunday. And finally, I want to marry you because the rest of our lives still doesn't seem like enough time to love you."

She stood there, a hand over her mouth as she watched me drop to one knee.

"So with all of that, will you marry me?"

"But, it's early and…."

"The pregnancy changes nothing. I want you to be my wife. Period. And I should tell you now, I'm not accustomed to not getting my way."

She smirked. "You do realize you're not doing yourself any favors by challenging me to say no."

I swallowed hard, my stomach flipping. "It's a joke. My way of masking the fear you're going to reject me." All this bravado and confidence had been a façade over the years. But in this moment, I was putting it all out there.

Unexpectedly, she got down on her knees, too, cupping my face. "The answer is yes, Liam. A hundred times yes."

I kissed her with relief, joy, and love. My heart was fuller than I'd ever experienced. Sealing the deal, I put the ring on her left ring finger. "Let's take this back to the bed to celebrate."

"Or we should christen the closet instead. You up for the adventure?"

"No. You're relegated to the bed while pregnant. This hardwood floor does not look comfortable."

She yanked down the puffy coat, spreading it down on the floor and making me laugh. "Spoilsport."

"Foreplay on the floor, sex on the bed," I compromised.

She laughed. "Such a negotiator. We'll see."

We did see. Which is why she ended up riding me on the floor. I was sure my back would pay for it tomorrow. Yet it was worth it for her smile. It was worth knowing this was only the first of many adventures to come.

EPILOGUE
Kendall

$\mathcal{T}$he funny thing about dreams was sometimes they came true in ways you couldn't have imagined. Watching my husband from our kitchen was pure bliss. He had our precious almost-three-month-old baby boy asleep on his chest while he perused his email on his phone. Although he still worked a good number of hours, he prioritized Charlie and me in the evenings and on the weekends.

I piped the eclairs, setting them on the baking sheet, excited to put my latest pastry class to good practical use. I was enrolled two days a week in culinary school while working at Stephen Walsh's restaurant another two days a week. The plan was to open a catering business someday, but first I needed to learn more about both cooking and the business side of things.

I hadn't returned to work at the law firm after having the baby. And I couldn't have been happier following my passion. Liam had not only been supportive, but he'd also adjusted his hours because he loved being a hands-on dad.

His new boss was more than supportive since he believed fully in a work-life balance. Yep, after not getting the coveted named partner slot, Liam had quit the firm and gone to work for Stephen Walsh directly.

It had been quite the scandal. Lowry and Anderson had lost a great deal of money with Liam's departure, especially since Stephen Walsh no longer needed the firm. But my husband hadn't looked back. Hadn't so much as considered it when the board had next offered him named partner if he would stay. Nope. It had been too late. He was now proudly serving Stephen's many companies with his talent. Considering our new boss was constantly in some sort of litigious situation, Liam was plenty busy.

I'd felt a bit of guilt at first about Liam giving up his longtime goal because the board hadn't wanted someone with a family taking over, but Liam assured me he didn't want to put his name on a firm that didn't value family. As if to prove it, before he'd left, he'd put a large, framed photo on his desk of us together. Tabitha couldn't have missed seeing that.

After washing my hands, I slipped upstairs and changed quickly. Between a baby who didn't quite sleep through the night and our busy schedules, adventures in intimacy hadn't been the priority. Hell, we were happy simply to have those precious hours together before we both passed out at night. So on this Saturday afternoon, I decided to spice things up. And I had just the thing to help me do it.

When I went back down into the kitchen, I watched while Liam put Charlie down in his bassinet. Perfect timing, I thought, turning around in the hopes of giving him quite the view. It wasn't long before I heard him suck in a breath and then his footsteps on the hardwood floor.

My heart was already beating in overdrive as it always did when I anticipated his touch.

"This is quite the surprise," he said coming up from behind me and kissing me on the neck.

I swear I could melt right there from the contact. "Mm, you like?"

"I more than like. You in nothing but a red frilly apron is the fantasy." His hand gripped my bare ass, making the point.

"Charlie is out, I'm assuming?" If so, it should give us about two hours.

"Like a rock. Best sleeping baby ever."

He really was. Although I still had to wake up to nurse him in the middle of the night, we often enjoyed four- to five-hour stretches of sleep. I wasn't complaining. "My mom said I was the same." I turned around to give Liam my full attention. "You know it's been a while since any of our counter-tops got some action other than cooking."

He lifted me up effortlessly, spreading me out on the granite surface. Then, ripping off the apron, he let his gaze roam down my body. "You're so fucking beautiful. It literally takes my breath away."

His hands followed his gaze, caressing my legs and up my sides, until gently cupping my breasts. Dipping his head, he kissed between them, before trailing his tongue down my stomach. "You comfortable?"

Nope. The granite was hard and cold. But I wouldn't be denied his touch, not even for a second. "I'm good."

"Excellent, because I'll be down here awhile." His breath fluttered over my clit, making my entire body shiver in antici-pation. But nothing could've prepared me for the way he buried his entire face in my pussy. He wasn't gentle. He wasn't careful. It was bliss. Because after I'd had the baby, he'd been cautious. Now, after a few months, he was no longer holding back. Thank God.

It wasn't long before my first orgasm crashed over me, then my second. By the time my third came along, I was ready to scream. It was only the thought of the baby sleeping which kept me quiet, making the climax that much more intense. I had to grab something from beside me and shove it into my mouth.

Liam peppered my inner thighs with kisses before glancing up and chuckling. "There are many visions of you burned inside of my brain, but this one, with you naked, glistening from me making you come, with an oven mitt in your mouth, will be by far my favorite."

I took it out with a wry smile. "It was either that or wake the baby."

He helped me up to a sitting position before stepping out of his jeans. "In that case, I'm putting oven mitts everywhere throughout the house."

The image made me grin. "I'm a fan. I'm also a fan of you inside of me." I gripped him, sliding my hand up and down on his hardened length and enjoying the way he shut his eyes with the sensation.

He scooted me forward, aligning himself and pushing inside of me. God, I'd never get tired of this feeling.

LIAM

My hips moved quickly. I knew I wouldn't last long. Not given the way she didn't mind tasting herself. Not given the way she was clawing the hell out of my back. But I wouldn't let go before she went over the edge one more time. I swallowed her groan with my own, taking her mouth while we both climaxed.

We both stayed there a minute, my cock still deeply seated inside of her. My wife felt incredible. But not as incredible as it was to call her wife. Or to have witnessed the birth of our baby son. Two of the very best days of my life.

Taking her face between my hands, I kissed her gently, laying my forehead against hers. "I love you. In ways I never knew possible. In depths I'm not sure I'll ever be able to fully express."

Her thoughtful brown eyes were on mine. "I love you, too. In ways you make possible and with the depths I see you express every day. You're an amazing husband. And an incredible father."

A few months ago, I wouldn't have believed her. Not truly. But thanks to my twice-a-month therapy appointments, I was becoming much more accepting of Kendall's generous love. Of hearing the good things and recognizing I deserved them. "You make it easy. So does Charlie. Speaking of which, I think we'll get another hour. What do you think about taking act two up to the shower?"

Her smile still got me square in the chest. Every time. "If you set up the monitor, I'll get the water warmed up for us."

I helped her down and swatted her ass for good measure before watching her walk up the stairs. Then I pulled up my pants and went over to set up the video monitor for Charlie. Taking a moment, I marveled at his chubby cheeks, button nose, and soft downy hair.

"Someday, when you find someone you love, ensure they are as understanding, patient, and kind as your mother. You will never want for anything else. And know that today, a year from now, ten years from now, there has never been a father prouder of his son than I am. You don't have to do a thing to earn it. It's just there. No matter what you decide to do with your life. No matter what you decide to become, it's always enough, sweet boy."

Climbing the stairs, I was greeted by Kendall on the last step with tears in her eyes.

"I take it you heard me?"

She reached out, entwining her fingers with mine. "I turned on the monitor just in time. Have I told you lately how much I love you, Mr. Davenport?"

I gave her a small smile, no longer hiding from my vulnerability but trusting her with it completely. Lifting her up with ease, I snuggled her against my chest and walked her in through the bedroom to our shower. "You have, but I'll never get tired of hearing it, Mrs. Davenport. Now what do you say we get to some non-pot holder-be-as-loud-as-you-want shower sex?"

Read the next book in the Miss Series! Chloe and Aiden's story is up next in Miss Typed.

ACKNOWLEDGMENTS

My favorite thing to write about is office romance. And I just love starting this new series with Kendall and Liam. I have so many more books planned to include Chloe's story next, so stay tuned for more to come!!

I want to take a moment to give a shout out to some of the people who made this book possible.

Alyssa Kress! You've been with me since the beginning and I can't tell you how much I enjoy working with you. You make my words better!

Thank you to Kelly Green, the best PA a girl could have! I'm so lucky to have you in my life!

Thank you to Marisa with Cover Me Darling for your gorgeous cover.

To Judy of Judy's Proofreading, Thank you for your eagle eyes!!

To Give Me Books: Thank you for your awesome team. You are so great to work with!

To all of the amazing bloggers who shared Miss Understanding, I thank you so much for your efforts! I've been so lucky to have met some of you in person over this last year and hope to meet many more of you!!

And last, but not least to my readers! I adore you all! I couldn't do this without you! Every share, every like, every note, and every review means the world!

ABOUT THE AUTHOR

Aubrey Bondurant is a working mom who loves to write, read, and travel.

She describes her writing style as: "Adult Contemporary Erotic Romantic Comedy," which is just another way of saying she likes her characters funny, her bedroom scenes hot, and her romances with a happy ending.

When Aubrey isn't working her day job or spending time with her family, she's on her laptop typing away on her next story. She only wishes there were more hours of the day!

She's a former member of the US Marine Corps and passionate about veteran charities and giving back to the community. She loves a big drooly dog, a fantastic margarita, and football.

Sign up for Aubrey's newsletter to get all of the latest information on new releases here.

Join her FB Group
Follow her on Instagram

Email her at aubreybondurant@gmail.com